Father of the
Bride of Frankenstein

Father of the Bride of Frankenstein

by Daniel M. Kimmel

To Jamie!
L'chaim!

1/28/18

Porto Sq. Books

© 2019

In-house Editor: Ian Randal Strock

Fantastic Books
1380 East 17 Street, Suite 2233
Brooklyn, New York 11230
www.FantasticBooks.biz

Trade Paperback ISBN 10/13: 1-5154-2379-4 / 978-1-5154-2379-9
Hardcover ISBN 10/13: 1-5154-2380-8 / 978-1-5154-2380-5

First Edition

Dedicated with affection and gratitude to

Susan Fendell

and

Kilian Melloy and David Emmert

"I get by with a little help from my friends"

Man plans and God laughs.
—Traditional Jewish saying

It's alive!
—Victor Frankenstein

PROLOGUE

Let me tell you, this is not how I imagined my daughter's wedding day. Of course, no father can truly imagine such an event. To do so cuts to the bone of the father/daughter bond, because it means having to accept the inevitable: that his little baby is undeniably a woman and is now ready to establish a home of her own. And it means much more than that. It means accepting some outsider, some interloper who clearly isn't worthy, as the person who will now become the primary focus of their shared lives, and that I, as merely the father, will forever after be reduced to just a supporting character.

It had taken me a long time and a lot of bumps in the road to get to this point and now, with the added support from the open bar I am paying for at the reception, I am planning on getting through it to the end. I would give my baby away, I would dance with her in celebration of that fact, and then I would see her go off with her new husband. My in-laws had had to deal with me. I suppose this would be payback.

Of course, today went far beyond anything I could possibly have ever done that required balancing the scales. Here it is, only a few hours before the ceremony, and where do I find myself? Not at the hotel where the wedding and reception is supposed to be taking place. Instead, I'm hiding out at a remote cabin in the woods with my daughter and her mother. Outside the cabin are several men with guns who were, in their words, "patrolling the perimeter." According to their leader, their job was to keep "unauthorized people" away. Samantha, my daughter, was comforting her mother, who was quietly sobbing into a lace handkerchief. Sam was in her bridal gown and Joanne, my wife, was smartly attired in a black and gray ensemble that had looked a lot better when she had put it on to pose for some photos a few days ago. Nearly an hour riding in a van, the last part on bumpy, unpaved roads, will do that to a person. Between the two of them they were wearing a couple of thousand dollars. I could only hope the chipmunk staring in at the window appreciated the fashion statement.

And where was the groom in all this? He was outside waiting for Rabbi Wheaton and Cantor Eisenstein, who would be performing the ceremony. No doubt they would be surprised at the sudden change of location. After months of detailed preparation, they would have been expecting to join our 200 or so guests who were in a ballroom at a downtown hotel. Indeed, I thought, glancing at my watch, they were there right now. At least that's what I had been told. They would have managed to get through the mob of protestors, media, religious fanatics, and curiosity seekers who were at all the entrances, outnumbering the invitees by a ratio of five to one, and then cleared a security checkpoint. There would be no party crashers at this wedding.

Outside, among the protestors, were a cadre surrounding a fringe minister who had decided that this wedding should not take place at all and that it was an affront to humanity. Add to this lively cast of characters the squadrons of police and nearly as large a contingent of hotel security, as well as a sizable showing from our friends in the media. I could only hope that our guests who made it through appreciated just how safe they were while being protected from the chaos outside. At this point, I was just hoping to survive the day and maybe get to taste some of the hors d'oeuvres ($21 per person), dinner ($39 per plate), and a piece of cake (which, at $800, better be the best damn cake I've ever eaten). At the moment, we had no idea if we'd even make it there, and since we were the wedding party, we were kind of the point of the whole thing.

My stomach started rumbling in anticipation. It was at that moment that the one door to the cabin opened and there he was: my son-in-law to be. Frank. The love of Samantha's life. Or, as you may have seen him referred to in numerous newspaper headlines, the Monster.

I suppose I really ought to start at the beginning. Not with my marriage or Samantha's birth, of course, although there are some wonderful stories to tell, but they're probably no different from the stories you tell in your family. Every family has a collection of lore about major catastrophes the family has confronted individually or collectively over the years that get retold at every gathering of the clan. The elements differ from story to story and family to family, but they're usually amusing, the result of tragedy becoming comedy in the retelling after many years.

"And your mother went into labor while we were stuck in the snow drift…"

"We hadn't planned on a Level 4 hurricane on the day of our wedding…"

"My best man had left the ring on his dresser… back in New Hampshire.…"

Years later, telling the children and grandchildren such stories would become a way to bring the family together through reliving shared experiences. But that's not what you want to hear today. Like everyone else, you want to know how—of all the families in the world—we were the ones who got to welcome Frank into our lives, altering our trajectories in ways that are still being measured.

Suffice to say, as the father in the story, I was usually the last to know anything. Indeed, right from the start I was out of the loop. In accounting where Frank came from and how he was created and set loose on the world, I probably learned the details around the same time you did.

CHAPTER ONE

I had been sitting in my private office at the bank doing my job, busily approving or disapproving loans, when the news came in. We're a community-based bank, so we avoided the shenanigans that the "banks too big to fail" had engaged in. Our clients were local start-ups, or established businesses looking to expand, or retailers looking to remodel. If they seemed like good risks—and most of them were—they would be approved. My desk was the end of the line. The weeding-out process had mostly already taken place. I had put in my time in the trenches. Now I was upper management, which came with a nice office, a nicer salary, and the ability to delegate work to others. I liked to think of my life as being similar to the bank: strong, stable, predictable. All of that was about to change.

It had been a quiet day and a bank is, by nature, a quiet place, so when I heard a loud shriek and then a shout of, "Turn it up," followed by the blaring of a newscast loud enough for me to hear behind closed doors, I imagined the worst. A terrorist attack or a plane crash. Unless it was taking place nearby, there was still little cause for this level of noise. I went down the hall to the conference room and saw most of our employees watching a newscast streaming on a computer monitor. It was playing on the big screen on the far wall as well.

No doubt you remember where you were when you first heard about it. It was one of those news stories that cause everyone to stop in their tracks. My introduction to the story that would literally transform my life and that of my family was an anchor breathlessly reading a hastily written news report surrounded by graphics that screamed "Breaking News" and "Authorities on High Alert." To the immediate left of the avuncular anchor—the elder statesman of this particular outlet which put him at about 45—was a graphic of a test tube with the caption "Life from the Lab."

"What's going on here?" I demanded in *my* authoritative voice, which was greeted by calls of "Be quiet!" and "Shh!" which is not how I'm used to being addressed by our employees.

On screen, the anchor was conveniently providing a recap. "For those of you just joining us, we have confirmed reports that researchers at the State University Medical Center have been conducting illegal experiments involving the reanimation of human tissue. According to people on the scene these experiments have been going on for a period of more than a year and have come to light because the scientists have succeeding in bringing to life a sentient human being."

"It's like something out of a movie," one of the tellers watching said, making me wonder if she was in here, who was minding the customers? I walked out to the main area of the bank. It was deserted. I looked out on the street and the only activity seemed to be at the sports bar down the block. If the TV screens in the window were any indication, no one was watching the ball game if there was even one being played. I locked the bank's doors and put up a sign indicating we were closed. Someone had to take care of business.

I returned to the conference room, where the anchor was clearly at a loss for words, as if he couldn't quite believe what he was saying himself. He paused to get some instructions through his ear piece. "I'm being told that a press conference is taking place at the university, and we're switching over there live."

The scene shifted to a conference room not unlike this one, only packed with reporters and camera crews, as an obviously harried and clearly uncomfortable spokesman came to the microphone. "I have a statement to read and will be taking no questions at this time. The administration of the State University Medical Center was shocked to learn that a team of doctors has been conducting unauthorized and possibly illegal procedures using tissues obtained from our morgue. As soon as we confirmed that this was real and not a hoax, we notified local law enforcement, and we are cooperating fully with their investigation. Questions about what they discovered and what arrests have been made should be directed to them."

The spokesman turned to go amid a roar of questions from the assembled press. One reporter with a particularly loud voice could be heard above the din.

"Did they actually bring a dead person back to life?"

The spokesman stopped, hesitated, and then returned to the microphone. "We wish to avoid any panic. It does appear that the latest of these unauthorized experiments involved a corpse, and that they had some success in bringing it to life. I have no further information on this except to say that all of the people involved, as well as their experimental subject, are now in police custody. Let me make this absolutely clear: The public is in no danger whatsoever." And with that, he beat a hasty retreat from the room, ignoring the continued shouting.

This was the stuff of horror stories, of course. Indeed, it was so much the stuff of horror stories that the head of the project—who had some mundane name like Smith or Jones—was quickly dubbed "Dr. Frankenstein" in the headlines. Looking back at it from a few years later, I'm not sure I could recall what his actual name was without Googling it. There's really no need to go through that part of the story at this late date, given that the details have became so widely known that there's not only a shelf full of books about the case, but Brad Pitt won his Oscar for playing the Monster in the popular—if somewhat inaccurate—movie version.

You'll probably recall that the doctors and scientists involved all went to prison on a variety of charges ranging from stock fraud to perjury to misappropriations of funds to misuse of human remains. The experiments, as it turned out, had been going on for several years and involved a number of people who had to arrange for hospital facilities to be used after hours without leaving any trace behind. They had begun with mice and worked their way through the animal kingdom before finally turning to human tissue. This last phase involved the appropriation of body parts from the morgue which then either had to be returned or destroyed. One of the nurses who had been a willing participant got cold feet when the human experiments began. (Indeed, she literally got cold feet having to procure several limbs from the morgue.) When the reanimation of a full cadaver proved successful, she decided she had had enough, and made her way to the hospital administrators. It was one thing to bring a gall bladder to life. An actual human being was something else.

The resulting scandal nearly shut down the university and did lead to the temporary closure of the entire medical center. As you might imagine, no one wanted to get so much as a tonsillectomy at a place that was now deemed in the public mind as a "Chamber of Horrors." The local media coverage couldn't help but be lurid given the nature of the story, but initial reports referring to "crimes against nature" were changed when several fact checkers pointed out that the legal meaning of the term had to do with what were once considered sex crimes. Those were among the very few laws the scientists had managed to avoid transgressing.

Through it all there was one matter that kept getting deferred, and that was what to do with the human corpse they had brought to life. It couldn't be said it had been brought "back to life" since the Monster, as he—and it was definitely a "he"—had no conscious memories of the past life that had inhabited the body. Instead, while he gave every appearance of being alive, he came across as an amnesiac. He retained language skills but had no memory of any life prior to the moment he had awoken in the operating room.

Given the popular culture's confusion over Mary Shelley's mad scientist and his creation being interchangeably referred to as "Frankenstein," the Monster was inevitably dubbed "Frank." As he was able to communicate, it was a name that he accepted. Although it was an adult body that had been animated in the university hospital, his mind at the time of discovery by the authorities was about as well-developed as a four-year-old. And therein lay the problem.

As far as a number of people were concerned, Frank's creation was a crime, not to mention blasphemous, and could not be allowed to stand. It violated dozens of laws that had been broken on the way to his "birth." Dozens more were hastily enacted to explicitly ensure that such experimenting would be deemed criminal in the future. To let him live, to such thinking, would make a mockery of such prohibitions.

Yet there was still the fact of Frank. He was not a hypothetical devised by some cruel law professor. He was alive. He could talk and understand and, as would become clear over time, learn at a rapid rate. While he could not recollect memories of any past life, it was theorized that pre-existing pathways in his brain allowed him to easily reacquire language and other concepts. By the time the government was ready to deal with his fate, more than a year after his discovery, he was as articulate as—and much better behaved than—your average teenager. When the government proposed that he be destroyed as an "abomination," the public seemed torn. His court-appointed attorney arranged for the media to have unfettered access to Frank, along with a variety of officials, spiritual leaders, and cultural figures. *People* magazine named him the most fascinating non-person of the year. Frank told reporters he had mastered the internet and was now enrolled in an online college, where he wanted to get a degree in bioethics. In interviews it seemed he had developed a sense of humor. Asked who his role models were in learning human behavior he cited the Dalai Lama, Nelson Mandela... and Boris Karloff.

Where the convictions of those responsible for his creation had happened swiftly, there seemed to be no rush to get to a resolution of the case of *In re: Frank*. There was speculation that the government hoped that his reanimated body was so unstable that he would quickly die a natural—or near-natural—death. Instead his skin, while remaining an ashen gray, had become increasingly supple. It was reported that his hair and nails were actually growing. Medical reports indicated that he was breathing, sleeping, and otherwise acting like a human being should. Could a court rule him non-human and order him summarily executed? Was he like a rabid dog that could be put down? There were those who thought so. The debate raged on with all the subtlety and openness to opposing views that were the hallmarks of every other dispute over the last few decades of American life. But then the Pope put his two cents in, and that was a game changer. Given the unprecedented nature of the situation, his remarks served to dissipate the fog of uncertainty.

It was, unquestionably, the most historic interview Oprah had ever done. The Pope was a major "get" for any interviewer, and the media savvy pontiff, knowing he was about to make news, wanted to reach the widest possible audience. Oprah had been informed that she could ask anything she wanted, but His Holiness would welcome a question as to the fate of Frank. A veteran media star and interviewer, she didn't have to be told twice.

"One of the greatest moral debates of our time is how we should deal with the Monster known as Frank," she began. "He was created by illegal experiments but now has been 'alive'—if that's the word—for three years. Should he be killed? Should he remain locked up? Should he be set free? What are your thoughts?"

The studio audience had not been primed for the topic, although some might have anticipated it. The Pope sat back and tented his fingers as if he was considering the question for the first time, even though he had long known what he wanted to say.

"The Church believes in the protection of life in all cases. This has not always been a popular decision, and people have disagreed with us on different points. All we can do is try to persuade others to share our view of the sanctity of life, whether it is someone facing the death penalty where we would prefer a life sentence, or the product of a violent sex crime where we would argue that there are not one but two victims."

These were contentious points, and there was some rustling in the audience. The Pope put up his hand.

"I will not try to convince anyone on these matters today." He turned to Oprah, "You asked about Frank. Whatever the circumstances of his creation, I see in him another example of the miracle of life. And where there is life, there is evidence of the hand of God. I think your government is right to prevent such experiments in the future. The creation of life in this manner is presumptuous and beyond the natural order of things. And yet the fact of Frank's existence says to me that he, too, has a part in God's plan. Frank has indicated that he not only wishes to acquire knowledge, but to be a moral creature, to know right from wrong and act accordingly. Thus, while we cannot know if he has a soul as you and I do, it is clear he is neither an animal nor an object. If we are obligated to honor all life as sacred, then we must honor Frank's life as well."

Having delivered himself of his homily, the Pope sat back and favored both Oprah and her audience with a smile. There were a few moments of silence as the pontiff's words sank in. And then the audience burst into applause. He had cut the knot. By separating Frank from the illegal experiments which had brought him to life, he allowed the condemnation to fall where it belonged, on those who had conducted the illicit activities. It was perfectly in keeping with the Pope's views to make the distinction between criminals and the life produced by their actions. But by keeping the focus on Frank, he managed to unite people who disagreed with his church's position on other issues. The tide had turned. Public sentiment now strongly favored sparing Frank's life.

Two months later, the court hearing *In re: Frank* ruled that Frank was a sentient creature capable of taking care of himself. They said there was no valid argument for his continued confinement and that, therefore, he was legally free. Beyond that, the court said it was unable and unwilling to rule any further. Upon his release, the State University offered him a scholarship, an on-campus apartment, and a stipend. Considering their personnel were responsible for his existence, it was the least they could do. He graduated summa cum laude that spring and finished up his masters' degree in record time. He entered the school's doctoral program that fall. And that's where he met Samantha.

CHAPTER TWO

Let me tell you a bit about my daughter. If Samantha was a different person, this story would have played out quite differently. But Joanne and I have just the one child and, as anyone who knows me knows, Sam is the light of my life. As often happens with fathers and daughters, we have a special bond. As I enjoy telling her, I kind of have to love her. That's my job. But I also like her. She's smart and determined, but not at all full of herself.

When she was little, I could make her laugh and get through to her when the other adults, including her mother, could not. When she was older, she could make me laugh. She would often present an odd or offbeat take on whatever subject we happened to have under discussion, which made our conversations endlessly fascinating. As a parent, naturally, I never stopped worrying about her, but even when I was concerned over one thing or another, I would never be too worried. She had a good head on her shoulders.

That was confirmed for me when she dumped one boyfriend in high school for being too controlling. He was jealous of her male friends even after she reassured him that she had one boyfriend, and the rest were just friends who happened to be boys. When he didn't get it, he was history. I asked her how she felt about that.

"You told me to watch out for the red flags, Dad," she said.

"Oh yes I did," I beamed, with a sense of satisfaction. She was nobody's patsy.

So, when she finished her freshman year of college and announced that she would be taking her degree in philosophy, I tried to respect her decision. It wasn't easy. My world is more practical. I'm a banker: I like things to be concrete. Money comes in. Money goes out. Everything went into nice, neat columns, and added up at the end of the day. So long as everything balanced out, I never had to worry about why.

Thus, when Sam announced she would be pursuing a path where all she would be asking is why, and then speculating on which answer might come closest to some ideal "truth," I got nervous. We weren't spending a small fortune to send her to college in order for her to become the smartest barista at the coffee shop. I regret to say that my initial reaction to her announcement was not as supportive as it might have been. Indeed, thinking back on it, I recall Joanne and I looked at her like she was insane.

"What are you going to do with a philosophy degree? Sit in the marketplace and carry on like Plato?" I asked. "You know, they ended up making him drink poison."

"Exactly," added Joanne, "What sort of job do you think you're going to get after graduation?" I didn't think she was being entirely unreasonable. In fact, I was making a mental note to check if one could get into business school with a B.A. in Philosophy.

Sam was having none of it. She looked at us not so much defiantly as confidently. "What sort of job? Any sort of job I want."

This was the problem with arguing with a philosophy major. As her college career progressed, we found that winning such an argument was easier said than done. Her maintaining a 4.0 average didn't hurt, either.

Eventually, I made my peace with it. It wasn't so much that I thought this was the path she ought to be on, as finally coming to the realization that I had the chance of the proverbial snowball in hell of talking her out of it. I have no idea where she got this stubborn streak. Probably her mother's side of the family.

"Look," I said to Joanne one evening, "she could go on to law school. Perhaps she'll want to pursue an academic career and teach philosophy. Maybe she'll become a great philosopher herself. She could write important works, weighty tomes that we'll leave out on the coffee table with pride and never actually read ourselves. Let's face it: she's smart and committed to her goals. When has she ever disappointed us?"

That was a question I probably shouldn't have asked. Sam no doubt could have offered me an extensive proof demonstrating that expressing rhetorical questions couldn't actually affect reality, nor were they even able to cause the situations that would refute the premise of the question. Just because I had indicated she had never disappointed us didn't create some perverse spirit which caused her to follow a path that would lead to her doing so. The logic on that was ironclad. I wasn't superstitious.

Meanwhile, if you refuse to walk under a ladder or toss salt that you accidentally spilled over your shoulder—"just to play it safe"—you may suspect what I had done. I had tempted fate.

It was a mere two weeks later that Sam came home for Thanksgiving vacation with her new boyfriend. For a father, meeting his little girl's new boyfriend is always fraught with tension. It's inevitable, I suppose. If this was to become permanent, he would supplant me as the most important man in her life, something I might not like but I was forced to admit was the natural order of things. All I could ask was that he was normal, sane, productive, and absolutely devoted to making Samantha the most important thing in his life, even at risk of forfeiting his own. I didn't think that was too much to ask.

So, with a smile pasted on my face, I was ready to greet this latest pretender to the throne. Joanne opened the door, and there was Samantha, scruffy in the current collegiate style, but still our beloved daughter. How many more times would she recognize returning to us as "coming home?" I wanted to treasure every moment. And then I noticed she wasn't alone. Of course not. She said she was bringing a guest. The figure hulking behind her was immediately recognizable by his ashy gray skin. Joanne and I stood in the doorway, frozen in place. There couldn't be two people in the world who looked like him.

Beaming, Sam made the introductions. "Mom, Daddy. I want you to meet Frank," she chirped, with a smile overlaying a tone of voice that made it clear that we had better get used to him. I was more than stunned. I was completely frozen in place. It was Joanne who had the presence of mind to realize that by keeping them at the front door, we were as much as announcing his arrival to the entire neighborhood. She quickly and deftly pulled me back to allow them into the house.

After they were inside, and Joanne had shut the door, Frank put down their luggage and took my hand to shake. It was cool and somewhat leathery to the touch. "I'm very pleased to meet you," he said, his voice much more adult and modulated than in those earliest interviews. "Sam has told me so much about you."

"And she hasn't told us anything at all about you," I blurted out.

"Daaaad," she said, in a tone that hadn't changed since she was four.

Frank now took Joanne's hand and leaned over to give her a kiss on the cheek. Turning to me, he gave me a broad smile indicating either that he was happy to be welcomed into our home, or else would soon be bringing it all down in a fiery apocalypse. "It's a pleasure to meet Sam's parents. I truly look forward to giving you both every opportunity to get to know me."

We would soon learn a great deal about him. Given his unusual and very public history, there was no need to keep secrets. He was very open, often volunteering information before Joanne or I could gather our thoughts enough to formulate a question. We learned that although he had no memories of whatever life his body had lived before being reanimated, the neural pathways already established allowed him to learn things the previous inhabitant of his body would have known. Thus, he had an adult command of English within weeks of his "birth," but had to struggle with higher math as he otherwise breezed his way to a college degree. As we shared meals, we learned that he ate and digested food just like any other human although he was occasionally surprised by things we took for granted. At our Thanksgiving meal, he seemed fascinated by the cranberry sauce whose shape indicated its origins in a can, but he savored every dish, complimented Joanne on the turkey, and even had seconds.

He shared with us that he wasn't going through the motions, but truly enjoyed the experience of eating just as we did, perhaps more so, as he commented on the variety of tastes and textures.

"My digestive system is human from one end to the other," he volunteered, adding that, indeed, all of his bodily organs functioned normally.

"Do they ever," said Sam with a not quite suppressed giggle.

"TMI, dear," Joanne replied, quickly cutting off that line of discussion.

When we finished that initial dinner, Joanne suggested that Frank and I go out on our enclosed back porch for some brandy and cigars. This was an affectation of mine that she generously and kindly indulged me out of respect for the fact that I had spared her a lifetime of the more typical male time-wasting pursuits of golf or watching televised sports. My limited athletic activity consisted of the billiard table we had in the rec room. If a few times a year I wanted to indulge in a cigar, that was perfectly fine with her… as long as said indulgence was outside.

Thanksgiving came during an unseasonably mild November, and the evening was rather pleasant. This was the first time the two of us had been alone together. I could tell the conversation was going to be awkward. I offered Frank a snifter of fine brandy that I kept on hand for such occasions. He made a show of inhaling the aroma of the amber liquid within. Whether he was actually enjoying it I couldn't tell, but it was clear he knew what was expected of him.

"I suppose I should ask if you're allowed to drink," I said, breaking the silence.

"By whom?" he asked. "Legally I'm an adult. The only one I answer to is me—provided I obey the same laws that apply to everyone else."

Wonderful. This was going to be another exercise in walking through a conversational minefield. "I'm sorry, I didn't mean to offend," I said, trying to smooth things over. "I was just considering how alcohol might affect you."

"You mean am I going to go on a rampage and frighten the villagers?" There was a pregnant pause, and I must have looked at him blankly, because he broke the tension with a laugh. "Actually, because my blood flows a bit more slowly now, it takes much more liquor for me to get tipsy. I should be absolutely fine, although I promise you that I will not to operate any chainsaws or other machinery while I'm under the influence." There was another pause while I tried to digest what he was saying. And then he laughed again.

This was certainly turning into my most memorable Thanksgiving. Here I was, sharing a brandy with a monster with a sense of humor. Even more complicated, he was a monster who was dating my daughter. I was at a complete loss for words. Not sure what to do next, I lit up my cigar. It suddenly occurred to me that he had been invited out for brandy *and* cigars, and so without really thinking, I offered him one. It was clear that he had either been prepared for this or had, amazingly, been exposed to it prior to coming into my home. Perhaps the previous occupant of his body had been a cigar aficionado.

He expertly cut off the tip and inserted it in his mouth. I lit another match and brought it to the front of his cigar. I had not anticipated his reaction.

"Arrggh! Fire bad!" he shouted, waving the flame away. Oh no, what have I done? As I looked on in shock, wondering whether the brandy had, indeed, gone to his head, Frank burst out in a roar of laughter. "That joke never gets old. Now you're supposed to say, 'Wait, wait, I was going to make espresso.'"

Great. That's what I really wanted to make this Thanksgiving complete: a monster who likes brandy *and* cigars *and* Mel Brooks movies.

Frank took my hand with the still-lit match and applied it to his cigar, then sat back and exhaled a perfect smoke ring. In the dusk, I could almost imagine he was normal. Almost.

We sat in silence for several minutes, puffing on our cigars and sipping the brandy, both activities proving to be helpful in taking the edge off the moment. Finally, he broke the silence.

"Samantha is a wonderful girl… woman. She's made me see things in my studies that have opened my eyes. I'm sure you must be very proud of her."

I have to admit it: you can never really go wrong praising a child to his or her parent. Feeling the warmth of the brandy, I relaxed and took in his praise. "I am. I always have been," I said. "But I can't say I always understand her work. Tell me, how has she helped you?"

Frank paused as if he wasn't quite sure where to begin, and then he just plunged in. "My creation is arguably the biggest crisis in the field of bioethics. There's no avoiding it. Even after the court's decision was made to recognize my right to continue my new life, the experiments which led to my creation have remained universally condemned… and rightly so. Please understand, I have no desire to create a humanoid army to conquer the Earth, no matter what you may have seen on the internet."

"Well, if it's on the internet, it must be true," I offered. I think I was feeling the effects of the brandy myself.

Frank chuckled. "However, I don't think the experiments were entirely worthless. I'd like to establish rules to allow strict parameters for certain types of tests, and Sam has shown me a philosophical structure that can be used to do so without crossing over into those things…" and here he paused dramatically, "…that man was not meant to know."

"I'm not sure I'm following," I said, taking another puff on my dwindling cigar for want of anything else to do.

"We need to clearly state what sorts of experiments can and cannot be permitted. Anything involving consciousness should not be allowed, obviously, but what about body parts?"

I poured myself a touch more brandy, not quite sure where this was going, and not so sure that I wanted to know. "Body parts?"

"Particular organs. A heart, a liver, a pancreas. If we could reanimate organs that could be used to replace diseased or damaged ones, would that not be serving the public good? Is a person with a reanimated liver any less human than one who receives a traditional transplant?"

"I suppose not," I replied, fairly certain this was a candidate for the most unusual Thanksgiving evening conversation ever. I don't know who would give out such an award, but I was sure we'd be eligible for it.

"I'm glad you agree," said Frank, oblivious to my bafflement. "While my focus has been on the consequences of such work in medicine, Samantha has focused on its impact on society. It's something that's very close to her heart. Indeed, our hope is to work closely together after we get our degrees."

"She hadn't mentioned anything to me."

"No, she asked me to broach the subject. You see, it's not just a combination of career interests. She and I have fallen in love. We'd like to have your blessing to get married."

You know how there are certain incidents in one's life that are just like great historic moments in leaving an indelible mark on your memory? This moment might have been one of them, but not for me. For the life of me, I couldn't remember much of anything that happened after that. However, Joanne and Sam said they'll never forget rushing out to the porch because there was a madman screaming incoherently. I was hoarse for the next several days.

CHAPTER THREE

I'm sure you can see what the immediate problem was. This being the 21st Century, my options were somewhat limited. I couldn't have Frank kidnapped and impressed into service on a ship heading to Australia, tempting though that might be. And as we're Jewish, sending Sam to a convent was right out. I suppose I could have sent her on a Birthright mission to Israel, but they were co-ed, and with my luck, she'd come back with a new peace initiative by announcing she was engaged to the son of the leader of Hamas. I was also up against the ruling that Frank was to be considered legally alive. So shooting him— assuming I was even capable of such a thing—was not only not in the cards but putting my life at risk as well. I'd probably end up missing and wind up in prison for attempted homicide. Not getting to go to the wedding would be small compensation.

Joanne and I stayed up late into the night, trying to figure out how to respond to this new state of affairs. We were all adults. Well, the jury was out on Frank's actual age, but he did have a college degree and he had been issued a driver's license, so I suppose we had to consider him one as well. What needed to be done now was a family discussion where we, speaking as the voice of experience, would try to get them to see the light of reason. We were certain that by treating this calmly and maturely and with a minimum of screaming (I had learned my lesson) we could get them to see the folly of their ways.

It would just be the four of us. Frank, of course, had no family. His previous identity was unknown and unknowable, and it was believed his remains had been selected for just that reason. We hoped that that imbalance would work to our advantage.

We gathered in the living room after Sunday lunch. Sam and Frank sat side by side on the couch, holding hands. Joanne and I sat on the opposite side of the coffee table in separate chairs facing them. We tried to look serious but loving, concerned but not worried. The message was that we wanted to have a conversation, not lay down the law. Sam saw right through us.

"Uh-oh, family council time," she said, turning to Frank. "They're going to try to reason us out of this."

"Now dear, we simply wanted to talk to you about—" I began.

"What about children?" Joanne blurted out, apparently having decided that there was no need to ease ourselves into the conversation that we all knew we were having. She had made it clear that she longed to be a grandmother someday, sometime in the far future, when she might finally admit her age or something close to it. If she still fancied that people mistook her and Sam for sisters, she realized that eventually that would no longer be the case.

"What about them?" replied Sam, apparently having decided she was going to make us fight for every inch of ground.

Joanne pressed ahead. "Do you know if the two of you can even have children? Would you really want to deny yourself the blessings of motherhood?" This from the woman who was reviewing nanny applications as soon as the epidural had worn off.

Frank chuckled. "If we can't, we can always make some in the laboratory."

Sam slapped his leg. "Not now, dear," she turned to us. "Frank's an amazing person, but he's still learning things like…" she turned back to him, "the appropriate times for humor." The smile left Frank's face as he put on a serious and sober expression that looked as if he had spent several hours practicing it in front of a mirror.

"Your mother raises an excellent point," I said. "Don't you want children? What if it's just not possible?" It's not the point I would have opened with, but it was important to maintain a united front.

"We'll worry about the alternatives if they become necessary," Sam said, ever the practical one. "We don't have to settle every last real and imagined problem before we even get started. Now, look, I know both of you love me and are concerned we're rushing into something without being aware of all the possible consequences."

Joanne and I nodded in agreement.

"Don't ever doubt that we're speaking to you out of love," I said.

"Daddy, I don't. I've told Frank all about our family…" Joanne raised an eyebrow, but Sam plunged on. "I told him that I never, for even one moment, doubt that I have your full love and support. It's made me what I am today."

I wasn't so sure that was a ringing endorsement, under the circumstances, but pressed on. "We're simply concerned that you can't even begin to imagine the problems that lay ahead, and you certainly can't be sure how things will turn out."

"Which is exactly the same way every couple goes into marriage, including the two of you. Daddy, if I remember, you told me Grandpa Joe was highly skeptical of your ability to earn a living."

The old buzzard nearly talked Joanne out of the marriage. I wonder what he would have made of this. "Well, I certainly proved him wrong," I replied, his face full of scorn passing before my mind's eye.

"Exactly. Two people deciding to get married should have their eyes open to potential problems, but in the end, it's about faith and hope, not a spreadsheet."

This is what I get for having a daughter who's a graduate student in philosophy. Why couldn't she have been a theater arts major? I felt we were quickly losing control of the conversation, but Joanne, as it turned out, was only getting started.

"You're absolutely right. It is a matter of faith, and that could be another problem," she said. "Have you given any thought about what rabbi would marry the two of you? Frank, do you even have a religion?"

Frank's answer was utterly without guile. "I'm barely four years old in real time. I'm trying to be an ethical and moral person, but in terms of a particular tradition, no, I haven't gone so far as to affiliate with one religion or another. I'm researching it, but there are so many."

For Joanne, who is the classic "three days a year Jew" who shows up for the Rosh Hashannah and Yom Kippur services, this was the wedge for which she had been waiting. "Well, then, we may be rushing into something without knowing all the details. Let me suggest we just put everything on hold until we get a chance to meet with Rabbi Goldblum. He's a very learned man, and he'll be able to tell us if such a marriage is even possible."

Sam perked up, as if she had just scored a point in her favor. "Rabbi Goldblum retired last year, Mom," she offered helpfully.

Joanne was not the least slowed down. "Well, then whoever the rabbi is."

Rabbi "Whoever" turned out to be Rabbi Wheaton, who was apparently the very model of a modern American rabbi. If the Fletcher School of Diplomacy was ordaining rabbis, Rabbi Wheaton was whom they would have turned out.

In the interim between our Thanksgiving conversations and the secular New Year, when Rabbi Wheaton joined us, Frank had taken some time to read up not only on Judaism, but on many other human faith traditions. Sam told us he even explored secular humanism.

"An atheist? My grandchild's father is not going to be an atheist," Joanne declared with finality, "Why can't he be an agnostic or Unitarian, like normal people? And is being Jewish so bad?"

"Mother," was all that Sam said in reply to this mash-up of a variety of contradictory schools of thought.

What impressed Frank was that nearly every tradition he examined was built around a variation of the Golden Rule. In the Talmud, that vast compendium of Jewish learning, the great sage Rabbi Hillel is approached by a scoffer who demands to be taught the Torah while standing on one leg. Hillel's response has come down through the ages, "What you find hateful, do not do to others. All the rest is commentary. Now go and study it."

That quirky response appealed to Frank's own quirky sense of humor, and he announced that, after careful consideration, he was going to embrace the faith of Sam's father, which was to say, mine.

"That's all well and good," Rabbi Wheaton replied, when the situation and Frank's decision was explained to him. He looked pleased, as if he had just found out the clergy placard under his windshield was getting him out of a speeding ticket. "Of course, it's not just a matter of paperwork. There's a process including some intensive study, and you will have to appear before a Bet Din—a religious court—to be questioned about your knowledge and the seriousness of your commitment, but I don't foresee any problems there."

Where I had been hoping to hear about objections and delays, Sam was hearing the "all clear" signal. "Then we can set the date for the wedding?" she asked.

"Well, there's also the matter of the circumcision."

"I think I hear the phone," said Joanne, going off to the kitchen before anyone could tell her that nothing had rung.

"Is that really necessary? It's seems to have already been done."

The rabbi sat back in his seat and tented his fingers. I don't know if he had picked this up from the Pope's TV appearance, or if it was something all clergy did. "Now we get into a touchy area."

"I'll say," I said to no one in particular.

"No, not because of the procedure itself, but of its necessity," explained the rabbi, clearly warming up to the subject. "We don't know the circumstances under which this body was circumcised. Was this the body of a Jew? We don't know, and it doesn't really matter. We are treating Frank as a new inhabitant of this body. Therefore, it is he, and not merely the body, that requires the ritual."

Sam started looking a little squeamish. "You're not taking anything more, are you?"

I turned to the kitchen. "Joanne, you need any help in there?"

The rabbi went right on. "No, of course not. While Frank's situation is unique, the conversion of someone already circumcised is not. The ceremony requires a symbolic drawing of a drop of blood, that's all."

"It may take a little longer than usual," Frank volunteered. Rabbi Wheaton looked quizzical. Sam beamed. I looked around to see if there was any of the brandy left from Thanksgiving.

Rabbi Wheaton explained that the flow of Frank's blood notwithstanding, this was not going to be a fast process. The conversion studies would take several months and would also include weekly meetings of Sam and Frank in his study to discuss what was learned and how they planned to make a Jewish home. Once that was completed, a date could be set for the circumcision and the hearing before the rabbinical court that would lead to the conversion. When Rabbi Wheaton pointed out the conversion might not be accepted by all streams of Judaism, I tuned out. I was not interested in internal religious politics. I was interested in my daughter and her future happiness.

And what I saw was, if there had ever been any doubt once Samantha set her mind to something, there was going to be a wedding.

CHAPTER FOUR

Conversations around the family dinner table became more and more peculiar. One evening, apropos of nothing, Frank announced, "I can't wait until we celebrate Hoshanah Rabbah next fall." It turned out that Frank was very enthusiastic about the conversion studies he was undergoing with Sam. For my own part, I had no idea what he was talking about.

"What's that?" I asked, politely, hoping we could quickly change the subject.

"See, I told you," said Sam, "There's a lot of the Jewish calendar that most Jews don't know anything about."

Frank seemed baffled. "Then how do you mark the transition from Succot to Sh'mini Atzeret?"

"I thought our congregation was Conservative," said Joanne, picking at the shrimp in the Chinese takeout we had ordered for dinner. "Have they suddenly gone Orthodox? I'm not sitting in a sex-segregated balcony."

"Mom, Daddy, we're learning a lot more about Jewish observance than we did in Hebrew School. There's a lot of stuff that's kind of interesting, especially if reinterpreted for modern times," said Sam, enjoying her vegan lo mein. "It's like I'm rediscovering something that I had taken for granted."

Frank started to explain the rituals of the obscure holiday with which he was so taken, but I cut him off. "Frank, it's wonderful that you've chosen to join the, er, chosen people. But not everyone follows every last observance. As we used to say growing up, Conservative congregations are made up of Reform Jews who hire a rabbi to be Orthodox on their behalf."

"I don't understand," said Frank.

"And that statement is the first sign that you do understand," I replied. "If you and Sam learn things and choose to be more observant than we are, that's fine with us."

"I'm not so sure…" said Joanne.

"Well, within reason," I said, plowing on. "The important thing is that the two of you follow the path that's right for you. Don't try to get her mother and me to change what we do, and we won't try to change what you do. Live and let live."

Frank seemed baffled, but Sam—bless her heart—got it. "Dear, we'll follow our own path. If Mom and Daddy are inspired by our example, that's great. But we have to respect the commandment to honor our parents, and not criticize them for not meeting the standards that we accept. Does that make sense?"

Frank pondered it for a moment, and then smiled. "I see the logic here. I'm fortunate to have you as my partner on this journey."

Joanne was having trouble following the conversation, but I picked up the gist. Moses had just come down on our side. Defusing the potential conflict may have been a greater miracle than parting the Red Sea, Cecil B. DeMille notwithstanding.

Of course, come Passover, we'd be clearing our house of leavened goods at a level we'd never before experienced, but for the moment, peace prevailed.

Now that the wedding was inevitable, it meant actual plans had to be made. I had suggested flying out to Las Vegas, to one of those chapels where the Justice of the Peace dresses up as Elvis, figuring it was no more absurd than Sam's fiancé being a reanimated corpse, but before Sam could respond, it was Joanne who shut down the discussion.

"Absolutely not. Sam is our only daughter, and this will be our only opportunity to plan a wedding," she got this dreamy look in her eyes, then turned to me and took my hands in hers. "Don't you remember our wedding day? I had imagined it since I was little girl."

Yes, I remembered it all too well. The limo driver disappeared with the maid of honor, and my best man short-sheeted the bed in the honeymoon suite. At the end of the reception, my new father-in-law came up to us to give his blessing. After embracing Joanne and kissing her on the cheek, he turned to me and said, "I give it six months."

"All too well," I said, much as I had tried to block it out.

"It was the happiest day of my life. And ever since Sam was born, I've looked forward to the day when I would get to plan her wedding." She turned to our daughter, "I want to make it the most special day you'll ever have."

Sam seemed a bit taken aback by all this new enthusiasm for planning a wedding, as Joanne was the one who seem to be raising objections about it from the start. It seemed that now that she had accepted the impending nuptials as inevitable, she could go ahead with her plans to make this the wedding of her dreams. "Um, Mom? Don't I have any say in this? It is *our* wedding, after all," she said, putting her hand on Frank's knee.

"I'm having trouble following this," Frank said to me. "Am I supposed to tag you now?"

Joanne and Sam exchanged glances and seem to come to an understanding. This was going to be a joint mother/daughter project. Joanne had the experience of having been through a wedding, while Sam would steer things in what she felt was the appropriate direction. I wasn't quite sure where that left Frank and me, but I was sure they'd be letting us know.

The two women rose as one. "We've got work to do," said Joanne.

Several days later, I came home to find a huge time chart taped up on one wall of the dining room. This provided the battle plan for the months ahead. It was a week-by-week schedule of what needed to be bought, ordered, reserved, mailed, or what have you. It was slightly more detailed than the quarterly economic reports we received at the bank from the Federal Reserve.

"When do we invade Normandy?" I asked, overwhelmed by all the things that would have to fall into place to bring this off. I idly wondered aloud how much this was all going to cost.

"It's too early to know what the final price will be. You can't put a price on happiness, after all," Joanne said reassuringly. "Besides, there's been some fluctuations on the futures market."

I wasn't sure I heard that right. "The price of soy beans is going to affect the cost of the wedding?"

"Don't be silly, I'm talking about lace. We have no idea what the wedding dress will cost."

On the far wall were pictures from various bridal magazines of a variety of gowns. Some were carefully crafted to show off the model's tattoos, an issue that had not come up when Joanne and I got married. I had to put on my reading glasses to make out the prices, which ranged from the mid-three figures to the low four figures. The most expensive was listed—before alterations—at $2,500.

"Why would anyone spend $2,500 on a dress that you would only wear for a few hours on a single day?"

Joanne insisted that they were being practical. "Don't look at it as an expense. Look at it as an investment. After the wedding, we'll have it carefully cleaned and stored, so that someday Sam's daughter or granddaughter could wear it."

"Now there's an idea," I said. "Sam, why don't you wear your mother's wedding dress? Then we won't have to spend anything on it."

Sam rolled her eyes. "Daddy don't be ridiculous."

Joanne, amazingly, agreed. "That's right. Don't be ridiculous. She can't wear my dress. It's out of fashion now."

Apparently, I was the only one here able to connect the dots. "So, if your wedding dress is out of fashion for Sam, what makes you think the dress you buy for her today is going to be in fashion twenty or more years from now?"

I was rescued from being told I was being ridiculous for a third time by the arrival of Frank, who had been given his own to-do list. First, he was to get a commitment from Rabbi Wheaton to perform the ceremony. According to Frank, the rabbi had a "window" from August 5 to August 19, and if we acted now, we could get a commitment. There was no mention if that came with a set of steak knives. Apparently, before that he'd be in Israel recharging his spiritual batteries while exploring Tel Aviv nightlife, and after the 19th, he would begin his major task for the year, of writing the only three sermons—two for the Jewish New Year and one for Yom Kippur—that most of his congregation would get to hear. It was hard work, requiring endless hours on the internet finding the right opening joke, the appropriate topical references and, if he could work it in, some reference to the significance of the holidays. We settled for August 17, a Sunday, with the rabbi performing the ceremony in the afternoon and then joining us for the celebration. We learned that if we wanted to do it on Saturday, we'd have to wait until after sundown, and thus dinner probably wouldn't be served until close to 10 P.M. Apparently a wedding disrupted the enforced rest of the Sabbath, which should have been a giveaway of what we were facing.

Frank's other task had been to scout out possible venues for the reception. Since we would be going from the ceremony right into festivities, they had to be able to hold the wedding there as well as the party. Naturally that would require a kosher kitchen—or a kitchen that could be "kashered" (a process that Frank explained involved blowtorches and a lot of washing). As we were trying to keep a low profile, Frank's research was all online. Joanne and Sam would then go and actually inspect the various sites. I offered to go along but was politely refused. Apparently, I would cramp their style. At least they didn't call me "ridiculous" again.

Then, just because our lives weren't complicated enough, we heard from one Frieda Guerrero. Ms. Guerrero knew nothing about the wedding plans, thank goodness. No, her agenda was something else altogether. She claimed that Frank was, in fact, her brother Hector, and she was challenging the court finding that Frank should be treated as an adult. She claimed that her "reanimated" brother was all of four years old, measuring his age from when he had been brought back to life and so, consequently, in the absence of her deceased parents, she should be awarded sole guardianship of Frank as well as control of any assets he might have acquired. Say, by selling the rights to his story to Hollywood.

Our bank's legal counsel recommended an attorney who had some experience with family law. I accompanied Frank to meet with him, given that lawyers were a set of creatures with whom I had a great deal of familiarity. Neal Kennerly dealt mostly with divorce and more conventional child custody cases, but his firm's practice apparently covered a wide range of law. When I spoke to him on the phone, he was not only conversant with Frank's story, but eager to take on the unique legal challenges the case presented. The fact that it might also get his name in the news might have had something to do with it as well.

We met in the library of his law firm's offices, with the matching volumes of court decisions lining the walls. We were surrounded by the majesty of the law or, as some might take it, the unending ability of people to argue about just about anything. Kennerly was a bulldog of a man in his forties, his hair showing the first hints of gray. He rose as we were ushered in and came around the long table to greet Frank with the warmth of brothers in arms who were about to go into battle together.

"I'm so very pleased to meet you," he said. "I've looked over the papers you sent, and I don't think she has a leg to stand on." He then turned his attention to me. "And you are…"

"This is Phil Levin, my father-in-law… to be," answered Frank. "He was the one who set up the appointment."

"Ah," replied Kennerly, indicating we were to take our seats. "Well, you understand that I will be representing Frank. And if there's any conflict of interest…."

"I fully understand. If you need me to leave…"

Frank interrupted. "I would be much more comfortable if he stayed."

"Very well," said the lawyer. "So, let's begin. Does this woman, Frieda Guerrero, mean anything to you? Does she stir up any latent memories of your past life?"

"None whatsoever."

"And the name Hector Guerrero?"

"Means absolutely nothing to me."

"Very good. Her complaint, such as it is, rests on the fact that her brother was a drifter who dropped out of sight several years ago, and that a blurry picture she has offered of him seems to have a vague resemblance to you. And, arguably, countless other men. We could move for summary judgment, arguing that she has failed to state a valid claim."

"That sounds very good," said Frank.

I, however, had much more experience picking up the nuances of the legal profession, and saw that this is not what he was recommending. "If I may, it sounds like that is not the course of action you think we should pursue."

Kennerly turned to me and tented his fingers. Apparently, this was not a gesture limited to clergy. "You are correct."

Frank looked puzzled. "Why don't we want to make this go away?"

Kennerly now went into full academic mode. "We do want it to go away. But we want it to go away permanently. If we get it dismissed on the flimsy record, she'll come back with more photos, or maybe some distant relative who'll claim you're the spitting image of this Hector. The last thing we want is for this case to be argued on the merits of her claim for custody."

Now notice that at this point he could have just said what his strategy was, but at $125 an hour he was in no hurry. I tried to cut to the chase. "So, Mr. Kennerly, what do you think is the best course of action?"

"DNA. We have blood samples from Frank here and from this Frieda woman, and we see if there's any genetic match up. When there isn't, case closed… permanently."

He seemed very pleased with himself. Frank didn't need me to see what the problem was. "What if there is?"

"Ah, then we have to go to our fallback position."

"And what would that be?" I asked.

"We would argue that the illegal experiments that granted Frank life had an effect on his genetic code, and that it is therefore totally unreliable."

Frank was following the discussion, if not quite the reasoning. "And how would you do that?"

"Well, here's the beauty of it. The people who conducted the experiments are all behind bars and not allowed anywhere near a laboratory. All their research has been erased and their equipment destroyed. To get them access to the material, at least so far as recreating the material at the genetic level could take years of legal action and years more of lab work, assuming they'd even be allowed to do so. In theory, we could drag this out to the point where you're legally an adult by whatever measure anyone cares to use, and that would render the matter moot."

Yes indeed, an absolutely brilliant strategy. At $125 an hour.

CHAPTER FIVE

The problem was that while Joanne might have had experience planning a wedding, and Sam had definite notions of what she wanted, and Frank was frequently consulted for his input, I was confined to my role as executive vice president of the bank. That is to say, every week or so I would be presented with a pile of bills, or amounts required to put a deposit on a hotel ballroom ($2,000), retain the future services of a photographer ($700), videographer ($1,000), florist ($200), and caterer ($900). This was a problem not only because I saw my dreams of a luxurious retirement for Joanne and myself turning into living in a one-bedroom apartment and cooking meals on a hot plate, but also because I seemed to be the only one who couldn't forget that this was not a typical wedding.

On occasion, even I slipped. One day Joanne asked me for a list of what family and friends I would want to invite to the wedding. I come from a small family, and have few friends that aren't hers as well, mostly some business associates where professional connections turned social. I gave her a list of twenty or so names, mentioning the friends I assumed she already had. I couldn't bring myself to ask how large the potential invitation list was, but I knew the invitations wouldn't be sent out until seven or eight weeks before the wedding, at the beginning of the summer. We were in the dead of winter now. There'd be plenty of time to pare the list down to a manageable size.

A week or so later, the president of the bank popped into my office—an unusual occurrence—and said, "Congratulations. Looking forward to it."

Before I could respond, she was gone. Then Harry, our internal auditor, did the same thing. Him I could question.

"Looking forward to what?"

"The wedding, of course. You must be so happy."

What I was was baffled. "How do you know about the wedding?"

If my question seemed odd to Harry, he let it pass. Instead, he reached into his pocket and pulled out a postcard. On the front was a color photograph of Sam and Frank. Frank, showing a bit more color than he did in real life, had his arm around her. She was holding a sign that read, "Save the Date!"

On the reverse was a request that the addressee mark August 17 on their calendar, so as not to miss the celebration.

"Yes, of course," I said. Playing the clueless father of the bride was not a stretch. I had no idea that they were planning these. I returned the card to Harry.

"I survived two weddings. You'll do just fine." He gave me a manly slap on the arm—sharing the experience of marrying off children had apparently made us brothers, rather than my being the person who countersigned his paycheck—and he was on his way.

"Hold my calls," I shouted to whomever was in the outer office as I closed my door. It took me a few moments to stop the throbbing in my head. When I called home, I got Sam.

"Hi, Daddy. Mom and I are leaving soon to look at floral arrangements."

"That's wonderful. Did you know about these 'Save the Date' cards?"

She laughed. "Of course I did. Frank and I had to pose for the picture."

Yes, that's right. So, everyone knew about these but me. "Why didn't it occur to you or your mother to tell me about them?"

"What was there to tell? We're just telling people to save the date."

"And everyone you sent a card to will now be expecting an invitation to the wedding."

"Hold on a second, Daddy." I heard Sam explain to her mother who was on the phone, and what I was questioning.

"Give me the phone," I heard Joanne say. "Hello, dear, there was nothing to discuss. I asked who you wanted to invite to the wedding. They were all added to the list. You got what you wanted."

I tightened my grip on the phone. "What I wanted was to see the whole list before anything went out. How many people did you tell to save the date?"

"About 300."

"Three hundred! Do we even know that many people to invite to a wedding?"

"It's all right. The wedding is in August. They won't all be able to come, but Samantha and Frank might get some nice presents from those who can't make it."

My head was spinning. "This was a solicitation for gifts?"

"Dear, don't be so mercenary. We just wanted to share the happy news."

And this is where we get into the law of unintended consequences. The cards did much more than tell family and friends to "save the date." They provided each of the recipients with something to share with *their* family and friends: they were on the invitation list for what was likely to be the most newsworthy wedding of the year, between the miraculously re-animated Frank and our daughter. Here was a story in which the whole world had an interest and, what's worse, an opinion. Unfortunately, the opinion did not always involve wanting to toast the happy couple.

It was a sunny morning around 6 A.M. a week later when the first protestors with signs arrived. "Marriage is only for two humans" was the nicest any of them said. "Monster marriage makes moral morass" was the most alliterative.

The camera crews were out there, too. It had been quite a while since Frank was in the news, and his forthcoming marriage was a big story. We turned down all requests for interviews and photo shoots. There would be no spread in *GQ* on "Cummerbunds for the Stylish Monster," and—separately or together—Sam and Frank turned down invitations to appear on *Today*, *Tonight*, *Good Morning America*, *Morning Joe*, *The Daily Show*, and, inexplicably, *SportsCenter*. Rachel Maddow promised a subdued and dignified segment, and I could see Sam was sorely tempted, but I put my foot down. There was no reason to give any interviews. People might be curious, but that was their problem, not ours. We had nothing at all to gain from any of this, and no matter how Sam and Frank came off, more attention to the wedding would only serve to stir up the crazies.

"Once you're married, you can do what you like," I told them, "but until then, I'm in charge of publicity, and there isn't going to be any."

Joanne looked out the window at the mix of protestors and press that the overworked town police were trying to keep off what was left of our lawn. Unless I put a stop to it, I was going to be the clear winner of "least popular person in the neighborhood" for the next several months. So long as this went on, traffic was snarled as demonstrators—who by now had been joined by those favoring as well as opposing the marriage—picketed. To make matters worse, the demonstrations were now a draw in themselves, as curiosity seekers drove by to have a look at the pandemonium. Meanwhile, the police were trying to make it clear to the reporters and their respective crews that there was no First Amendment right for any of them to set up shop in our rose bushes.

After several minutes of taking in this chaos, Frank got up and left the room. I wondered if he was beginning to have his doubts about throwing his lot in with humanity. When he came back he was slipping his cell phone into his pocket. "I think I may have the answer," he said.

All three of us looked at him in surprise, as this was the first time he was taking a decidedly pro-active approach. Sam smiled and went to his side. "What is it?"

"We hire a press secretary."

I couldn't believe my ears. "I just said I didn't want any publicity."

"And I agree," he replied, amiably enough. "Unfortunately, they don't." He gestured vaguely to the mob outside. "If we do nothing, we lose control over it, and it could get worse. I just got off the phone with one of the public relations people at the university. His suggestion was that to rein in the beast, we have to feed it. That doesn't mean we have to do interviews, at least not now, but we should give them an occasional photograph, say of Sam in her wedding dress, with brief press releases so they can report *something*. He said we could even spin it to our advantage, such as announcing that part of our plans will include establishing a charitable trust for some worthy cause, like a scholarship, and it would be set up at your bank."

This was not a bad idea, but that mob out there didn't look like they could be controlled by a press release or a photo. "What happens when they start asking for more?"

Joanne stood up. "Then I could agree to do an interview, saying that the privacy of the bride and groom should be respected until after the wedding."

"I don't know…" I began.

"Frank is right," said Sam. "It's not a perfect solution, but it buys us some time, and gets the media off of our backs for a little while.

Eventually, Frank and I will have to decide how to handle this ourselves…"

"We're not going to abandon you after the wedding," said Joanne.

"I know that, Mom, and I know we can always count on your support, but it will be time for us to take on full responsibility for our own lives."

Frank continued, "The person I spoke to knows someone who's willing to work on a part-time basis, and I invited him to come over this evening, to see if it works." He turned to me. "If that's all right with you."

I took a deep breath. These days, this had become a major coping mechanism. "I want to scream and do a few other things unbecoming a bank executive, but instead I'm going to say two things. First, good job, Frank. You focused on the problem and a possible solution. We'll meet this person tonight and see what he can do. Second," and I turned to Sam and, especially, Joanne, "No more surprises. I want to know what's going on before it happens."

They nodded, apparently chastened. Of course, there would be more surprises.

We had taken to ignoring the doorbell, as it was inevitably some reporter or protestor or nosy neighbor who had somehow managed to slip through the gauntlet outside. However, Frank had received a phone call a few minutes earlier, and we knew who this was. Joanne went to the door herself, and even down the hall from the entranceway, we could hear the roar of the crowd, the shouted questions, the police struggling to hold people back. They had been told that Tom Hammer was expected. He was actually Thomas J. Hammer, III, of a long line of public relations people. I had no idea it was a hereditary job but, apparently, he was "of counsel" to the family firm that had been founded eighty years ago by his great-grandfather, Maxwell Hammerstein.

Joanne brought him into the living room, where we had the blinds drawn and were huddled like primitives around a cave fire, only in our case it was the television on which we had just seen Joanne wave to the crowd and then hustle the young man inside. Frank stood to shake his hand and introduce everyone. There was an awkward moment as we tried to figure out how to proceed, and it turned out that there was something to be said for genetics. Tom took control of the room, and immediately put everyone at ease.

"Thank you for inviting me to participate in your happy event," he said to Frank and Sam.

"Participate? Does that mean you're a volunteer?" I asked hopefully.

"Dad."

"No, it's okay. You're all undoubtedly under a lot of stress. You're not celebrities. Except for Frank here, you haven't any experience being in the public eye," Tom turned to me. "Probably the biggest public spotlight you've been in was representing your bank at a Kiwanis luncheon."

"Rotary Club, actually."

Tom smiled. "If I was buying a house and needed a mortgage, I'd come to you. You're the expert. When it comes to managing the press, I'm the expert. I'm here to help."

Joanne smiled. Frank and Sam nodded agreeably. After a moment, I realized they were all looking at me. "Okay, help. What are you going to do?"

Tom looked down at his shoes which, if I was any judge, suggested someone making an extremely nice living from his work. He caught his breath and began his spiel. "Tomorrow morning, I have a series of meetings with the cable news channels, the networks, and the local press. I explain to them that we are not looking for publicity and are not likely to be granting interviews or providing media access to the event itself."

"Not likely?" I said. "Not at all."

"Let me explain how this works. This wedding is news. There's nothing you can do about that. However, if you provide them with a trickle of occasional news items, you can keep them happy. A picture of the bridal gown or wedding cake. You're not doing any interviews, and that's fine, at least for now, but there are other people who we can send out. Would the rabbi performing the ceremony be willing to talk about the challenges raised, perhaps discuss the conversion process that Frank is undergoing?"

"That hambone? You'll be lucky if he doesn't demand his own show."

"Dear, I'm sure Rabbi Wheaton would be happy to help out," said Joanne.

"Wonderful," said Tom, leaning back on the couch and relaxing for the first time. "This should work for most of the time between now and the wedding, but eventually they're going to want to see the bride and groom."

Sam perked up. "Frank and I could do Rachel Maddow's show. I know she's interested and would give us a sympathetic hearing."

Before I could object, Tom shook his head. "Here's the problem with doing that too soon. You do MSNBC, and then CNN and FOX will want interviews as well. And when they don't get them, they'll start looking for other people, perhaps an old boyfriend, or a disgruntled supplier upset that he or she didn't get the contract. Then the broadcast networks have their morning shows and their magazine shows, and there are plenty of other cable outlets with special slots—the Discovery Channel is already planning on pre-empting 'Shark Week' for 'Monster Week'—and the feeding frenzy starts all over again. My suggestion is that we hold off on any interviews until closer to the event, when everyone understands how to deal with someone getting an exclusive because of time limitations. Somebody wins and everybody else has to report second hand. That's the way it goes."

Joanne looked frazzled, as if the rug had just been pulled out from under her. "Is it really that complicated? What can we do in the meantime?"

Tom beamed. "We do a press conference. Each of the major outlets gets a seat, and the feed is offered to all media. Everyone gets the exact same material, and you do it one fell swoop. I think Frank, or maybe Frank and Sam, can do thirty to sixty minutes. Everyone will be so busy cutting and recutting the material to make it unique to their brand that they should leave you alone for a while. After the wedding, when you're back from your honeymoon, if you want to give Rachel an exclusive interview, that can probably be arranged."

They all looked at me again. "I don't like it," I said. Everyone started talking at once, but I put up my hands to silence them. "I don't like it, but I don't see that we have another alternative. Tom, my question for you is this: if we follow your plan, does that make *that*"—and I gestured beyond the curtains—"go away?"

"As far as the press, yes. I will make it clear that there will be zero availabilities on site, meaning here, and that those outlets that continue to infringe on your privacy will be locked out of any information down the road. This is a feature story, not the outbreak of war. As long as the press is fed, they'll play by the rules."

Frank spoke up. "What about the rest of them?" Good question. I was beginning to see that he might be an asset to the family after all.

"The protestors, pro and con, have the right to demonstrate, but this is a residential neighborhood, and you are doing nothing to make your home the locus for this event. With the cooperation of the local police, we can probably get them to enforce reasonable time, place, and manner restrictions. However, I suspect that once the press is gone most, if not all, of them will depart as well."

For the first time in days, I felt like things were getting under control. Tom's schedule would not survive, but we could not know that. I may have been living in a fool's paradise, but for the moment, the chaos would be pushed back.

I turned to Frank. "Son, it looks like you got us a press agent."

CHAPTER SIX

This wedding was turning into a series of fires. No sooner had we put one out than another one would flare up. One would think it couldn't possibly be this complicated. As Tom had promised, the press had faded away, happy with the tidbits he tossed them every few weeks. He knew that I really didn't want any part of it, but I reluctantly agreed that a scholarship fund in honor of the newlyweds could be set up at the bank. To my amazement, people were so eager to have some connection with Sam and Frank that donations started flooding in as soon as it was announced.

Within a month, we had half a million dollars in a trust, according to the press release Tom drafted, complete with quotes that were attributed to me. It went on to explain that it would be the source for an annual grant to a student looking for an ethical way to apply cell regeneration for the good of humanity without crossing over into "things man was not meant to know." I thought that was a bit melodramatic but, as it turned out, Tom was right. Somehow, it kept everyone happy, including the board of directors at the bank, as they watched the fund continue to grow.

And then, one day, we heard from one Rev. W. Allen Twitchell. After everyone else had given up demonstrating, he remained picketing in front of our house, showing up dutifully at 9 A.M. Taking an hour off for lunch at noon, and then returning for the 1 to 5 shift, Monday to Friday. According to the flyer he gave to the few people who were willing to engage him, he took Sunday off for the Lord's Day, and took Saturday off out of respect for our Sabbath, which put him one up on Joanne and me.

An evangelical minister from a group so obscure it seems to have consisted solely of his own congregation, his approach was unique. He claimed that the marriage was taking place under fraudulent purposes and could not be countenanced under the law. Twitchell believed that the only permitted marriage was between a man and a woman, but he had lost that battle when the Supreme Court ruled otherwise, and he reluctantly accepted that—at least so far as secular law was concerned—a marriage could exist between two men or two women. It was his contention that Frank was not a man.

At this point, I had come to the conclusion that there was a special place in hell for theologians and attorneys. According to Twitchell, the court in *In re: Frank* had not found him to be a man as understood in the law, but merely an independent being entitled to make its own way in the world, like a corporation. No one would argue that Dupont or ExxonMobil could marry a human being, or that a corporate merger was in any way akin to a marriage. And so, he was challenging the right of the state to issue a license to allow such a wedding to take place.

There were several problems with this. First, Rev. Twitchell could not show he was a party to the wedding or would in any way be injured by it should it be allowed to take place. In legalese, this meant he lacked "standing," although he seemed to have no problem with that in front of my house five days a week. Second, even assuming that his sect did not accept Frank as a man, that had no bearing on whether Rabbi Wheaton could so find and, indeed, the courts were loath to get into such disputes of religious doctrine.

Frank's lawyer, Neal "$125 an hour" Kennerly, saw the case as one that could be resolved quickly, while also paying for his daughter's orthodontia. With only three continuances—two from our side and one from Twitchell's—the matter finally had its day in court where. In under five minutes, the ruling came down against the minister. Indeed, the judge said that in all his years on the bench, he had never heard a case that required so much chutzpah to bring into court. Twitchell was not familiar with the word, which led to my witnessing an extraordinary scene where I heard "chutzpah" explained by Judge Ramkumar Murgadoss. How a judge whose parents came from Mumbai explained the Yiddish word often simply translated as "nerve" or "gall" to an evangelical minister from Oklahoma might have rendered the case an amusing footnote. Unknown to us, Twitchell was spending less time laughing and more time trying to figure how to redefine his case.

Meanwhile things were getting marked off the checklist as orders were placed, decisions were made and—especially—checks were written. A few days had gone by without any major shocks or surprises, and it looked like I was going to be able to hold off reordering the economy-sized 200-pill supply of my favorite antacid. Things had returned to their normal routine, which should have been a warning sign.

It was end of the week, shortly before lunch, when I heard some sort of uproar down the hall, towards the tellers lobby. I glanced at the security screens to make sure I shouldn't be hitting an alarm. Standing in the middle of the lobby was Frank and, as happened nearly everywhere he went, he was creating a fuss simply by his presence. Whether it was his standing at over six feet or the grayish, leathery pallor to his skin, he looked out of the ordinary, and with everyone in town following the wedding plans—insofar as Tom had made them public—he wasn't easily mistaken for a basketball player having an off day. I figured I better find out what this was all about.

When I came out into the lobby, there were the usual gawkers, including a few among the tellers. It's not like Frank had been a frequent visitor to the bank. Off the top of my head, I couldn't recall him ever coming here by himself. I walked over to where he was shyly signing autographs for a trio of giggling teenage girls.

A fourth girl, not part of the group, stood to the side as if awaiting her turn. Her glasses and baggy sweater suggested that her agenda was different than that of the autograph hounds. After returning the signed notepads, Frank turned his attention to the loner, as she nervously pulled a strand of dirty blonde hair back from her face.

"You're really him?" she began somewhat bluntly.

Frank had become an old hand at these public encounters and realized that most people simply wanted to share a moment with him so that they'd have a story they could tell others about how they "met the monster." Well, perhaps it was kinder than that. Frank smiled and said, "The one and only." When she said nothing further he added, "They tore down the lab after that."

It was a way to speed the conversation to its conclusion, but instead she lit up. "Yes, I know. That's why I want to go to the university next year to study bioethics." She paused, and then said in a quieter voice, "Will you be teaching there?"

"Why, I don't know. There's been some talk about getting me into the classroom, but nothing definite. Perhaps I should go ask. Thank you for prompting me."

The girl looked like she was ready to teeter over into a giggling fit and I thought I'd better rescue them both. "Frank were you looking for me?"

He turned to me with an expression I couldn't quite read, and then reached out to shake my hand. He had gotten better at it since we'd first met. Not too hard, not too weak. A firm "hail fellow, well met" handshake.

"Ah, where are my manners? This is Phil Levin, my father-in-law to be," he said, indicating me, "And this is…"

"Madelyn Teich," she said, "I'm hoping to study with Frank this fall at the university."

"And I must introduce you to Sam, my beautiful bride. She's doing research there as well."

I don't know if that's the answer she was expecting, but I took her silence as an opportunity to whisk Frank away. "Pleased to meet you. You might want to pick up an application for our scholarship fund on your way out."

Before either of them could say anything further, I put my arm around Frank and directed him down the hallway to my office. It was an awkward moment, but there wasn't much I could do. In a short time—growing shorter by the day—Frank would be family. It wouldn't be right to tell him not to come to the bank, as if my association with him was a source of embarrassment. If Sam was marrying some big movie or sports star who was instantly recognizable to the public, his appearance would prove disruptive as well, although perhaps a bit easier to take. As they say, you have to play the cards you were dealt.

When we got to my office and I could close the door, I asked him what brought him to the bank, hoping he wouldn't say, "My feet." His humorous repartee still needed a lot of work.

Instead, he seemed a bit nervous. Maybe it was the fact that he was sitting in the seat usually taken by a prospective home buyer or small business owner seeking a loan and worrying about not getting it. If a piece of furniture could absorb nerves, this chair would have been reduced to a pile of tinder. I walked us over to the sofa and chairs on the other side of the office. They were rarely used because reviewing a loan application isn't supposed to be a social event, but my position warranted a large office, and situations arose, like now, where conversation shouldn't be held across a desk.

When we were settled, I decided to try to help Frank ease into whatever was troubling him. "So, what new territories have our brides conquered this week?"

"Pardon?"

"What's off the checklist?"

"Oh, right. The take home gifts."

I asked him to repeat it, as I knew I couldn't have heard that right. "Take home gifts? I assumed we'd put them all in the car. Shouldn't be hard. It'll be mostly envelopes anyway, and anything really outsized will be shipped—"

"No, no, these are gifts that Sam and I give the guests."

Now I was genuinely puzzled. "Why are we giving them gifts? They're supposed to be giving *you* gifts. We're feeding them, entertaining them, running an open bar through the whole thing. Why are we giving them gifts, too?"

I suddenly had a nightmare image of Joanne and Sam joined by Oprah saying, "And you get a car… and you get a car… and *you* get a car…"

"Joanne said it's the custom now. Everyone will get a small glass filled with candies that says, 'Sam and Frank forever' with the date."

"What kind of candies?"

Frank smiled. "Joanne said if they weren't chocolate you'd never let us hear the end of it."

"That's right. Chocolate is dessert."

"But the chocolatier was afraid they'd melt, so they're chocolate inside hard candies."

Chocolatier. I shuddered. It couldn't have been the hotel or some novelty supplier. Just that word alone probably added $300 to the bill.

Frank reached into his pocket and gave me a little cloth bag with hard candies. "Thank you. I think I'll save these for after lunch." I put them on the coffee table and then turned to Frank. "So, you didn't come all the way here just to give me candy."

"No…" he began, as if not quite sure what to say, and then evincing a look of resolve which was clearly visible across his face, he said, "I wanted to discuss the wedding party."

"What part of it?"

"No, not 'what.' Who. Sam has decided that she doesn't want a whole parade of ushers and bridesmaids, so we're each picking one.

She's asked her cousin Susan to be maid of honor, and Susan has accepted."

Susan was the daughter of Joanne's brother, and she was also an only child, a couple of years older. They'd always been like sisters growing up. "Good choice," I said.

"And the nice thing is that the maid of honor pays for her own dress."

"Well, I guess we can afford those going away candies now."

Of course, that wasn't why he'd come, either. Sam could have told me this over dinner some night. It's not like there would be other friends or relatives who would be put out that they hadn't been picked or made to buy hideous bridesmaids dresses.

"So, what I can do to help you, Frank? Have you picked your best man? One of your professors or fellow grad students?"

"Yes and no. I've picked someone, but I haven't asked him yet. I'd like it to be you."

That was not what I had been expecting. After the initial shock of meeting and discovering his relationship with Sam, I'd come to like Frank, and appreciated his methodical way of thinking things through. If this bioethics thing didn't work out as a career, there could be a place for him at the bank. Still, this was out of the ordinary.

"This comes as a complete surprise, Frank, and it's somewhat unusual. No, let me correct that. It's entirely unusual. I'm not even sure what the protocol is."

"Sam and I are going over the wedding ceremony, and while we're going with the traditional Jewish service, we don't feel bound by some of the customs that have accumulated across the years. So instead of the father 'giving away' the bride, Sam will walk down the aisle with her mother, so Joanne will have her moment in the spotlight. As for you, you'll already be up there with me, and just have to make sure you have the rings. That's a pretty important job. You think you can handle it?"

Even I couldn't miss the twinkle in his eye. "My job is handling the bank's assets. I think I can hold onto a couple of rings for a few hours."

"Oh, and you'll have to give a toast at the reception."

"I've done my share of public speaking. I think I can do that."

Frank stood. "Then it's settled. Thank you."

I stood, and Frank gave me a hug. It was getting a little less awkward. "And I'll already be in a tux, so it's not like I need special clothes."

Frank started to head out. "Thank you… Dad. You're really the one male friend I've developed a close bond with these past few months. You've been showing me what it's like to be human, or human again."

Now I may have started to blush. "It's nothing any loving father wouldn't do to welcome a new member of the family." I turned to my desk. I really did have some work to get done today. "You and Sam will be joining us for dinner?"

"Yes, of course." He strode to the door, and then hesitated. "I almost forgot. The best man does have one other responsibility."

I gave him a big smile. "Anything, son. What is it?"

"You'll be throwing the bachelor party."

CHAPTER SEVEN

Two days later, I still hadn't quite assimilated the idea that I'd be responsible for Frank's bachelor party. I had a nightmare that I hired a stripper, and when she got down to her G-string, she started taking her body apart to shouts of, "Take it off, take it *all* off." Monday morning, I was going to quietly look into whether seeing a therapist was covered under my medical insurance, because I was beginning to wonder if I was going to make it to the finish line.

Joanne had no such problem. The "list" was her anchor, and as long as we were getting the things done that it said we needed to get done, she was happy. No, she was more than happy. She was as content as I'd seen her in all the years of our marriage. This was the moment she had been waiting for, and with the guidance of the list assuring her that she was accomplishing everything she needed to, all was right with the world.

Over the last few weeks she had ordered her dress, carefully designed so that she would stand out from the crowd as the mother of the bride, yet not upstage Sam. Somehow, for all the problems they had had during Sam's adolescence, they were now closer than ever as Joanne deftly negotiated her role as family elder and bedrock support for the bride. They had sampled hors d'oeuvres, selected the champagne for the toast (Piper Heidsieck—a personal favorite that made me cry as I realized how many glasses would get but a sip before being poured down the drain), and made sure the hotel had put aside sufficient rooms for our out-of-town guests. If General Eisenhower had had Joanne planning D-Day, I had no doubt World War II not only would have ended sooner, but each of the POWs would have gotten a lovely going away gift.

The afternoon was to be devoted to a major facet of both the wedding and reception: the music. My suggestion that we simply use Bernard Herrmann's score for *Psycho* was not even dignified with a laugh, which was just as well, because I wasn't sure I was kidding. However, I soon learned that I would not be the only one disappointed today.

It turned out that when it came to the music during the wedding, Sam and Frank would be answering to a higher authority than Joanne: namely, Cantor Eisenstein. The cantor is the musical director of Jewish services and, as such, not only is a performer, but must be an expert on liturgical music and what is and is not appropriate. Thus, although "everyone" knew what music should begin and end a wedding ceremony, neither piece would be a part of Sam and Frank's wedding.

"I don't understand," said Joanne. "Why can't they play 'Here Comes the Bride?' Don't they know it?"

"Alas, all too well," said Frank. "Cantor Eisenstein made it clear that under no circumstances would it be played at any wedding where he and Rabbi Wheaton were officiating."

"Because…" I said, hoping we could avoid several more verbal volleys before getting the answer.

"Because it was written by someone named Wagner."

"Who's Wagner?"

Frank and Joanne both pronounced the 'W' as if it was in English. It took just a moment, and then I knew what the cantor's objection was, and why nothing anyone would say could overcome it. "Vagner, dear, Richard Vagner. He's a composer remembered for two things: he was a brilliant musician—"

"Yes," said Joanne, "So why can't we use him?"

"And he was a notorious Jew hater. Worse, he was Hitler's favorite composer."

Frank nodded sadly. "I did some research after our meeting, and Sam and I agree we really shouldn't have him at our wedding."

"I'm sorry, Mom, but he was a rather nasty piece of work," added Sam.

Joanne looked like she was going to argue the point, but I think she knew it was already over. "And if Hitler's favorite dish was chicken, would we have to change the menu?"

"According to my research, he was a vegetarian," said Frank, "So you don't have to worry about that."

"Well, at least you'll go up the aisle to the traditional 'Wedding March'…"

The look on Sam's face indicated that Felix Mendelssohn's universally beloved march was also going to be barred from the ceremony.

"So, what is he going to allow? 'Hava Nagila?' What's wrong with the 'Wedding March'?"

This turned out to be a bit more complicated than Wagner. "Well, according to Cantor Eisenstein, Mendelssohn was a convert."

Joanne sat up with a start. "What's wrong with that? Frank is a convert, or soon to be, and once you're in, you're the same as anyone else."

"That's right, Mom," said Sam, who had had to attend the conversion program with Frank even though she was already Jewish. "But Mendelssohn was born Jewish and was then baptized. He converted out."

Joanne was about to say something further when Frank interrupted. "Plus, the music was written for something called *A Midsummer Night's Dream*. I don't know the whole story, but apparently the bride marries a jackass, and the cantor suggested that was not the best message to be sending our guests. I have to say that I agree with him."

I had nothing to add. From the day of our marriage to this, I don't think I've ever given a second's thought to what music ought or ought not to be played at a wedding. Joanne, on the other hand, seemed to have scored the entire soundtrack, only to be told it would all have to be replaced.

Sam reached into her carryall and pulled out a CD. "The cantor gave me a recording of Jewish wedding music that includes klezmer, Israeli music, and some modern compositions. I was hoping you could go over it and let me know what you thought."

"I suppose it wouldn't hurt to listen…"

The sun broke through the clouds. Joanne would get to orchestrate the wedding after all, and was probably already imagining friends and relatives coming up to her and demanding to know where she had found such original music for the ceremony. I didn't know how much of the credit she'd be willing to share, but I did know this: Under no circumstances were she and Cantor Eisenstein to be left alone together.

"Well, I'm glad that's all settled," I said, getting up.

All three of them looked at me. "We haven't even gotten started," said Joanne.

Sam now pulled a stack of CDs from her bag. "We have to audition the band."

Three hours later. Many versions of "Isn't She Lovely," "Celebration," and, of course, "Hava Nagila." One person threw in "Hatikvah," although I doubt even the Israeli ambassador would request his national anthem at his child's wedding.

The band leaders on some of the CDs even suggested when a song would be played. "This would be for the groom dancing with his mother," an anonymous voice hesitantly indicated, followed by "I Can't Get No Satisfaction." That was an easy reject.

"I'm afraid I'm not much help here," said Frank. "The music is unfamiliar to me, and I really can't tell much of a difference between the different versions."

"It depends on how many people are in the band and what instruments they play," explained Sam.

"And how much they cost," I muttered.

"I guess your musical memory didn't transfer," said Sam to Frank. "Does it all really sound the same?"

"Well, there was that one version of 'Sunrise, Sunset' that was very different…"

"Yes, on the electric guitar," said Joanne. "I promise you we will *not* be using that band, even if Cantor Eisenstein says that it was Moses's favorite instrument."

"Mom, I hardly think that…"

I didn't know how much more of this I could take, and there were several more CDs in the pile. Of course, this was just to get the choices to a manageable level and then go meet with the finalists. I picked up the next one in the stack. It seemed somewhat cruder than the others, as if it had been individually made, rather than mass produced as part of the band's marketing strategy. "Frank and Sam Mix" was scrawled on the front.

"What's this?"

"Oh, that's from one of the guys in my department," said Frank. "He has a band and wanted to know if we'd consider him."

Samantha reached out and took his hand. "Dear, you didn't tell me one of your friends wanted to audition."

"Well, I haven't heard it yet. I don't know if they're any good. But after listening to these others, I don't know if I would even know what 'good' sounds like."

I slipped the disc into the machine. After a moment it began. "Hi, Frank and Sam. This is Mike Mulvaney, of Mike's Madcap Music and Mayhem. As I've gotten to know the two of you, I realized that your wedding should be something extraordinary. Sure, you'll want some of the things that they play at all weddings, and we can do that, but I don't think you want your guests going home—I don't think *you* want to go home—thinking, 'Well, that was like every other wedding I've been to.'"

"I don't remember any wedding I've been to," said Frank.

"So, here's a few selections I don't think you'll be hearing from anyone else."

And with the strum of a guitar, the recording roared to life. I couldn't quite place it at first, but it sounded awfully familiar. The volume dropped as Mike said, "This could be used for the arrival of the wedding party at the reception."

The music now went full throttle, and Sam and I recognized it at the same time. It was theme from *The Munsters*, a 1960s television sitcom about a family of monsters and vampires—and a normal looking daughter.

Before I could say anything, Mike was back, "And how about this to get everyone out on the dance floor?"

Even Joanne picked up on this after the intro, as he segued into "The Monster Mash."

"Over my dead—"

"You know," said Frank, "I kind of like it."

When the song was over, Mike came back. "Here's one more to show you just how serious we are about this. Then we have some of the more expected pieces, so you can hear that we can do it. This is a song by En Vogue that was done for *Sesame Street*, and I'll bet there won't be a dry eye in the house for it as Sam and Frank have their first dance together."

After a soft introduction, it took off, as he sang about wanting a monster as a playmate and a friend. I don't know, maybe it had been a long afternoon, but it was charming. Frank and Sam were enchanted. Even Joanne seemed to melt a bit.

"I think we need to meet with them," said Samantha.

"Mike will be so pleased," Frank answered with a smile. As with picking me for best man, Frank was starting to assert his own viewpoint a bit, and he seemed happy it was so well-received.

For several months, Frank and Sam had been meeting with Rabbi Wheaton to prepare for Frank's conversion. Ordinarily they would have gone to a class as well as meeting with the rabbi, but there was no program going on at the moment, and Frank proved such an eager student that even the rabbi had trouble keeping a step ahead of him in preparing materials. Sam was amazed at how much about being Jewish she didn't know and wondered if they had made the right decision.

One Friday night, we were invited to their apartment for what we were informed was "Shabbat dinner." It turned out to be just like a regular dinner, only with a lot of blessings, including the candles, the bread, the wine, the meal itself, and even washing our hands. I was going to pass, as I had already showered before we came over, but Sam insisted. "It's easy, Daddy, and we even have the prayer transliterated into English."

So, the three of us—Joanne smiled, but would not be moved—trooped into the kitchen, where Frank picked up an odd cup with two handles, recited some Hebrew, and ceremoniously poured water over his hands, drying off before returning to the table. I picked up the cup, not certain what to do.

"Let me," said Sam, as she handed me the card with the blessing to read, and then poured the water over my hands. As she handed me the towel, she said, "It's traditional not to talk between the handwashing and the *motzi*, the blessing over the bread."

I was about to respond, but she put a finger to my lips. "Go take your seat," she said. "I'll be right in."

When she joined us, Frank stood and uncovered two braided loaves of bread that had been sitting in front of him. Holding them up, he said a blessing, and then asked Sam, "Did I do that right?"

"Perfect," she beamed. He gave us each a piece of bread he tore off from one of the rolls, and said, "It's customary to dip it in salt."

Joanne had a funny look on her face. "I remember doing this at my grandparents' when I was a little girl." She nibbled on the bread, and then said, "Are you turning into my grandparents? There's a limit to how much I can take."

"Mom, part of the process for Frank is for us to try to observe the various customs and rituals, so he'll get to see what it's like living a fully Jewish life. There are some things that are really quite meaningful."

Joanne looked at the beautifully set table and the candles that Sam had previously lit, and seemed to accept it all, but then suddenly her face stiffened. "You're not going to do that thing with swinging a chicken over your head at New Year's, are you?"

"What?" I had never heard of such a thing.

Frank laughed. "No, we're not going to do that. Rabbi Wheaton explained that it's not even a ritual. It's a superstition." Chalk one up for modernity.

After dinner, Frank led us in an abbreviated version of the Grace After Meals in English. "I'm still learning the Hebrew," he said apologetically.

"That's quite all right," I allowed. "What I'm more concerned about is whether this is all too overwhelming. You've got so much to do in reconnecting with the world. Do you really need this?"

Frank and Sam exchanged looks, and I thought this was the moment they would agree to fly to Vegas and get married by Elvis. Instead, Sam turned to Joanne and me and said, "We talk a lot about what we've learned and how it fits into our lives, and how it's a good fit."

"We didn't raise you like this," said Joanne. I wasn't clear if it was a challenge or a confession.

"Each generation has to make its own way," replied Sam. "The nice thing about our path is that we're not expected to be perfect, and if there are things that are difficult or that make no sense, or even seem antithetical, we're not rushing to adopt them. A philosopher named Franz Rosenzweig was once asked if he followed some observance which he did not. He didn't say, 'No.' Instead he answered, 'Not yet.'"

"And what about you, Frank? Are you having any second thoughts?" I had had enough anxiety preparing for my bar mitzvah. I couldn't imagine what he was going through on top of planning a wedding on top trying to figure out how to be accepted as human.

"Of course. Rabbi Wheaton says that my questions are signs I was meant to be Jewish."

"That's a cute response," I said, "but it doesn't really address the point."

"What I have found is that I have a quirky, some say ironic, way of looking at things, and as I'm reading the various Jewish texts and commentaries, I'm finding myself in sync with much of it."

"Really? I don't recall a lot of laughs in the Bible."

"Maybe you could join me at services some time. I'm constantly finding things that are amusing and make me think at the same time."

"Including some of the other congregants, no doubt."

"Let me give you an example…"

Samantha rose and started collecting the dishes. "If we let Frank get started, this can go on all night, and I think Mom wants to get going."

"Just the one…"

"Go ahead, Frank," I said, "I'm interested. And Sam, if it starts a whole new discussion, we can adjourn for the night."

Frank went to a side table which was covered with books. He picked one up. "This is our weekday prayer book." He flipped a few pages and found what he was looking for. "This is from Psalm 30. We say this every morning. 'What profit is there if I am silenced? What benefit if I go to my grave? Will the dust praise you?… You transformed my mourning into dancing…'"

We all looked at him. He looked back at us. "Don't you see?" he asked.

"I'm sorry, dear," said Joanne. "See what?"

"It's about me." He had a big smile on his face.

"And Rabbi Wheaton thinks so, too? What did he say when you told him?"

The smile left Frank's face. "He said we'd need to study further."

"Words of wisdom," I said. And that's what my life was like: a minefield. No matter what direction I went, there was the potential for something unexpected to blow up.

The following Thursday found me wandering around the university campus. I hadn't been there in a while—not since my last reunion—and I was awash in memories of simpler times. When I was an undergraduate, the drinking age had been 18, and there were more than a few beery nights at the student union. Now most of the undergraduates were underage, and liquor was harder to get. I assumed it was at least as hard to get as the marijuana I caught a whiff of as I passed one of the dorms.

Samantha had agreed to meet me at the faculty club for cocktails. As a graduate student, she was old enough, but this was hardly a place she and her peers would choose to hang out, assuming they could afford the membership fees. For me, it was all a part of doing business. I would meet clients of the bank here once or twice a month for lunch or dinner, dispensing with the nostalgia walk across the grounds that I had indulged in today.

Sam was standing at the entrance when I got there. It was no secret where it was located, but the non-descript doorway practically screamed, "Not a student hangout." As opposed to almost every other exposed space on campus, there were few if any notices taped to the walls. Professors and alumni didn't really care about the midnight showing of *Pink Flamingos* or someone seeking roommates in Florida for spring break.

"Hi, Daddy," she said, giving me a warm hug.

"I see you put on your good jeans," I noted.

"And socks," she teased, holding up one foot. "I know they have a strict dress code."

We headed upstairs to the lounge where the dress code, if it existed, was presumably less strict. I wouldn't know. The only times I ever came here I was in a suit and tie. The décor in the lounge was a lot of wood and red leather, although the deer heads and antlers that used to be part of the room's décor were long gone. *We'll join the modern age,* the room seemed to be saying, *but we won't like it.*

"Would you like to see a menu?" asked the fifty-something waiter who arrived at our table. He definitely looked old enough to remember what this lounge used to be like. At this hour, he was just going through the motions, not really expecting much business at 4:30. The dinner rush, such as it was, would be an hour or two away.

"I don't think so," I said. "I'll have an Old Fashioned, and…"

"Chardonnay for me," said Sam.

"Can I see an ID, miss?"

Sam pulled out her driver's license and university ID with a practiced flip of the wrist. She was at an age where this was still a frequent occurrence. The waiter gave a perfunctory glance at the cards and handed them back, not having expected any problem.

As he turned away, I asked, "Don't you want to see my ID?"

He looked at me as if even reacting to my small attempt at humor would be too much of a strain. "I don't think that will be necessary, sir."

When he was gone, Sam patted my hand. "I'm sure he just assumed you were comfortably over the age limit."

"By about four decades."

The waiter returned with the drinks and a silver bowl of mixed nuts. Nothing but the best for us. When he left, I raised my glass and said, "To smooth sailing ahead." We clinked glasses, and there was an awkward silence. These days, every gathering of two or more family members seemed to have a purpose, had to be carefully scheduled, and then have its agenda cross-checked with "the list." Since I hadn't said why we were meeting, Sam was concerned that I was bringing bad news.

"Sam, you can relax. I'm fine. Your mother's fine. Well, what passes for being fine these days. I just wanted to have a little father/daughter time."

"I'm *so* relieved. Let me just tell Frank." And then, with the practiced ease of her generation, she pulled out her phone and, barely looking at the screen, tapped out a message to him. It might have said, "No problems." Or it might have said, "Pckeqdj dq32dj;" Without checking, who would know?

"Were you two worried?"

She took a sip of her wine. "We couldn't tell if something was bothering you. You're not always the easiest person to read."

I took a slightly bigger gulp of my cocktail. "I am no more—and no less—nervous than any other father preparing to marry off his only daughter. With all the added excitement Frank brings to the equation, it's hard for me to imagine what would be 'normal'."

"Frank's full of surprises," she said. "Yesterday I came home and discovered that he wanted to surprise me by cooking dinner."

"How was it?"

She made a face. "We sent out for pizza. I told him after the wedding he could sign up for some classes if he wants to learn how to boil water without using every pot in the kitchen."

This was just like old times. When Samantha was little, we would go out and have adventures. It might be a movie, or a trip to the museum. And she would share with me what her world was like, whether it was the bossy friend she had in second grade or the boy she had a crush on in eighth. By the time she was in high school and college, though, hanging out with her parents wasn't cool and, truth be told, I didn't blame her. It's not like I wanted to hang out with my parents at that age. But now that she was truly entering adulthood, I was hoping we could reconnect and recapture the special relationship we had. It wasn't so much that I was jealous of Frank, which would have been foolish, as that I was resentful of the Event. The wedding had sucked up all the oxygen in the room, and I was left gasping. For the next hour, at least, we could put that aside. With luck, our time now would be a down payment on a new chapter in both our lives.

"So, let's not talk about the wedding. How is school going? When do I have to start calling you 'Dr. Sam'?"

She allowed herself a giggle—it may have been the wine—but then jumped in feet first. "You know how you used to quote that corny expression about lemons?"

"When life hands you lemons, make lemonade."

"That's it. Well, the university took what might have been a crisis that brought the whole school down and turned it into something where other research institutions are now studying us. Turning biology, medicine, and philosophy into a single cross-disciplinary study is going to transform medical procedures here and, eventually, around the world. And the best part of it is that Frank and I are in on the ground floor."

"That sounds like it calls for another drink." I signaled the waiter, but Sam indicated she was standing pat with her still half-full glass.

Instead, Sam was so enthused that she plowed right on. "We're working on cloning organs that come from the recipient's own tissues. There's no rejection because there's 100% compatibility."

I tried to keep up, instead of making her go over the things she took as a given. "Okay, that sounds promising. But what if the donor is too sick or the organ is too diseased to be cloned?"

"That's where I come in," Samantha said. "If it were possible to manipulate cells from one part of the body to grow into an organ for another part, should we do it?"

Made sense to me. In my job, money is fungible. Birthday checks that some teenager deposits in his or her bank account can be turned around and given as loans to a start-up business. I couldn't see why cells shouldn't be treated the same way. "Why not? If I need a new heart, take my thigh muscles. I'm just sitting on them."

"It's not quite that simple. And we're nowhere near being able to do that yet. But if we could, are we moving into forbidden territory? That was the whole argument over stem cells, whether life was being taken to grow new organs."

The waiter came out with my drink, and Sam looked at her now-empty glass, "Well, I suppose one more would be okay. I'm not due back in the lab until the morning." I nodded, and the waiter was off to fetch another glass of wine, and perhaps to run an ID check on the middle-aged woman sitting by the window on the other side of the lounge.

"This is way out of my league, but if I follow you, then I don't see what the problem is. Hasn't everyone already agreed on the lines that shouldn't be crossed?"

"For human life. There'll be no more reanimated corpses, so it's a good thing I got mine," she said with another giggle.

I looked at her with some parental concern. "Are you sure you need a second glass of wine?"

"Daddy, listen, the question comes from cloning animal cells. Do we allow experiments that would improve the intelligence of chimpanzees?"

"Bad idea. I saw those movies."

"What about dogs? What about squirrels who could plant explosive devices without being detected?"

Now I was getting nervous. "You can do those things?"

"No, not at all. This is all theory. And Frank, of all people, pointed out why it never has to get that far to achieve the results that we want in creating needed tissues and organs."

I was afraid to ask, but this is what happens when you invited Frankenstein's monster into your family. Things spin out of control, and even a pleasant conversation with my daughter could suddenly turn macabre. "Okay, I'll bite. What did Frank figure out?"

Sam accepted the second glass of wine, and said, "It's like the kosher pig."

Okay, even I knew that pigs weren't kosher, but how that had anything to do with cloning was beyond me. "Of course, it is. And I think you've had enough to drink now."

She brushed my comment aside. "Daddy, listen. Rabbi Wheaton had Frank studying what makes something kosher or not. For a mammal to be kosher it has to have cloven hooves and chew its cud. A pig has split hooves but no cud."

"I'm not even sure I know what 'cud' is and I don't know that I want to know this close to dinnertime..."

"Some scientists in Israel have been growing pork in a vat. They're growing cells without having an actual animal. Religious authorities have been debating whether it's technically alive at all.

If they decide that the law is inapplicable here, you could end up with perfectly kosher bacon. And if we can develop vat-grown cells that can be turned into various organs without ever having been part of a living thing until its surgically implanted, we avoid the ethical issue entirely."

Out of the corner of my eye, I noticed that our waiter was having a problem with the woman on the other side of the room. She stood up and started yelling.

"Ma'am, I'm sorry, but this is a private club, and if you're not a member I have to ask you to leave."

The ranting woman headed in our direction. "There you are, the woman who's trying to steal my brother." Samantha, who was about to go into further detail, turned to me in confusion. I stood up, ready to keep this person away from my daughter. At that moment, two members of campus security arrived, grabbed the woman by the arms, and briskly escorted her out of the lounge. A third officer came over to us somewhat apologetically.

"Do you know who that woman is?"

Sam looked blank, which left it to me. "I'm afraid I do. She's a crackpot attempting to interfere in my daughter's forthcoming marriage. Her name is Frieda Guerrero. It's somewhat complicated, but I think I best get my daughter home." I reached into my wallet for a couple of business cards. "If you call our lawyer he can fill you in on all the details. And if you need further information from me, I'm easily reachable."

As he had no reason or, really, authority, to hold us, he let me escort Sam out. When we got outside, there was no sign of Guerrero or campus security, and Sam relaxed.

"Are you okay?"

"Next spring."

"Excuse me?"

"You asked when you'd have to start calling me 'doctor.' If I keep to my schedule after the wedding, I should be defending my thesis next spring."

I looked at her for a moment, and then held her close. Right now, next spring seemed very far away.

CHAPTER EIGHT

At Sam's insistence, we went up to her department's offices instead of heading straight home. It was a short walk across campus and, at this hour, the undergraduates were largely in the dining halls. The sun hadn't quite set, but various lights started to turn on across the campus. When we got to the biology building, Sam led the way to the second-floor graduate lounge where Frank was hanging out with several other students. There were a couple of pizza boxes on the counter, and the four male students were washing down their dinner with bottles of beer.

"I can't believe you're going to let Mike play at your wedding," said one of them, daintily wiping crumbs from his blond beard with the sleeve of his shirt.

"It's not certain," replied Frank, chomping down on a slice of mushroom pizza, "but we liked the CD."

"Thank you," said a thin young man with an unruly mop of dark hair and black framed glasses, giving a little bow. "Wait until you hear our version of 'Rumania, Rumania'."

Before Frank could respond, he noticed Sam and me in the doorway. He smiled but then, as the look on her face registered, he hurried over. "Sam, what's the matter?"

She said nothing, but hugged him tightly, pressing her face against his chest.

"There was some trouble at the Faculty Club, but everything's fine," I offered, not waiting to be asked or be introduced.

Frank looked at me. "Trouble?" He gave Sam a reassuring squeeze, and then moved her back a step. "Someone was bothering you?"

"It was this strange woman...." she said, not quite sure how to explain what had happened so quickly.

"Frieda," I said, not sure how much to say under the circumstances.

Frank got very calm. Eerily calm. And then with a voice that would have cracked marble said, "What did this woman do to you?"

"Nothing, really," replied Sam. "Security hustled her out of the club before I even knew what was going on."

"She was stalking you?" Frank clenched his fist around the bottle of beer, which shattered with a sharp crack.

"Frank, take it easy," said Mike the musician, "Don't start rampaging against the villagers. You're better than that."

Frank looked as tense and angry as I had ever seen him. And that's when he suddenly saw me. We locked eyes. "You were there?"

"Yes, and Sam was never in any danger."

"You saw this woman come after her?"

"It was over before she could do anything."

Sam looked at Frank with a bit of fear. "I've never seen you like this, dear. I'm fine. I'm okay. Please don't get upset."

"No!" he shouted, "I *will* get angry. This will *not* stand."

He looked at me, and in a low and intense voice said, "Call Kennerly. I want him to get a restraining order against her."

The room became so quiet that you could hear the proverbial pin drop. Finally, Mike broke the silence. "A restraining order? Wow, they don't make monsters like they used to."

The next morning Frank, Sam, and I arrived at the lawyer's office. He had already been filled in as to what had happened, and obtained the report filed by university security. Unfortunately, the guards had let her go outside, and there was no telling where she was now. The address she had used in her initial filing turned out to be a dead end, and it was not clear that she could be easily located. Kennerly said the best we could get at the moment was a TRO—a temporary restraining order—which could be litigated once she could be served with the appropriate papers. The important thing, as far as I was concerned, was that should she appear again, we had a court order that would necessitate her being taken into custody until we could figure out how to make her permanently leave us alone.

When we left, Frank said to Sam, "I'm sorry for losing my cool. I know you can handle yourself, but you wouldn't even be having this problem if it wasn't for me."

She gave him a hug and a kiss. "We're in this together, partner. Don't you ever forget it."

I took my leave, certain I had something to do at the bank regardless of what my appointment calendar said.

That evening, we gathered in our living room for what Joanne insisted was an important session having to do with wedding invitations. I was beginning to regret demanding that no action be taken without my being part of it. After all, how hard could a wedding invitation be? You take the form, you put in the proper names, place, and date, and it's done. How little I knew.

After dinner was cleared, Joanne came out a pile of binders and envelopes. "Tonight," she said, "we're going to construct the invitation." She then handed Sam, Frank, and me thick envelopes. Without even looking inside, I recognized them as invitations to weddings we had attended.

"You saved these?" I asked, somewhat surprised.

"Of course," said Joanne, "I knew that they'd come in handy someday. Now, before we begin, I'd like you to look inside your envelope and tell me what it says."

I opened my envelope. It was for my nephew Bobby's wedding last year. "It says Bobby and Janet are getting married on June 16 at the Springfield Country Club, reception to follow."

Frank opened his envelope. "Guido and Stan are pleased to take their vows on October 10 at the Unitarian Church," he read. "In lieu of gifts, please consider a donation to the Human Rights Campaign."

Joanne looked at us without comment, then turned to Samantha. "And what does your invitation say?"

Samantha had spread out the contents of the envelope in front of her. "It says that Nita and Richard will be getting married on November 14 at 2 P.M. Both his and her parents are paying for the wedding, which will be a religious service. The bridesmaids will be dressed in light blue, possibly aqua. The floral arrangement will include peonies. And they planned ahead long in advance of the wedding."

Joanne beamed. Sam smiled with satisfaction. Frank and I looked like we were watching a foreign movie without the benefit of subtitles. I refused to say anything, but I couldn't control Frank. "How did you get all that?"

"It's obvious," she said with a cryptic smile.

Frank took the invitation from Sam and held it up to the light. "I don't see anything hidden."

Joanne took the invitation from him. "That's because it's not hidden. You just have to know how to read it."

My wife had apparently been freelancing with the National Security Agency, specializing in cryptography. "Okay, since nobody's leaving until we all understand this, please tell us how we use the right code for wedding invitations."

I'll say this for Joanne. She was not a sore winner. Having achieved surrender, she was ready to move ahead, rather than take a victory lap. "Let's start with the envelope. What do you notice?"

"It's addressed to us?"

Sam laughed. "It's handwritten, Daddy."

"And what does that mean?" asked Joanne.

I knew this one. "That I won't be addressing the envelopes."

"That's right," she agreed. My handwriting was somewhere between the Dead Sea Scrolls and a doctor's prescription. I was about to suggest some software for address labels we had at the bank, but Joanne went on, "I've already hired the calligrapher who'll do the envelopes. We want there to be a chance that they'll actually get delivered."

Frank started to go for the invitation, but Joanne put up her hand. "Not yet, dear. What else do you notice about the envelope?"

Sam gestured that he should look in the upper righthand corner, which I didn't think was fair, since no one was helping me. "The stamp?" he said.

"Precisely." The stamp was that year's treacly "Love" stamp, which was usually issued around Valentine's Day. Turning to me she asked, "And what stamp do you have?"

I looked, hoping it would be one commemorating the 300th anniversary of the backhoe. No such luck. "The 'Love' stamp."

"That's right. Those invitations went out at the end of August, and yet they had stamps that were issued in February. Obviously, they had foresight, just as I did. I have several sheets of this year's stamp, good to go."

"That's certainly planning ahead," said Frank. Thanks a lot, guy. Just wait and see what I have planned for your bachelor party.

"Now before we examine the invitation, let's take a look at the inside of the envelope."

Glued to the inside of each envelope was a piece of shiny, colored paper. "Notice that Sam's invitation has a light blue sheet. That's how she knew that the bridesmaids would be in light blue. It's a clue to the color scheme of the wedding."

"What do you call this?" asked Frank of the liner for his envelope.

"Magenta," answered Joanne. "And what a lovely wedding that was."

"Brown," I said, holding up my envelope.

"Yes," said Joanne, "And remember how I made you change your tie?"

I took the envelope that was inside the envelope and held it up. "And what does this mean?"

Joanne looked at me as if I was never going to master this. "It's an envelope, dear. It doesn't mean anything... All right, let's look at the invitation. Samantha, could you explain to your father and your fiancé how to read an invitation?"

"It's pretty straightforward. This invitation comes from both sets of parents, which means they're both hosting—and paying—for it."

That made sense. "All right, how do you know it's a religious service?"

"Read what it says, Daddy."

"Joseph and Muriel Barkowitz request the honor of your presence..."

"Exactly," said Joanne.

"Exactly what?"

"'The honor of your presence.' If it wasn't a religious ceremony it would say 'the pleasure of your company.' That's because you can't invite people to a religious rite which is a public function open to anyone."

I couldn't believe what I was hearing. "How do you know this stuff?"

"Everyone knows it," sighed Joanne. "You just have to pay attention."

"Frank, did you know this?"

"Don't go by me. This is the first time I can remember actually seeing a wedding invitation."

I'm sure there were more secret messages hidden, but I was only going to ask one more time. "What about the peonies?" I asked Sam. "Where did you get that?"

"That was the easiest thing of all." She held up the invitation, and in one corner was an artistic rendition of a peony. "If it's on the invitation, it's a safe bet it's one of the themes for the wedding."

I knew when I was licked. "All right, run all the information through the Enigma machine and put the invitations together. There's nothing you're including I don't know about, right?"

Joanne rolled her eyes. "Of course not," she said. "Where did you get the idea that we'd be hiding things in the wedding invitations?"

The actual drafting of the text didn't take long. There was a brief discussion over response cards which would, of course, require more stamps. Joanne, who had immersed herself in various books on the subject, was momentarily taken with the idea of not including one. It was apparently a modern invention, and those who had been properly brought up knew to send their acceptance or regrets via a personal note, possibly written with a quill on parchment and then sealed with wax. In a rare instance of sanity, I prevailed when I noted that some people, such as Frank and Sam's fellow students, might not be aware of the custom, and draw the wrong conclusion from the lack of a return card.

"What would that be?" asked Joanne.

"That they weren't actually invited to the wedding and had been sent the invitation simply as a notice," suggested Frank.

"As well as a hint that they still should send a gift."

"That's won't do at all," said Joanne. "We'll go with the return cards."

An hour later, Joanne and Sam were happily discussing floral designs, fonts, and whether the front of the invitation should be covered by a sheet of tissue paper. This last was because when invitations had literally rolled off a printing press, the tissue kept the ink from smearing. That was not the case today, but they decided to go with the tissue paper, perhaps to honor several centuries of the printer's art.

Meanwhile, Frank and I slipped outside for cigars. It had been a long day, and I had never really gotten the break from the wedding planning that I had hoped for with Sam. I thought Frank might appreciate some time to talk about what had happened in the lab yesterday. It turned out that was on his mind as well.

We went out on the patio and on the edge of what would be a lively flowerbed a month from now, but now was just an expanse of dirt surrounded by brick and slate. After he took a thoughtful puff, exhaling so the wind carried the smoke away from us, he said, "I want to apologize for losing my temper yesterday."

"You had every reason to be upset, and no real harm was done except to the beer bottle, but I do have to wonder what else might set you off."

He took another puff. Exhaled. "That's not really what you're wondering about, is it? You're wondering if Sam is in any danger from 'the Monster'."

"Well, I wouldn't put it quite like that…"

"You don't have to. I would sooner allow myself to come to harm than hurt Sam. The reason I was so upset was that she had been put in harm's way because of me."

"I appreciate that," I said, "Of course, we don't know that the woman meant to do her any actual harm—"

"And we're never going to give her the chance to find out. That's why I insisted on contacting Kennerly and getting the restraining order."

I took a puff on my cigar, flicking the ash off at the end. "Your friends seem disappointed. What were they expecting you to do? Tear down the building?"

"In a way, yes," he replied. "Don't get me wrong, Mike and the other grad students treat me like one of the guys. There's a lot of teasing and kidding around, but nothing malicious. Even though our whole academic discipline has been built up because of the experiment that created me, I'm a fellow researcher, not a lab rat."

He looked like he had more to say. I could've prompted him, but it seemed more important that he get around to it in his time. We sat quietly for a bit, saying nothing. When it seemed as if his cigar was going out, I handed him my lighter. He puffed it back to life.

Returning the lighter, he said, "Remember the first time we did this? I told you how Samantha and I had developed feelings for each other, and I thought you were going to have a stroke."

"You did take me by surprise."

"It wasn't the announcement. It was me. After all you had absorbed from the news coverage, in fact, after all you've absorbed from books and movies and TV shows dealing with creatures like me, I could hardly expect otherwise."

"But then I got to know you…"

"And yet I still get the reactions. Even Sam sometimes looks at me as if she's not quite sure who or what I am."

I didn't know if I was necessarily the best person to talk to about this and told him so. "Have you discussed this with Sam?"

"Of course. We're committed to being honest with each other, and if there's something one or the other of us doesn't understand, we talk it through. I don't know if you've noticed, but I find you pretty baffling sometimes."

I looked at him in the moonlight. He looked perfectly human and perfectly enigmatic. "Me? Really? How so?"

"Like when I show up at the bank, you're always in a rush to get me into your office."

Now it was my turn to vamp for time. After a couple of puffs, I said, "Yes, it's true. When we're around people who don't know you, I sometimes get self-conscious. You have to understand that a bank is a place where the primary focus is money going in and money going out. When you come in, you're a disruption…"

He started to object, but I cut him off. "No, it's true, Frank, and not because the customers want to get their pitchforks. You're instantly recognizable, and people assume they know you from the news or the movies or some magazine article. It's the price of being a celebrity. If you were a movie star or an athlete, it would be much the same."

"But not exactly the same."

"Of course not. As you said, we've all had a century or more of popular culture telling us to be afraid of the living dead, whether it's Frankenstein's monster or zombies or vampires. Then you come along, and you're different. You're friendly, you're articulate, you're warm—"

"Well, somewhat."

"—and people are curious. Someone coming up to you for reassurance may not even know if they want to be assured that you're safe, or that you really aren't. So just like we've had to learn to cut you some slack, you're going to have to cut us some slack as well. Everyone gets upset from time to time, but when *you* do it, they'll be wondering: does this prove he's normal, or is he about to reveal what he really is? It may not be fair, but it is what it is."

Some more quiet puffing. Finally, Frank stood up, ground the live end of the cigar against the slate walk of the patio. "You've certainly given me some food for thought."

"Don't overthink it, Frank. You've got plenty of time to figure out how to navigate the world. First, we have to get you through your conversion class and then the wedding. And then there's getting your

Ph.D. Anyone who knows what you're going through isn't going to be wondering why you snapped in the lab. They're going to be more amazed at how you're holding it all together."

I stood up just as the back door opened and Sam came out. "Frank, it's after 11. It's time to go home."

Yes, it was time for my baby to go home with the monster. Maybe the real story here is how *I* was holding it all together.

CHAPTER NINE

A couple of weeks of peace and quiet. The wedding plans were going full steam ahead, but the crises were all in normal parameters. The wedding invitations were ordered. Joanne and Sam and Susan, her maid of honor, went to a fitting for the wedding gown and helped Susan select her outfit, with the promise it would not be some monstrosity she'd want to burn after the wedding. Sam and Frank planned their honeymoon.

"I'm thinking two weeks in the Carpathian Mountains," said Frank at dinner one night.

"Is that like the Catskills?" asked Joanne, spooning some red sauce onto her pasta.

"It's in Eastern Europe," explained Frank, "running through Romania, Slovakia, and Poland. It's the source for stories about Baron von Frankenstein and Count Dracula."

Joanne dropped the serving spoon. "You're joking."

"It's supposed to be lovely in the summer."

Sam interrupted. "Perhaps we could save this conversation for later."

Frank looked confused, as he did when he got a reaction to something other than what he was expecting, but he got the message. "Of course, dear."

Joanne went to get a damp cloth to wipe up some of the sauce that had spattered onto the table.

"There's a lot to be said for Niagara Falls," I said. Sam gave me a look that signified something other than, "Thank you, Daddy," and I turned my attention to the parmesan cheese.

Those days, that was what passed for normal, so I was happy to be moving forward. The list said it was time to book the reservation for the rehearsal dinner, even though it was still months away. Since we were going to be a significantly small group, we made our arrangements at a restaurant at the hotel. Although it was still in the future, it seemed like the light at the end of the tunnel was coming into view. By the time we reached the rehearsal dinner, we would be following a tightly written script, and could stop worrying.

Which should have reminded me of an old expression that my Uncle Isaac used to say. "If you want to make God laugh, tell him your plans."

The following afternoon, I received a frantic phone call from Tom Hammer. The usually unflappable press agent was not happy.

"I can't believe you'd do this without giving me a head's up."

I felt like I had come into the middle of the conversation. "What am I supposed to have done? I've been reviewing business loans all morning."

"The website."

"I don't understand. How is the bank's website a problem?"

"Not the bank's website. The one for the wedding."

"I'm sorry, I have no idea what you're talking about. What website for the wedding?"

I heard some clicking over the line. "I've just sent you an email with the link."

"Tom, this is all news to me. Let me take a look and call your back." I hung up the phone and swiveled to my computer. I quickly opened his email and found the link. It was at something called WeddingCastle.

What it contained was pictures of Frank and Sam, details as to when and where the wedding would take place, their registries at several stores, and the phone numbers for the hotel, the caterer (for any special needs), their recommended airline (Southwest—"they won't treat you like luggage that talks"), and a space to leave comments to the happy couple. The comments quickly went from "See you in August, Sam, I'm so happy for you," to "Burn in hell with the other whores of Satan." And then it got really ugly.

I immediately called Tom back. "I knew nothing about this."

"Do you know what this does?"

"Besides giving every crazy person all the details for the wedding?"

"Let's not even go there," Tom said. "Everyone knew what they were opening themselves up for when they agreed to be part of this. The voice mail systems are screening the phone calls. And I would urge you to take down the comment section unread."

"Okay. It sounds like there's another problem."

I could hear him sigh over the phone. "You've just given everyone in the media—from the *New York Times* to the *Weekly World News*—a road map for your wedding. I've been trying to give out tiny morsels of information, but this opened the floodgates."

He was right, of course. This was another example of the law of unintended consequences, a subject that was going to be at the top of the agenda this evening. But for now, we had to figure out what to do after the proverbial cow had left the barn. I gathered that burning the barn to the ground wasn't going to do it. I tried anyway.

"Let me get them to take this website down as soon as possible."

"It's too late," said Tom. "The internet is forever. Even if you deleted it, there would be screen grabs and backups. No, once it's out there, it's out."

"So, what do we do?"

"Journalists are like cats. The only way to get their attention away from something is to provide something shinier or faster to distract them. If we give them a bigger story, the website will be no more than a footnote."

I was afraid of where this was going, but it's not like we had any choice. "I'm guessing you have something in mind."

"We have to give them Frank."

While Tom began the arrangements for the press conference we had sworn not to do until closer to the actual wedding, I tracked down Joanne. She was auditioning hair stylists. She'd been going to the same salon for 25 years, but as she said, "It's not every day you see your only daughter get married." I was beginning to wonder if I'd see the day at all.

It turned out that these websites were now part of the process and allowed guests one-stop connections to hotel and travel reservations and the like. Joanne hadn't mentioned it because it contained only information about things we had already decided.

"When did we decide to announce it to the world?"

I could barely make out what Joanne was saying over the phone. "Hold on, dear," she shouted. "Can someone please turn off the hairdryer?" What had sounded like a 747 taking off abruptly stopped. "That's much better."

"Yes, I can hear you just fine now."

"No, not you, dear, the permanent they're trying out. I think it looks quite good on me."

"Joanne, can you focus for a moment? Why did you set up this website?"

"Well, I asked Sam and Frank to do it, but they got caught up in some project at the university, and when I took a look, I saw how easy it was, so I just did it myself."

"Did you stop and think that once you put it up everyone could see it? There's a reason they call it the *World Wide* Web."

"But they can't. Only those with the password can get in."

I started to feel the familiar throbbing at my temples again. "What password? I was able to get right into the site."

"I can't understand it," she said. "I specifically remembered that it asked me to pick a password. It had to have letters and numbers and capitals and small letters and punctuation marks. And it couldn't be my email."

The throbbing picked up a notch. "And did it say that anyone who wanted to access the website needed this password, or that *you* would need it if you wanted to come back and make some changes or additions?"

There was a long pause. "Come to think of it, I wondered how other people would know the password if we didn't tell them… You can't blame me. It's very confusing."

She had me there. "Yes, it is. That's why I leave this stuff to the IT people."

"The 'It People'?"

"Information Technology."

"Is there a problem?"

There was no use yelling now. The damage had been done. "No, dear. Not if your intent was to tell the entire world every detail about the wedding."

The following morning at 10 A.M., Tom, Frank, and I met at the university. I would not appear at the press conference itself, but the idea was that Frank should have some friendly face there besides Tom, who was going to be too busy orchestrating the event. And if, somehow, my presence became known, it was less likely to cause a feeding frenzy than if Frank was accompanied by Sam.

It had been a while, but Frank had given many interviews at the time of the court proceeding to determine his fate, and so was comfortable under the hot lights and before the camera. It was one of the few things that went right. The university let us use a small classroom in the business school, chosen for its comfortable seats, wood paneling, and limited space. There were maybe two dozen reporters there representing the major cable outlets, the broadcast networks, the local stations, several news magazines, the local newspapers, and a handful of what Tom called "wild cards." I wasn't sure why we needed anyone who wouldn't ask safe, predictable questions, but he said they had played ball so far, and inviting them was a way ensure their continued cooperation. The still and video cameras operated as a pool, with the feed going to all the participants.

At a minute past ten, Tom strode out to the podium. I was with Frank, who was looking somewhat uncomfortable in a blue suit, white shirt, and silver necktie, in an adjacent classroom with a connecting door. While the press conference would not be carried live, we had a monitor that was getting the same feed as the various TV outlets.

"Good morning. We know there has been a tremendous amount of public interest in the forthcoming wedding of two students here at the state university. Although the wedding is several months away, we've called you here today to meet with the groom-to-be, who will take some questions. As you've been told, the wedding is a private event and there will be no public access to it, nor are the bride and groom interested in giving individual interviews at this time. They're focusing on planning their wedding and the start of their lives together. However, they're grateful for all the good wishes from the general public and wanted to satisfy some of the curiosity surrounding the event."

With that, he turned to side door. That was Frank's cue to head out. In the smaller room, Frank seemed to hesitate.

I patted him on the back. "You're going to do just fine. Just smile and be yourself."

Without looking back, Frank strode into the room. By prearrangement, the reporter from the local daily would get to ask the first question, so none of the big feed reporters could feel they were being snubbed.

"Wow," said Frank, looking over the crowd. "Imagine if I was announcing a run for president."

Someone from the back of the room shouted out, "Are you running for president?"

Tom, who stood to the side stepped forward and touched Frank's arm before he could answer. He then turned to the reporter and said, "Arnie, please wait your turn. And, no, Frank here is not running for president."

He then turned to Frank and muttered something that the microphones didn't pick up, but which I imagined was something along the lines of, "Enough with the jokes."

The next few questions had all been anticipated, and Frank handled them with ease. Yes, he and Samantha (not "Sam") were very much in love. No, she would not be answering questions at this time. Yes, his prospective in-laws had welcomed him into the family with open arms, compressing several months of complicated history into a sentence or two. No, he had not recovered any memories of who he might have been. I would have stopped there, but Frank was warming up, and kept going.

"Every once in a great while I might hear a song or see a name in the news and have a sense of *déjà vu*, but at no time during the wedding plans had anything like that happened," he said. The specialists he still consulted told him that it was likely he had never married.

When we hit the half-hour mark, I started to send signals to Tom and Frank to wrap it up. Of course, behind a closed door, these signals had no effect. Unfortunately.

"We have time for one more question," said Tom. "Arnie, it's your turn now."

"Could you talk about your upcoming conversion to Judaism?"

"Of course. Samantha and I have completed our studies—"

"Isn't she already Jewish?"

"Yes, but with a conversion connected to a marriage, it's usual for the Jewish partner to share in the experience."

"But why become Jewish at all? Why not become Christian?"

Uh oh. I didn't like where this was going.

Frank didn't blink. "Well it didn't make sense to me to join a different religion than my wife. Marriage is about starting out on a journey together."

I don't know if that last came from Frank's heart or a greeting card, but if the press conference had ended on that note, it would have been fine. Arnie, however, was just getting warmed up.

"So, if your bride-to-be was, say, a Wiccan, you'd become a witch?"

Tom stepped forward to cut it off—a little too late for my taste—but Frank put up his hand. Now I was really getting nervous. Frank had something to say.

"When the court declared me human, I embraced my humanity. Part of doing that was finding a moral code to live by. I don't know what I would have done if Samantha was a Wiccan or a Buddhist or Muslim or atheist or any of the other hundreds of flavors of theology the world has to offer, but I looked at some of the major traditions, and I found the ethical teachings of Judaism is where I was most comfortable."

"So, what you're saying is that you think Judaism is more ethical than Christianity?"

At this point, Tom leaned into the microphone and said, "Thank you," and led Frank out of the room. Most of the reporters were appalled at this line of questions, but at least a couple saw they had just been handed a far meatier news story than they had anticipated, and it had nothing to do with being pro- or anti-Jewish.

The reporter from FOX shouted, "Did you rank the world's religions in deciding which one was right for you?"

One from a local station wanted to know, "Did God appear to you and tell you which religion was the one true faith?"

If there was one blessing in what had transpired it was this: it hadn't been going out live.

CHAPTER TEN

"Mazel tov. Now you know what it's like to be an outsider."

I didn't think Rabbi Wheaton was being very helpful, but Frank—who had seemed a bit shaken after the press conference—seemed more like his old self after meeting with his religious teacher.

"I think I already knew that, Rabbi," he said. He seemed to have recovered somewhat from the press conference. We were in the rabbi's book-lined office at Congregation Sons of Israel v'Tzedek v'Tefila, the awkward name the result of a merger of three synagogues, none of which was willing to erase their history in the process. The result was that it was universally referred to as "the Temple."

I had assumed that Samantha, who had joined us, and Frank would want to have a private meeting with the rabbi, but he wanted to meet with all of us. Joanne was in deep consultation with her makeup artist and couldn't get away, while Tom elected to pass after wresting a promise from everyone—including Rabbi Wheaton—that none of us would do or say anything publicly about the wedding without going through him. That done, he went back to his other current client, a charity carnival coming to the county fairgrounds next month. At the moment, I couldn't say which was the bigger circus.

"I couldn't believe those questions. It was like they were daring me to attack other religions."

Sam took Frank's hand. "I didn't think we'd have to face anything like that in this day and age."

The rabbi frowned and shook his head. "We have it easy in America. We're widely accepted here in ways that have been rare in our people's history." Turning to Sam he asked, "Have you ever felt singled out because you were Jewish?"

"Not since that time in summer camp when I was 8 and one of the other girls asked to see my horns."

I didn't know whether to be shocked or appalled, and so I chose to be both. "You never told us about that."

"She was from the South, and heard Jews had horns," Sam explained.

"Horns? Where did she get that idea?" asked Frank.

Before the rabbi could launch into his lecture on the subject, Sam replied, "From the Bible. Fortunately, our counselor was an art history major, and explained it. When Moses received the Law at Sinai, his face reflected God's radiance to the point that the Israelites found it difficult to look directly at him. The Latin version of the text mistranslated the rays of light as 'horns.' That's why Moses has horns in Michelangelo's famous sculpture."

"Fascinating," said Frank. I was still balancing myself between shocked and appalled.

The rabbi stepped into the moment of silence that followed. "The important thing, Frank, is that you handled yourself well. You expressed confidence and pride in your choice to become Jewish without falling for the bait those unscrupulous reporters were setting out."

Some of the stories were already hitting the internet, and the religious brouhaha even eclipsed the news about the wedding. Most of it was straightforward, but a couple of the seedier outlets were running headlines like "Can a Monster be 'Chosen'?" One of the cable outlets had put on a roundtable of clergy, plus a Wiccan and the head of the local chapter of American Atheists, all of whom agreed that Frank's life was his own, and no one had the right to second guess him. It was the Unitarian minister who summed up the consensus, "There are many paths to a good and righteous life, through various beliefs or"—acknowledging the atheist on the panel—"non- or disbelief. I'm less concerned with which path he has chosen than that he has chosen to be a force for good in the world."

It would turn out to be a one-day wonder, except for the cranks and haters, and the news soon moved on to other stories that captured people's attention, only one of which seemed to involve kittens. Rabbi Wheaton concluded our meeting by saying that he now felt confident that the time had come for Frank to undergo the formal conversion process, which would consist of three things: circumcision, the rabbinical court, and the ritual bath. As Frank had arrived pre-circumcised, as it were, the circumcision would consist of drawing a single drop of blood before three witnesses. Rabbi Wheaton invited me to be one of them, but I took my inspiration here not from Moses but from Mary Shelley, author of *Frankenstein*: there are some things in this universe that man is not meant to know. I don't know what a complete list would be, but I'm pretty sure it would include not knowing what one's son-in-law's penis looks like.

It would take several days to line up the rabbis for the *bet din,* the court of rabbis who would question Frank and determine if he was a suitable candidate for conversion. Meanwhile, the long march toward the wedding continued.

I may never eat cake again.

According to the list, it was time to lock down the cake. Of course, it wouldn't actually be made until just before the wedding, and the number of tiers would be determined by the number of guests. The very top tier, which would have the miniature bride and groom, would be put aside for Frank and Sam to take home, to freeze and defrost as they marked various milestones in their first year. After that, it could be used as a doorstop.

The question before us now was threefold: the frosting, the filling, and the cake itself. Marsha, who introduced herself to us as the "hotel's liaison with the caterer," brought us to a lavishly set table in the otherwise empty ballroom. At each place setting was a tiny slice of cake, proportionally designed to give us an appropriate sampling of each element.

"This is our traditional wedding cake," beamed Marsha.

We each took a forkful. It was vanilla frosting and vanilla cake, with more frosting between the layers of cake. Joanne savored her piece. "It reminds me of our wedding cake."

"Me too," I said. "Took me years to get the taste out of my mouth."

"What was wrong with it?" Joanne pouted.

"It was vanilla."

Sam and Frank laughed, and then said in unison, "Chocolate is dessert."

"We can't have a chocolate wedding cake," said Joanne. "It will seem like a six-year-old's birthday party."

Marsha, having negotiated this terrain many times, moved us forward. "You're certainly right that you wouldn't want a Devil's Food Cake at a wedding. But things have changed in recent years, and bakers have brought all sorts of flavors into play."

She raised her hand to signal the next entry, and suddenly four waiters appeared as if from nowhere, took our half-eaten vanilla cake away, and replaced them with new slices. These consisted of a white frosting, a dark brown filling, and yellow cake.

"This is our Magnificent Mocha cake. The frosting is a white chocolate, and the filling is a cream cheese base pureed with espresso beans."

We took our tastes.

"Wow, this would be a big hit in the lab," said Sam.

"One bite of this and my mother would need a defibrillator. I think it comes on a bit strong."

"No worries," said the still-smiling Marsha. "We have many more to go." Indeed, we did. Nearly two dozen. There were cakes that featured strawberries or coconut. There was a red velvet cake with a frosting so that thick my arteries hardened just looking at it. There were cakes decorated with chocolate chips, and cakes decorated with floral arrangements including real flowers.

At one point, Marsha—whose spirits never flagged, although she wasn't sampling the cakes—simply announced "The Hummingbird." As I did not see any feathers on the plate, I wasn't sure what she was telling us, but after we had each forced down the sugary sample, she explained, "This is a Southern classic. It contains pecans, bananas, pineapples, and an assortment of spices."

"And a Confederate flag?" I asked.

Joanne shot me a look.

"Next, the Grasshopper."

Plates were exchanged for the umpteenth time, and I was beginning to wonder if we had run out of fruits and were now moving on to other ingredients. Before I could say anything, though, Frank started choking and coughing. "I think someone sabotaged the cake."

Marsha took her heretofore untouched fork and took the tiniest offering from his plate. "Why, no, this is how it's supposed to taste. What's the matter?"

Frank gulped down a goblet of water and frantically looked around for more. I put my untouched glass in front of him. He drank half of that, and then said, "It tastes like someone replaced the frosting with toothpaste."

"Oh, you're tasting the mint."

"Is that what that is? The only way we should serve this cake is with dental floss."

After several more rounds, including Pink Champagne, Nutella, Amaretto, and Peanut Butter, I was about to suggest that if we really wanted to be different, we shouldn't serve *any* cake. Why couldn't we be the trendsetters for a change?

Even Marsha seemed ready to throw in the towel, when a new cake arrived. It was a marble cake mixing chocolate and vanilla, with a snow-white vanilla frosting and a chocolate almond ganache filling. It wasn't too vanilla. It wasn't too chocolate. And there wasn't even a hint of mint. As each of us took a taste, there was a silence followed by a smile.

Marsha looked around the table. "I think we have a winner."

After the paperwork was done, Marsha thanked us for persevering through the process, telling us we had been comped for dinner at the hotel's restaurant. I was sure the cost would be hidden in the multitude of bills I was writing checks for somehow, but for the moment, it was a nice gesture. After Joanne and Sam had "freshened up," we descended to the lobby restaurant, and were immediately seated.

A waiter came to take our drink orders.

"Chardonnay for me," said Sam.

"Sounds delightful," said Joanne, "I'll have the same."

"Manhattan on the rocks," said Frank, who had clearly gotten more adventuresome since our brandy and cigars moment last Thanksgiving.

"And you, sir?" asked the waiter, looking at me.

Two hours of cake tasting had done me in. "Mylanta. Straight up."

The following Monday afternoon, we reconvened in Rabbi Wheaton's office. He then walked Frank downstairs to the chapel, where three other rabbis were sitting as a court. They would question Frank about his sincerity and intent, and if they were persuaded, he would be welcomed into the fold, pending his completing the third step, going to the *mikveh* for ritual immersion. After making introductions and presenting the rabbis with documentation of the symbolic circumcision, Rabbi Wheaton took his leave.

"Why didn't you stay with him?" Joanne asked upon the rabbi's return. "In fact, why can't we be there to support him? Suppose he needs character witnesses?"

Rabbi Wheaton smiled reassuringly as he took his seat behind his desk. The top was cluttered with papers and books, but in neat, almost picturesque, piles. I wondered if they were just for show, and he had another office down the hall where he did his actual work. "Frank will do just fine," he said to Joanne, Sam, and myself. "He'll be asked some questions about Jewish practices and the Jewish calendar, but it's not really a quiz. If he can't name all the fast days he won't lose any points."

"*All* the fast days? How many are there? I thought it was just Yom Kippur," I blurted out.

"There's also *Tisha b'Av*, and then there are the minor fast days, each of which has its own story…"

Before he could tell us the story of however many fast days there are, Sam spoke up. "If Frank isn't being quizzed on his knowledge, then what are they asking him?"

That's my daughter. When it mattered, she could cut right to the heart of things. Three pairs of eyes focused on the rabbi, and three pairs of ears were ready to catch every word. "They'll be questioning the one thing I have absolutely no fear about Frank being able to address: his sincerity. Does he intend to commit to continued learning, and taking steps to climb the ladder of *mitzvot*?"

"The what?" asked Joanne.

"The commandments," explained Sam. "Rabbi, tell them the story about Zusya."

"Sousa? The March King?"

"No, Rabbi Zusya. It's a much beloved and instructive story. Facing the end of his life, Zusya said that when he finally appeared before the Almighty for judgement, he did not expect to be asked why he was not like Moses. After all, who among us could measure up to the greatest prophet and teacher of our people? No, said Zusya, what I will be asked is, 'Why were you not like Zusya?' In other words, what is expected of each of us is to strive to be the best person we are capable of being."

"What does this have to do with Frank?" I wondered.

"Don't you see, Daddy? They'll be asking Frank how he sees his life ahead, not as a picture of perfection, but as someone always striving to be better. Will he help me make a Jewish home and observe the Sabbath and holidays? If we have a family, will he ensure they receive a Jewish education? Will he be a member of the community and attend services and support worthy causes?"

I was about to say that's a lot more than I ever did, when we heard loud laughter in the hall. Annoyed, Rabbi Wheaton got up to see who would disrupt his synagogue. When he opened the door, much to his and our surprise, there were Frank and three men whom I assumed were the rabbinic court.

"Stu," called out one of them to Rabbi Wheaton, "bring out the schnapps. And not the cheap stuff. We want to welcome Frank home."

"Home?" I asked.

"It's so obvious to us that Frank has a *neshama*, a Jewish soul, that it's likely he was Jewish in his previous life as well, although he has no memory of it."

Sam got up and went to the door to let the group in, greeting Frank with a big hug. "You made it!"

"Well I still have to go out for the dunking."

"What?" said Joanne. "Why do you have to have go out for donuts?"

At this, the rabbis burst out laughing again. Joanne started to turn red, and the eldest of the rabbis raised his hand to silence his colleagues. "Frank is referring to the *mikveh*, the ritual bath. It's the ease of his humor, utterly lacking in mockery or disrespect, that convinced us. The family that welcomes him in is very blessed indeed."

This seemed to mollify Joanne, but I still wasn't clear what had happened. "Frank has a very peculiar sense of humor, that's true, but we were hoping that as he became better connected with the world, he would calm down."

"No, no," said the third rabbi, "His humor is part of his gift to the world. It is an antidote to the fear and hate that continues to plague us. As miraculous and disturbing as his appearance among us may be, it makes him more human, and thus better able to address the very issues he raises. His disarming humor can reassure us that reason and being attuned to God's law will show us the way."

I had no idea what they were talking about. Later Frank told me that they had discussed the holidays and the Jewish life cycle as expected, and then focused in on why he wanted to be Jewish, other than marrying Samantha. He said it was learning about the Jewish holidays. On Purim, he said, Jews are encouraged to drink and celebrate to the point that they can't tell the difference between Haman, the story's arch-villain, and Mordechai, the story's hero. And yet just a few weeks later, at the Passover seder, these same Jews have four glasses of wine and celebrate the liberation from Egypt without a hint of drunkenness or levity. He loved the contrast. He felt he had a serious contribution to make to the world, yet he never wanted to forget that he could laugh and make jokes and act silly. Judaism would allow him to do both.

It was at that point that the discussion turned to Jewish humor. It turned out that along with all his serious reading, Frank had also been studying Jewish comedy from Sholem Alechem to Woody Allen, as well as books by rabbis like Joseph Telushkin and Moshe Waldoks, who had written quite a bit on the Jewish contribution to comedy. And then one of the rabbis made the mistake of asking Frank what his favorite Jewish joke was.

It was a joke so old that even I knew it, involving a parrot that could say the Hebrew prayers being brought to synagogue on Rosh Hashanah, and the owner betting the other congregants whether it could really do so. The parrot remained silent and the man slunk off in shame, knowing he'd have to make good on his losses after the holidays. When he berated the parrot, the bird replied, "But just think of the odds we'll get on Yom Kippur."

I couldn't believe the rabbis didn't know the joke as well, but apparently Frank's rendition was of such a caliber that the rabbinic court turned into several rounds of "Can You Top This?" Which led them to Rabbi Wheaton's office in search of the schnapps.

The trip to the mikvah the next day was anticlimactic. It wasn't on the official list, so Joanne wrote it in, and then checked off "Frank converting." It was a major milestone on the way to the wedding.

CHAPTER ELEVEN

Saturday morning found me in the last place I expected to be: back at the Temple. Frank was going to be called up to the Torah for the first time, and it was a big honor. Indeed, it was such a big honor he was being called up third. Why that was a big honor escaped me, but Josh, the head usher, assured me it was.

We arrived at the nearly empty synagogue shortly before 9:30 when Frank and Sam, who apparently had been attending regularly in recent weeks, introduced us to Josh, a tall, taciturn figure who Frank said could be quite friendly once he warmed up to you. We sat midway in the sanctuary, just off the center aisle, where we could admire the décor, which was 1950s suburban, with light brown seats, red carpeting, and stained-glass windows which pointedly avoided depicting anything. The array of geometric shapes reminded me of when Joanne had dragged me to the Mondrian retrospective at the museum.

As Josh went over his clipboard, he said to me, "And you'll have the fourth *aliyah*."

"Excuse me?"

"You'll be called up after Frank."

No one had warned me. The last time I had been "called" to the Torah was when I was 13, at my own bar mitzvah. I didn't even know if I remembered what to do. "No, no. I'll pass. This is Frank's day. I don't want to do anything to draw attention away from him."

"Hmm," Josh reflected, "I was told to give you an honor."

"It really isn't necessary."

"I'll tell you what. You can open the ark. All you have to do is pull the cord on the curtains and slide back the cabinet doors. I'll be right there to assist you."

"Daddy," said Samantha, "It's easy. Last week the 95-year-old great-grandmother of the bat mitzvah girl did it."

Now there was a vote of confidence. "Okay, I'll do it. How will I know when it's time?"

"Either I'll come get you, or I'll send one of the other ushers."

"Wonderful," said Frank. "Now let's get our *tallisim*."

Frank and I had put on yarmulkes—the traditional skullcaps—when we entered the synagogue, but now we went back to the outer foyer where there was a rack of prayer shawls. I saw a number of men had brought their own, but this way everyone was covered... literally. Frank muttered what I assumed was the appropriate blessing, and briefly wrapped his upper body in the shawl before adjusting it to rest on his shoulders. His blessing would have to count for two. I put mine around the back of my neck and draped the two ends in front.

When we returned to our seats, Joanne looked at us and said, "If my father could see you now."

Rabbi Wheaton and Cantor Eisenstein made their entrance at that moment, greeting people along the way as they worked themselves towards the front of the sanctuary. When they got there, the rabbi surveyed the room, and then signaled Josh to come over. "Go get the kibitzers in the lobby to come in so we'll have a minyan," he told the usher, who hurriedly went out to round up the errant congregants.

As they came in, Rabbi Wheaton—assuring himself we had the requisite quorum of ten—officially welcomed us. "Shabbat shalom. We begin our service on page 65. Please rise."

With that began more than an hour of Jewish aerobics. We stood. We sat. We read responsively in English. We sang in Hebrew. Well, some of us did. Even with transliterations, not knowing the melodies were a barrier to participation. Somewhere in the second hour, Josh came up the aisle and stopped by our row, signaling me, "It's time."

I followed him to the front of the sanctuary, where he indicated I was to go up and take a seat on the opposite side from Rabbi Wheaton. There was someone there I vaguely knew from the bank. I think he was a customer. We shook hands, and I took my seat as we watched the cantor in action. When he concluded, he was joined by the rabbi, who announced, "We now come to the centerpiece of Shabbat morning: the Torah service. Please turn to page 139."

After a few minutes of singing, the rabbi lifted both hands skyward, which was the signal to rise again. Josh magically appeared at my elbow and led me to the side of the ark, the cabinet containing the Torah scrolls.

"Pull the green cord," he whispered to me. I did, and the embroidered curtain slid back, revealing the carved wooden doors guarding the scrolls. "Now slide them to the left and right." This was not dissimilar to the mornings I was in charge of opening the vault at the bank, and I got through it without mishap. When I was done, Josh led me down the two steps to the main platform, and had me stand beside the cantor, who was singing up a storm. To my left was the fellow I knew from the bank. Josh then took one of the Torah scrolls out of the ark—there were several of them—and handed it to the cantor. There was some more singing as we first turned to face the congregation and then turned back to the ark to bow our heads. I kept looking to Josh for cues, and he didn't steer me wrong.

At the end of the singing, Josh took the Torah from the cantor and handed it to the fellow whose name I finally remembered was Max something-or-other, who proceeded to walk off with it. Josh gave me a gentle push on my back, and I realized I was to follow Max. Soon Max, Cantor Eisenstein, Rabbi Wheaton, and I were parading around the sanctuary. People touched the cover of the scroll with their prayer books or the fringes on their prayer shawls, which they then kissed, presumably as a sign of respect. This custom fortunately did not extend to the people in the line, so I merely had to endure many people shaking my hand while wishing me "Shabbat shalom" or "*Gut shabbes.*"

When we returned to the front of the room, Josh relieved Max of the Torah, and the rabbi and cantor shook hands with both Max and me. Clearly, we had discharged our functions, and could return to our seats. It took me a moment to get my bearings, as there were now many more people in the room than had been here at 9:30 when services began. I finally spotted Joanne and Sam and returned to my seat. Frank had already been moved to the front of the room to get him ready for his *aliyah.*

The first two people were brought up with quick dispatch. And then it was Frank's turn. The cantor started chanting something, and then paused so Frank could either tell or confirm something, and then the cantor's voice loudly rang out with "Ephraim ben Avraham v'Sarah."

He then chanted the blessing before the Torah reading, and I found myself joining in the congregational response—I guess it had remained in my memory after all—and then the next few verses of this week's portion were chanted by the cantor. Frank then did the blessing *after* the Torah reading, because you can't have enough blessings. I'm surprised there wasn't one to be said on the occasion of saying a blessing. We could easily be here all day.

Before the service could proceed, Rabbi Wheaton stepped forward. "Most of you know the unusual route Frank has travelled to get here this morning. This week, following a visit to the mikvah, he officially joined us. As it is written in the Book of Ruth, 'Your people shall be my people.' He has taken the Hebrew name Ephraim, and it is a pleasure to welcome Ephraim ben Avraham v'Sarah—Ephraim son of Abraham and Sarah—for his first aliyah. Ordinarily, we would treat this as his bar mitzvah, and have him chant the haftarah as well, but with his wedding to Samantha—who is here this morning with her parents—he already has a full plate." Taking Frank's hand, he added, "*Yasher koach*—may you be strengthened as you go forward in your new life as a Jew." The other people around the scroll—there were several of them—shook hands with Frank, and finally the service was allowed to continue.

When the next person had completed his turn at the Torah, Frank was sent back to us. Sam gave him a big hug and kiss, "I'm so proud of you."

Joanne was a bit more circumspect but was beaming with pride nonetheless. I gave him what I hoped came across as an approving handshake, and said, "Well done, Frank."

As we all sat down, I noticed someone in the last row in the back of the sanctuary who I had not seen earlier. He wore a hat, not a yarmulke, and no prayer shawl. He looked familiar, but out of context, so I couldn't place him. Several minutes later, my mind started to wander as someone who looked considerably older than I started mumbling through the *haftarah*—the week's selected reading from the prophets—stumbling through the text as if he had just become acquainted with the Hebrew language earlier that morning. Suddenly the stranger's face emerged from the mist of my memories. It was Rev. W. Allen Twitchell, the minister who had tried to get an injunction against the wedding. What was he doing at the Temple?

I didn't think it wise to confront him directly in the middle of services. At least, I hoped it was the middle. If we were still in the preliminaries, we might be here until nightfall. I saw Josh coming up the aisle and beckoned him over.

"The man in the back with the beat-up fedora and no prayer shawl is someone who wants to stop Frank and Sam from getting married. He's a Christian minister, and I don't know if he's here to cause trouble."

Josh gave a quick glance to the back, and then turned to me. "I'm on it."

He went up to the front of the room and took the empty seat next to the rabbi as the man who was celebrating the 70th anniversary of his bar mitzvah by destroying his *haftarah* was going into the home stretch. Josh and the rabbi quickly conferred, and then Josh came down and summoned his assistant. For all most people knew, they were discussing future honors, like who got the first piece of herring at the kiddush, but then they split apart and went up the aisles on opposite sides of the sanctuary. Out of the corner of my eye, I saw Twitchell look nervously back and forth between the two of them and then rise, hurrying toward the exit directly behind him. With that, I got up and went up the center aisle, not wanting to risk losing him and not finding out why he was here.

However, by the time Josh, his assistant, and I all made it to the lobby, he was gone. I ran to the front doors, but there was the usual foot traffic outside, with no sign of Twitchell to be seen.

I thanked the two ushers, and said, "I don't know what he's up to, but if he shows up again, don't let him anywhere near Frank or Sam. And if he tries, call the police."

I returned to my seat, not explaining where I had been. Forty-five minutes later, the service finally came to an end, and we were all invited into the social hall for *Kiddush* (technically, the blessing over the wine) and a luncheon for the congregation that we had contributed to in honor of Frank's being called to the Torah. After some lox and whitefish as well as joining Frank and the rabbi and several others for a series of "*l'chayims*," I calmed down enough to note that, come Monday, attorney Kennerly was going on the meter again.

With the wedding now only a few months away, there wasn't going to be a lot of downtime. Sunday afternoon, however, was relatively quiet. Sam and Frank had gone off to meet with Mike to discuss the play list for the reception, since they had decided to hire his band. Joanne declined to join them, "All I ask is that there be some normal music that the rest of us can dance to."

"Don't worry, Mom," answered Sam before leaving, "He's played weddings before. He'll make sure everyone gets something to dance to... even Daddy."

I was lying on the couch with the Sunday paper, doing the crossword puzzle, as I always did, in ink. "I'm a bank officer," I called out, without looking up. "I can stop payment on all those checks I've written."

"I love you too, Daddy."

And now it was a quiet Sunday afternoon at home with just Joanne and me. I focused on the puzzle. "A seven-letter word for 'union.' Workers? Bargain? Laborer?"

"Try 'wedding', dear," called Joanne from the dining room.

She was right. I couldn't even escape it in my crossword puzzle. I threw the paper down. Maybe I'd come back to it later. Maybe I wouldn't. I got up off the couch and padded barefoot into the dining room. There Joanne sat at a table covered with what looked like the inventory of a stationery store. Maybe two of them.

"What's all this?"

"The invitations. I spent the week putting the envelopes together and making sure the calligrapher did everyone's address right. Now I just have to seal them, stamp them, and get them to the post office in the morning."

"What can I do to help?" I asked, feeling a bit guilty at how much she had taken on her own.

"You can keep your filthy, ink-covered hands away from the invitations," she snapped, and then immediately softened. "I'm sorry, dear, I'm juggling a lot of things at the moment."

"I think we'll all be glad when this over."

Joanne gave a look of surprise. "What do you mean? I'm looking forward to the wedding. I think it may be one of the greatest days of my life, right up there with Samantha's birth and the day we got married."

I was touched. After all these years. We may have had our ups and downs, but we'd weathered the storms together. "Is it all right to sit at the table and keep you company if I agree not to touch anything?"

"I'd like that... you know, between the surprise of Frank himself, and then everything with the wedding and the conversion and the protestors, the two of us haven't have much time together in months."

"Maybe you and I should be the ones who go off on a honeymoon. Of course, I'd have to rob the bank to be able to pay for it."

"That's not a bad idea."

I looked at her. "Robbing the bank?"

"No, silly. You and I getting away for a little bit. When was the last time we did that?" I began to think about it, but Joanne interrupted. "Don't try to remember. It'll just make us more depressed."

All the while she was talking, she was sealing envelopes with a wet cloth and putting stamps on them. I suddenly had a horrible thought. "Did you put the stamps on the return envelopes?"

"I'm way ahead of you, dear. Samantha and I put the return cards, envelopes, and stamps together the other night."

I looked at her with admiration. "You're a lot more on top of things than I think I give you credit for. I don't how we'd have gotten through this process if it wasn't for you and that crazy list."

Flick, seal, stamp. "It's all about being organized." She got up and took a pile of completed invitations over to a box on the sideboard. On her way back, she checked the list on the wall. "Are you and Frank all set with your tuxedos?"

"Getting measured on Tuesday."

"And the rings?"

"Already purchased and in our safety deposit box at the bank."

"And the horse-drawn carriage?"

"It's reserved and… wait a second! I didn't approve any horse-drawn carriage. Whose cockamamie idea was that? I told you not to do anything without discussing it with me."

Joanne came over and kissed the top of my head. "There isn't any horse-drawn carriage. I just wanted to see if you were paying attention."

She sat down and waded into the pile of invitations again. After a few moments, I said, "In this rush to get everything checked off, there's something you and I haven't discussed. Are you *happy* with the choice Sam is making?"

"After the initial shock wore off? Yes. I think he's a good man who's devoted to Sam, and the two of them share so much from their field of work to the seriousness with which they undertake anything. I think that's why they connected. Whether it's medical research or a *Shabbat* dinner, they take whatever they do seriously, but they don't take themselves too seriously. There's a playfulness Samantha has never lost, and I wondered if she could find someone who would share it rather than tell her she has to grow up and be a 'grown-up.' It's what attracted me about you."

"What are you talking about? I'm Mr. Establishment Banker. Serious. Responsible. No nonsense."

"Yes, at work you take your responsibilities seriously. You don't cut corners or do anything but your best. But your colleagues don't know the real you: the man who does crossword puzzles in ink or has his three-or-four-times-a-year cigar on the back porch so as not get me upset. Or who watched reruns of *The Munsters* with his daughter all the way through high school."

Another stack of invitations had somehow piled up in front of her, and she got up to put it with the others. She then came over to me and gave me a hug from behind where I was seated. "You know we don't have to wait until after the wedding for a second honeymoon. Samantha and Frank won't be home for hours."

I couldn't believe what I was hearing. "In the middle of the afternoon?"

She came around and kissed me on the lips. "We don't have to let anyone from the bank know."

And with that, she left the room. Was this for real? I heard her footsteps heading upstairs to our bedroom. "Don't keep me waiting, dear. This may be our last chance for months."

I may be only a vice president at a local community bank, but never let it be said I didn't recognize when an offer was too good to refuse.

CHAPTER TWELVE

I'd been putting it off long enough. One of my responsibilities as Frank's best man was to arrange for the bachelor party. However, just as I had no desire to see Frank's circumcision, I really didn't think it was my place to host a bacchanalia with strippers and lewd jokes. During lunch I went over to the campus, figuring I didn't need to have this discussion at the bank. Unfortunately, Frank was off in the library doing research, and no one know precisely where he was or when he'd be back. In fact, the department office was empty except for Mike.

"I keep forgetting you're one of their colleagues and not just a bandleader," I said by way of awkward greeting. "What's your part of the project?"

"You know how Frank wants to see if we can reanimate organs to see if they'd be suitable for transplant? I'm testing animal organs to see if they are capable of being reanimated independently of their bodies."

"Are you having much success?" I asked.

"Some days are better than others. I'm working on the lower gastro-intestinal tract right now. On the best of days, it's a challenge."

"And on the worst of the days?"

"We open all the windows."

"Sorry I asked. Look, Mike, I'd like to get your input on something."

Mike got up from where he was eating his lunch. "Can I get you some coffee? Juice?"

"That's quite all right. I didn't mean to interrupt your lunch."

I thought we'd have to go through a couple more rounds of who could outdo the other in courtesy, but then Mike was a grad student; he didn't have to be told twice to go eat. He resumed his lunch and indicated I should take the seat across from him.

"I don't know if Frank told you, but he's asked me to his best man."

"Yeah, he mentioned that," said Mike between bites of his tuna fish sandwich. "Kind of unusual."

"That it is. In fact, it's more than that. I'm expected to host the bachelor party, and I'm uncomfortable with throwing a party like that for the person who's going to marry my daughter."

Mike laughed. "I'm guessing it's been a long time since you've been to a bachelor party. What did they do at yours, hire a stripper or show some X-rated videos?"

I may have turned a bit red, "I don't really remember the details…"

"Probably because you were all drunk or stoned or drunk *and* stoned. Am I right?"

Not answering I said, "You see what my problem is."

Mike took a swig of his caffeine-free, sugar-free cola. Before I could ask him what the point of the beverage was, he said, "You've come to the right person. Frank and Sam are an unusual couple in a lot of ways. They're figuring out their own way of doing things. Their academic careers are groundbreaking. Their wedding will be unique."

"I understand you'll be playing a part in making that happen."

Mike smiled. "I'll do my best. And it stands to reason that Frank's bachelor party should be one-of-a-kind as well. He told me he just wanted to have a nice evening of male bonding, the way the two of you bonded over brandy and cigars."

Well, that's one way of putting it. "Did he tell you what he had in mind?"

"He wasn't quite sure. which is why he was looking for suggestions that he could pass on to you. So now we've eliminated the middleman, and I can give you my ideas directly. I like the idea of the cigars. Never actually smoked one, but it's something I've meant to try someday. Brandy seems a little high-falutin' for this crowd. Other than you, will there be anyone there who's not a grad student?"

I hadn't really thought about a guest list. "Are there any professors we ought to invite?"

"One or two. Don't know if they'll come. Anyone else?"

"Perhaps a relative or two… of Sam's. Frank's lawyer and his press agent. They've been doing enough work for him that they should have a bit of fun." Especially when they're not on the clock.

"Okay, then," said Mike. "Consider this: how about a scotch tasting?"

"How would that work?"

"My father is a liquor distributor. He knows all the local players. One of the reps for a bunch of distilleries does a whole show, complete with wearing a kilt and playing bagpipes. He then brings in samples of his distilleries' wares while talking about how scotch is made, how to distinguish different types, single malts versus blends, the whole shebang. At the end of the evening, everyone is pleasantly buzzed, they've learned something useful, and everyone's kept their clothes on."

I liked it. This was the sort of male-bonding exercise that would discharge my obligation with regard to a bachelor party without embarrassing me, my family, or the bank. And Frank would have a memorable celebratory evening in anticipation of the wedding.

I smiled. "Mike, the minute I heard the *Munsters* theme on your demo, I knew you were a good person."

"Yeah, Sam, told me about that. Wouldn't have figured you for a *Munsters* fan. It was Lily, wasn't it? That Yvonne De Carlo: rowrrr!"

That was quite enough male bonding for me. "Do have a number for this scotch expert?"

"Don't worry about it. My dad will take care of it. You set up the time and the place, and I'll make the arrangements."

Well, that went better than expected, and I didn't even have to have an embarrassing conversation with Frank, although who would have been more embarrassed I couldn't say. Arranging the room for the event at our local country club was easily done. One of the outer buildings was specifically designated for events where smoking would be permitted, and as both the bank and Mike's liquor distributor father had long-standing relations with the club, there was no issue about bringing in our own liquor for the tasting. Of course, the fact that we were ordering all our food from them was helpful as well. Here I was in my element, cutting deals to our mutual advantage without having to worry about public attention or controversy. Tom was happy to receive the invitation and agreed there was no reason to alert the press about a private party. Should there be any questions after the fact, he'd have the advantage of actually having been there.

Meanwhile Mike's father, Oscar Mulvaney of Mulvaney's Liquors, contacted me to coordinate with his scotch expert. Ian MacLellan, a real estate broker by day who had a sideline sharing the history and celebrating the world of scotch. He was extremely knowledgeable, and apparently put on quite a good show. Mulvaney assured me that we would not be disappointed. As part of the package deal for MacLellan and his pours, there would be little gift bottles for each of the guests, and full-size bottles for Frank and myself. Things were going so smoothly I should have been wary, but I decided after all the bumps in the road that we had hit head on, it was about time something happened where everything fell neatly into place.

The invitations went out, and replies came back in short order. In addition to Frank, Mike, and myself, there were four other grad students, Tom our press agent, and Neal Kennerly our lawyer. A cousin of Sam's sent his regrets but said he would be flying in from San Francisco for the wedding. We had also invited the professors who worked with Frank, but none seemed to feel that the professor/student barrier was worth breaching for a bachelor party. Sam, of course, was sitting this out, just as Frank had absented himself from the "bachelorette" party that Susan, her maid of honor, had thrown for her. Joanne was there as a guest, but I didn't question either of them about it, figuring that these things were simply part of the tradition. Which brought us to Evelyn.

Evelyn was a grad student in the bioethics program and, as such, was friendly with both Frank and Sam. She had been invited to Sam's party and went, but when she got wind of the bachelor party, she wanted to know why she wasn't invited to that. Mike explained that it was a "stag" party, but even the terminology was half a century or more out of date. The party was to celebrate Frank's coming transition to married life, and there really was no logical reason she should be excluded from her classmates, given the line-up for the night.

A few days before the party, Sam and Frank talked it over, which was apparently how they handled everything. Sam's argument was that, while she found some ironic enjoyment in the "all-girl" bridal shower, it really was an anachronism. Frank agreed, and so an invitation was extended to and accepted by Evelyn for an evening of cigars and scotch. If this was what they wanted, I saw no need to object.

So, on a Saturday evening, the ten of us convened in the enclosed gazebo at the club, where I got to welcome everyone on Frank's behalf. "By his request," I said, "this is less an evening about a bachelor leaving his single status than about someone doing something alone for the last time before he begins his lifetime partnership with… well, with my daughter Samantha." I turned to Frank. "Did I get that right?"

"Perfect," he said.

I took my seat at the round table that could easily have seated twelve. Where the two additional seats would have gone was set up with a microphone and a plaid cloth featuring yellow and red stripes crossing a field of blue, purple, and black. I had been told that particular plaid was the emblematic tartan for Clan MacLellan. Tom and Neal were in sports jackets and ties, I was in my usual business attire, and the grad students were in various states of "I don't have a full-time job yet" clothes. The conversation came to a halt as we heard the mournful wail of bagpipes not far away. Doors at the rear of the gazebo opened and there, playing the instrument in full regalia—including a kilt that matched the cloth at the head of the table—was Ian MacLellan. All six feet and two inches of him.

He paraded around the table and, when he got to the head of it, shifted to a somewhat lighter air. When he finished, he removed the mouthpiece from his lips and waited for acknowledgement, which was not long in forthcoming with an enthusiastic round of applause. It was quite an entrance.

"*Lang may yer lum reek*," he loudly declared to a baffled silence. "Ay. It means, 'Long may your chimney smoke,' or roughly, may your life be long and fulfilling. Now, where's the guest of honor?"

Frank's classmates were quick to point him out, directly across the table from the Scotsman. "So, you'll be tying the knot soon. That is a cause to celebrate, and there's nothing like a wee dram when there's a reason to be happy. So, before we begin tonight's history lesson and tasting, I'd like to begin with a toast." With that, he pulled up a leather case that had been under the table and opened it, pulling out a bottle filled with a dark golden liquid. Each of us had a small glass at his (or her) place, and he walked around the table giving each of us a generous pour.

When he got to Evelyn, he did a double-take. "I see we have a lass amongst us. Surely you're not our groom's intended?"

"No," she said, "Just a classmate."

"And are you sure you'll be able to handle the nectar we'll be sampling?"

She looked around the table. "Probably better than most of these specimens."

"You've got spirit, lass," replied Ian with a laugh. "I look forward to the evening ahead."

When he finished filling each glass and returned to the head of the table, he removed a large goblet from the bag to a big laugh, but then poured himself the same amount, or perhaps a bit less, than he had for everyone else. He then raised the glass and, holding it in Frank's direction, said, "May the Lord keep you and your bride-to-be in His hand, and never close His fist too tight upon you!"

As we put our glasses down, Ian said, "Let the tasting begin."

Three hours later, we had sampled half a dozen whiskeys, with a break for a hearty snack halfway through, and now I was passing around the Churchills I had brought for the cigar part of the evening. Before I could demonstrate how to prepare the cigar for smoking, Evelyn brought out a pocket guillotine and snipped off the end of her cigar, then offered to do the same for the others. Frank laughed and looked at me. "Looks like you're going to a circumcision one way or the other."

Ian presented each of the guests with an individual airline-sized bottle of scotch, while Frank and I got wrapped boxes along with the admonition not to open them tonight. "A fine scotch is to be savored," he told us, "not drunk when you can no longer tell one from the other." He began packing up his wares, and turned to Evelyn, "You're rather well-equipped—"

"Excuse me?" she said with an edge to her voice.

"Pardon, I meant carrying your own cigar cutter."

"Oh," she laughed. "Well, when you grow up in a house with five brothers, you're apt to pick up the odd vice."

"Nothing odd at all. Some of the finest women of my acquaintance enjoy the occasional cigar."

"Say, what happened to your accent?" shouted out Frank from the other side of the room.

"*A dinna ken,*" he said, and then, without a trace of a burr said, "It's all part of the act. The name is real as are my Scottish roots, but I was born in New Jersey."

This brought some hearty laughs from around the table. "That reminds me—" began Evelyn, but what it reminded her of was cut off by the crashing open of the doors at the rear of the room. We all turned to look.

Standing in the doorway was a young woman in a tight-fitting police uniform that could barely contain her proportions. Short but fiery red hair came down beneath her cap.

"Mike," said Frank, with a bit of a slur, "I thought you promised no strippers."

In response to that, the woman drew her gun and said, "I want everyone seated at the table with your hands where I can see them."

"Now look here, Miss, there's some sort of misunderstanding—"

"That goes for you too, Pops," she said, pointing the gun at me. Meanwhile, two more officers came in behind her, accompanied by someone in civilian clothes. As I turned my attention to the new arrivals, I realized who the non-officer was: Frieda Guerrero.

Neal recognized her at the same moment and got out of his seat. "Officer, you are making a terrible mistake. This woman is under a court order to stay away from my client, and you are aiding and abetting her and risking being found in contempt of court."

The officer, whose name tag identified her as "Moulton," turned to Frieda. "Is that true, ma'am?"

Ignoring the question, she said, "These people have been trying to keep me from my brother Hector, who was kidnapped and made to undergo horrible experiments."

The lawyer, keeping his hands raised, stepped away from the table. "Officer... Moulton. This deranged woman claims to be a relative of my client. We know for a fact that this isn't so. If I may..." he said, slowly peeling back his jacket and removing a sheaf of folded papers from an inside pocket. He took a step forward to hand them to Officer Moulton, but one of the other cops plucked them from his hand.

"You stay right where you are, mister."

While Moulton looked at the papers, I asked Neal what they were. "The result of the blood test," he said. "They have absolutely nothing in common."

"And you carry them with you?"

"Where Frank is involved, I'm finding it's better to be prepared."

Moulton looked at Frieda. "It says you're not related at all."

"Hah, how could a lab test know that?"

"Because DNA doesn't lie, does it Ms. Guerrero? You have no genetic markers in common," snapped Neal.

Moulton was losing her patience. "Well…"

"Of course, we don't," Frieda answered smugly. "Hector was adopted."

Moulton turned to Frank. "Are you or are you not the creature who was reanimated on the state university campus?"

Neal snapped, "Don't answer that!"

But it was too late. "The only 'creature' I see here is someone who took the word of a crazy person to pull out a gun and threaten people at a private party."

"He does look like that Frank who was in the newspapers," said one of the other officers.

"I've about had it with you lot…" began Moulton.

Things were spinning out of control. "Officer," I said calmly, "Frank is going to be marrying my daughter in a few weeks. This was a private party to celebrate that. What possible interest could any of this be to law enforcement?"

"According to the affidavit filed by this woman, Frank or Hector, or whatever his real name is, was reanimated in a university laboratory four and a half years ago. The drinking age in this state is 21. I don't follow all the details, as this is way above my pay grade. So, I'm doing the only thing I can do under the circumstances. I'm taking you all in for contributing to the delinquency of a minor and you"—pointing at Frank—"into protective custody."

Neal immediately turned to Frank, "Do not answer *any* questions except by saying you want your attorney. You got that?"

"Take Perry Mason first," she said to one of the officers.

Under ordinary circumstances, we would have had to wait until Monday morning for a hearing, but Neal had made prior arrangements with the club that, in the event of any unusual circumstances related to our party, his partners were to be called at home. Apparently, one of the calls got through, because a local judge was persuaded to hold a special session of night court, convinced that an injustice would be done by making us wait 36 hours. The fact that the county would save money if this could be wrapped up Saturday night may have played a role as well.

At 11:30 P.M., there was a little crowd in the courtroom. I didn't know what Neal was going to do, but we agreed that for the purpose of this hearing, he would represent all of us. Frank, the nine party guests, and Ian McLellan, still in full regalia, were at the defendant's table. An assistant district attorney, obviously too low in seniority to get out of the assignment, sat alone for "the people." Behind the rail at his back were Officer Moulton and the two other police officers, Frieda, and the last man I expected to see: the Rev. W. Allen Twitchell. What was he doing here? Further back in the courtroom were Joanne and Samantha, who insisted on coming when I made my proverbial one phone call, as well as a small rabble Tom seemed to recognize.

"Don't file anything before you speak to me," he said. One of the bailiffs instructed him to be quiet and face front.

We were then all told to rise and greet the judge who would be presiding over this special session. It was none other than Judge Ramkumar Murgadoss who, the moment he saw Frank, started to roll his eyes as if not quite believing what he had gotten into. Everyone started shouting at once. The judge rapped his gavel repeatedly until he got the silence he was expecting. "I understand there are a lot of conflicting claims here, but we are going to do this by the rules. Let's begin by hearing the charges."

The young prosecutor, perhaps noting the presence of several reporters, rose and began his formal presentation. "May it please the court, now come the people in response to a complaint registered on—"

"Get on with it, counselor. I have an early tee time in the morning. What are the charges?"

"Ten counts of contributing to the delinquency of a minor, to wit, by providing an underage youth with intoxicating liquor."

"And that underage youth…"

"That would be me, Your Honor," said Frank, half rising in acknowledgement.

"I was afraid of that. And how do the defendants plead?"

Neal and the rest of us stood at his direction. "We plead, 'Not Guilty,' Your Honor."

Judge Murgadoss sighed. "All right, let each of the defendants state their name for the record, and then we can proceed."

After we had each done so and resumed our seats, young Mr. Hawke, the prosecutor, rose to deliver his opening statement. The judge was having none of it. "Mr. Hawke. Mr. Kennerly. In the interests of time and getting to the point, is there any objection to reducing the present issue before this court to a determination of the alleged minor's legal age? If, in fact, he is over 21, there is no case, is there?"

"No, Your Honor," mumbled Hawke.

"And, Mr. Kennerly, if it is determined that, as a matter of law, Frank here is deemed less than 21 years of age, then the matter becomes sufficiently complex that it will have to be bound over for a full evidentiary hearing. Do you agree?"

"I don't believe it will get that far, but I don't dispute Your Honor's description of the parameters of the case."

"Thank you, Mr. Kennerly, I'm glad I have your permission to proceed."

"Now hold on, I'm not agreeing to spend the weekend in jail." Evelyn blurted out, looking not at all happy.

Murgadoss rapped the gavel sharply. "Young lady, I will allow no such outbursts in my courtroom. However, I will note that any questions of release on bail or personal recognizance will be addressed if, and only if, I determine there is a case at all. Does that answer your objection?"

A much more subdued young woman replied, "Yes, Your Honor."

"Now then, this court has already dealt with one challenge to Frank which was dismissed as we are bound by the decision of *In re: Frank*, where it was held that he is a free and autonomous being, not subject to destruction or control by the state. Is the prosecution proposing to relitigate that?"

"No, Your Honor. I simply note that the issue decided by the court was Frank's liberty, not his age or when he was deemed to be born. There is nothing in the court's ruling that bars you from determining he was 'born' at the moment of his reanimation, rendering him four and a half years old, and thus subject to child protective services."

"Yes," said the judge noncommittally. "And your response, Mr. Kennerly?"

"Putting aside the issue of this complaint being brought by someone under a court order to stay away from Frank—"

"For the moment."

Kennerly allowed himself a slight smile. "Her complaint itself is flawed on its face. On the one hand, as outlined by my learned colleague, it claims Frank is a child. On the other hand, it claims Frank is in reality one Hector Guerrero, who would be 29 years old. His age would not change because he has been resuscitated—"

"Objection. Reanimated."

Kennerly didn't miss a beat. "A distinction as yet unaddressed by law."

"I'm afraid he's got you there, Mr. Hawke. Objection overruled."

Kennerly continued. "Further, the court in *In re: Frank* clearly did recognize his implied adulthood in ordering him freed. Had they thought him a child, even a particularly unusual and gifted child, he would have been placed under the supervision of a guardian. So, where the complainant seems to be arguing that he both is and isn't a child, there was no such confusion by the court which clearly recognized him as a self-sustaining adult."

The judge turned to Hawke. "Anything in rebuttal... No, I would think not. You've done your best with a bad hand, Mr. Hawke. As the song says, you have to know when to hold them and know when to fold them. I am dismissing all charges against the defendants. Officer Moulton, please take Ms. Guerrero into custody for violating a court order. We'll have a hearing on a possible contempt charge Monday morning at 11 A.M. Otherwise, the rest of you are free to go."

He banged his gavel and rose. MacLellan rose from his seat and shouted, "Freeeedom!" Everyone stopped and stared, including the judge. More quietly he said, "I apologize, Your Honor. It's just that I've always wanted to do that."

Judge Murgadoss did not react. "Mr. MacLellan, is it? Come see me in my chambers. I have your bagpipes and your case of samples. I was hoping you could examine them and make sure everything was intact."

"Ay, Your Honor, it would be a pleasure. Might I bring my assistant along?" He put out a hand in Evelyn's direction.

"It would be an honor to accompany you, laddie," she said, in something approximating his accent.

"Very well," said the judge, rolling his eyes. "The more the merrier."

CHAPTER THIRTEEN

"...with the judge ruling that he is an adult and is entitled to a bachelor party as much as any other person preparing for a forthcoming wedding. Tonight, in an exclusive, we have the couple-to-be themselves, talking about life in the public eye, and how a forbidden experiment may lead to countless lives being saved. Stay with us."

When we got out of the court house, Neal arranged for transportation back to the country club for people to pick up their cars. Frank and I left with Sam and Joanne. Tom held an impromptu press conference, trying to spin things the best he could. The story, of course, was "Defying Court Order, Deranged Woman Disrupts Party." Much of the media covered it that way, if they paid any attention to it at all. Then there were the ones looking for the lurid headline, such as "Monster's Co-ed Bash Raided by Police."

As Sam drove Joanne and me home, we were too tired for any post-mortem. I did decide that I would no longer complain about Neal's hourly rate. As the saying goes, everyone hates lawyers... until they need one. The following afternoon, the four of us convened with Neal and Tom at our house. The demonstrations seemed a little noisier today, but by now had faded into the background noise. We were just a few months away from the wedding, and the ending was starting to come into sight. Hopefully, we had seen the last of Guerrero, but Twitchell's showing up in court following his appearance at the temple concerned me. What was he planning?

"I'm afraid feeding the press tidbits is no longer going to work," Tom said.

"We're not doing another press conference," I insisted. "We can't go through that again."

"Agreed," said Tom, pacing our living room while rest of us sat. "It's time for the next step."

"And what would that be?" asked Frank.

"You and Sam agree to be interviewed."

"How will that help?" This was Joanne, who had gotten very serious since last night in court. "If they do one show, isn't everyone going to demand equal time?"

"Of course," said Tom. "But they also know how the game is played. The closer we get to the event, there may or may not be any further opportunities, and obviously we're going to look for a sympathetic—or, at the very least, friendly—venue. Someone with no axe to grind."

"And who might that be?" I asked.

Before Tom could respond, Sam spoke up, "Rachel Maddow."

"Yes," said Tom, "That's who I had in mind. Smart, fair, hasn't ridden this story like a hobbyhorse, and whose questions will be probing but not an attempt to trip you up."

Neal, who had been taking this all in, sat up. "This isn't really my area, and I'm sure she will give them a good platform to express themselves. But why won't every other cable outlet, magazine, and newspaper demand equal access?"

"You're right. They will. And they'll also understand—whether they'll admit it or not—when they don't get it. And the reason is that the interview itself will give them all fresh grist for the mill. The cable channels will have roundtable discussions. The print magazines will interview psychologists, theologians, lawyers, and doctors, asking them to react to the interview. The newspapers will have op-eds, as well as having their regular columnists weigh in. If we're lucky, they'll start playing off of each other. An expert on CNN will say something that a columnist in the *Wall Street Journal* will respond to, leading to a symposium in *Mother Jones*, which will be analyzed and torn apart on FOX News…"

"How can you be sure they'll fill up all this space and time with commenting on the interview and then commenting on the commentaries, and so on?" asked Joanne.

Tom quit his pacing and smiled. "They haven't let me down yet."

"…and did you have no qualms about Frank's background?"

Frank and Sam were in the studio with Maddow, who was devoting two segments of her nightly show to the issues raised by their marriage.

Her tone was of that of a friend looking for insight, not a grand inquisitor and, as a result, the two were relaxed and open.

"Actually, the first time she saw me was in the student union, which has a magnificent view of the lake. I couldn't have picked a better background," said Frank, smiling.

Sam patted his knee, and then addressed Maddow. "Of course, but that was only until I got to know him. He can't be held responsible for the people who conducted the experiments which brought him to life, any more than you or I are responsible for being born. In each person's life, one's own existence is a given."

"That's why she calls me her little postulate."

Maddow laughed. "I didn't think we'd be discussing high school geometry tonight."

"See," continued Sam, "that's what I mean. Once you get to know Frank as a person, there's nothing monstrous about him at all. In fact, it was his acknowledgment that the experiment that brought him to life must be forbidden, but that the technology—brought down to a lower level—might be useful to humanity which forms the basis for our bioethics project."

"Now dear," interrupted Frank, "it was really you who brought things together."

Sam turned to Frank. "But I couldn't have done it without you."

"And I never would have thought it all the way through without your help."

Maddow laughed again. "We'll try to get these two lovebirds back on topic after this. Stay with us."

The morning they were to do the show, Tom spent a few hours going over possible lines of questions. It was less about having them scripted than in avoiding surprises. He wanted them prepared and ready for whatever direction the conversation took. He asked them about their falling in love, about sex, about whether they could have children, about their work at the university, about how Frank felt about those members of the public who feared and even hated him, about converting to Judaism, and about whether they had any curiosity about who he once was. It was grueling, and there were moments I wanted to get up and make him stop, which is presumably why he put Joanne and I in a separate room, where we were watching it on closed circuit television.

"So, what's it like making love to someone who isn't as warm-blooded as a normal human?" said the woman playing the interviewer.

Sam looked directly at the camera. "She's *not* going to ask that."

Off-camera we could hear Tom, "And what if she does? You don't have to answer the question, but what people will be looking at is how you react. Are you embarrassed that you're two adults with a healthy sex life, or are you ashamed of the relationship for which you're seeking the audience's approval?"

Sam seemed flustered. Frank turned to the interviewer and said, "On a cold winter night, I make her take a hot shower first. And if she's still not warm enough, I make her turn on the electric blanket."

The interviewer looked at Frank and, after a moment, laughed. She then turned off-camera, "I'm sorry, Tom, that's not the answer I was expecting."

"That's okay," said Tom. "Good job, Frank. If a question makes you uncomfortable, make light of it or pivot onto another subject. You're not bound by her agenda."

Sam turned to Frank. "I'm beginning to wonder if this is a good idea."

"I'd like to ask you a bit about your work. I realize it's in the early stages, but is it true that you're continuing part of the experiments that brought Frank to life?"

This was a question that they were expecting, and that they had rehearsed thoroughly. After a good deal of discussion, they decided that Frank would be the most effective spokesman. "Rachel, while I don't regret the fact of my birth—or regeneration, or whatever you want to call it—the fact remains that bringing dead people back to life raises a multitude of ethical and legal and moral questions that, honestly, we are not anywhere near being prepared to answer. While I am grateful for my own existence, it's clear that this is not a path that humanity should go down anytime soon, if ever. One of the questions of our bioethics project has been asking is whether being able to do something is enough of a reason to do it, and we have concluded that the answer to that is 'No.' So, I am the first and, in all likelihood, the last of my kind."

"Yet you are continuing the experiments?"

Now Sam spoke up. "No, and it would be misleading to say so. What we have agreed to shut down is any attempt to reanimate sentient life.

Frank himself is a good reason why. A person might want to bring a loved one back from death but, as we've seen, the new person has almost no connection with the old. So, the primary reason for doing so is insufficient."

"So, what are you doing?"

"Trying to save lives," said Frank.

"We're experimenting with reanimating the organs of the deceased. Too often, a person in need of a transplant dies because an appropriate donor cannot be found in time. What if we could find such a donor among the much larger population of the recently dead, as opposed to the merely dying? If we could bring a heart or kidney back to life again, making it fully functional, it could be transplanted into a living body needing that organ replaced."

Maddow looked thoughtful as she contemplated the possibilities.

The mood was broken by Frank saying, "Pretty cool, huh?"

She looked at Frank and laughed. "Indeed, it is. Thank you both coming onto the show. And a hearty *mazel tov* on your forthcoming wedding."

In our living room, Tom muted the sound. "That was perfect. That's the difference between working with a pro and dealing with crackpots."

"That seemed to go well," Joanne agreed, albeit tentatively.

"It did. It went very well. No doubt someone looking to stir up trouble will take things out of context, but then that's the beauty of this. We can refute any such claims with actual clips from the interview."

The thing that concerned me was that we still didn't know what that crackpot Twitchell was up to. He had seemingly abandoned his post picketing our house. Further, he had not shown up for the contempt hearing for Guerrero, where she was given a one-year sentence—suspended so long as there was not any further violation. It was made very clear that there would not be a third chance.

Things calmed down after the interview. As Tom had predicted, the media feeding frenzy consisted of consuming their own. The interview was hashed and rehashed from every angle, but no one tried to get around his firm answer that there would be no more interviews before the wedding. In fact, the major reaction at the university was over Frank's announcement that they were experimenting with reanimating organs.

However, before the newscasts could start showing film clips from old shockers like *The Crawling Eye*, Dr. Simonson, the head of the Bioethics Department, met with a few science reporters and explained that, so far, they had worked with the pancreas of a mouse and the lung of a hamster, so the zombie apocalypse was, in fact, many years off.

Indeed, when the dust settled, it turned out the biggest fallout from the bachelor party had been almost entirely overlooked. Ian the real estate broker/Scotch authority and Evelyn, Sam and Frank's classmate, had become an item. It was Sam asking her mother if we could add a "plus 1" to Evelyn's R.S.V.P. that led us to the next great hurdle of the wedding preparations: the seating chart. Adding Ian to the grad students' table was easy. They'd mostly met, except for the couple of spouses not in attendance that night.

The problem was that the only times extended family got together was for weddings and funerals, and our goal was to make sure that the one didn't turn into the other. This involved having an encyclopedic knowledge of who wasn't talking to whom, what grudges going back years had remained unresolved, which remarried spouses should not be seated at the same table and making sure none of these people were seated with anyone from the bank. As the special ambassador for the Middle East was not available to lend his diplomatic skills, it was left to Joanne and me to negotiate the territory.

Sunday afternoon, Joanne and I were in our dining room, the table no longer covered with wedding invitations but with R.S.V.P. cards. A few tables were already set. The small wedding party allowed a table for Frank, Sam, Joanne, me as best man, Susan as maid of honor, and her fiancé Gary. Another table consisted of the grad students and Dr. Simonson and his husband. My heart went out to Ian. I hoped he'd bring a flask with him to get through the shop talk. Two tables were set aside for people from the bank, with the tellers and loan officers at one table, and a handful of executives and their spouses at the other. I shuddered to think what would happen if the vice president for real estate was seated next to the person who serviced our ATMs. We designated another table for the "professionals": Rabbi Wheaton, Cantor Eisenstein, Neal Kennerly, Tom Hammer, and their respective spouses. I had no idea what the conversation would be at that table, but they all had to interact with the public professionally, so I was confident they'd do just fine.

Joanne looked at the layout of the ballroom and was pleased. We would be seated at what was designated as the "head table"—although it was as round as the others—on the opposite side of the dance floor from Mike and his band. Mike would get to sit at the graduate table between sets. The rest of the band would be well taken care of in a room off the kitchen. The location of other tables seemed to be at random, at least until we got to the family assignments. Then I saw that they had been shrewdly selected as buffers.

This seemed an excellent moment to open my gift bottle from Ian. It was a lovely 12-year-old. I poured myself a bit, and asked Joanne if she'd like some.

"No, dear. This is a time to keep a clear head," she said, as much to me as to herself.

We filled two more tables with our friends from the neighborhood and other social groups, and Sam's friends from college, high school, and one girl she'd known since they met at sleepaway camp at age ten. We managed to squeeze out one more table—this of cousins and second cousins of Sam—since they were all in approximately the same age range. We figured they could spend the evening trying to figure out how, or if, they were related.

We were lucky that Frank's list had been so short. In fact, other than the grad students, the only person he added was Josh, the head usher from the Temple. It was a toss-up between the grad students and the cousins, and Joanne decided that Josh, who was single, would be more likely to find a nice Jewish girl at the cousins table. I wasn't aware that matchmaking was among our responsibilities, but we had him seated, and that was the important thing.

What was surprising was the number of family members we had invited expecting them to say "No" who had instead said "Yes."

"You haven't seen your Aunt Paula in twenty years," I remembered complaining when reviewing the original invitation list. "Why are we inviting her?"

"Because we got invited to all of her children's weddings," said Joanne matter-of-factly. "And we had to send a gift to each of them. Now, maybe, we'll get a gift back."

Most likely the same gift. I think every large family has a large collection of useless gifts that go from wedding to wedding until somebody finally decides they've turned into valuable antiques and sells them on eBay.

With all these people coming, there was the problem that many of them had complicated histories. I expressed the hope that the wedding would be neutral territory, like Switzerland, and everyone would be on their best behavior. Dream on. The record turnout was because so many of them were curious to see, if not meet, Frank. The invitation was a pass to the most talked-about social event of the season, and therefore something not to be missed. That didn't mean that bygones got to be bygones.

"You can't put the Steins and the Helpmans at the same table, because they were partners in a Florida timeshare that went bankrupt, and your Uncle Henry never forgave the Helpmans." I took their return cards and placed them at separate tables. "That will do for the moment," she continued. "Of course, my cousin Molly is getting a divorce, and so we can't seat her at the same table as her sister Helen."

You would have thought that I'd learn by now not to question such pronouncements, but I didn't do well with missing pieces. "Why not?"

"Because Molly's husband ran off with Helen."

"Will he be coming to the wedding, too?"

"I'm not sure. We'd better put them on opposite sides of the room."

The obvious thing to do would have been to seat Joanne's family with my family, since most of them had never met, but it would have been too obvious that we were keeping them away from other people. I suggested giving each person their own table, but that idea went nowhere.

"You know, it's not too late. We could still send them to Vegas to elope," I said.

"Don't even think about it," Joanne answered.

Somehow, we got everyone placed, even though one of the tables would have to be enlarged to fit sixteen, while another one would consist of just five people. Joanne carefully wrote in the names at each table and collected the cards. It had been a grueling four hours, but we did it. I waited for her to check off "Assign seating" from the almighty list, but instead—before rolling the seating chart up—she carefully wrote at the top of it, "Seating arrangements v.1.0."

I looked at her. "Are you kidding? What more has to be done?"

"We've got another few weeks, dear. A few more response cards could require us to start all over again."

CHAPTER FOURTEEN

It was the day of the wedding. The guests had risen from their seats as Samantha made her way down the aisle. There was a murmur of excitement. Under the chuppah—the traditional wedding canopy—stood Rabbi Wheaton and Cantor Eisenstein. Frank and I smartly dressed in our tuxes with elaborate white boutonnieres affixed to our lapels, stood on one side. Across from us was Susan, the maid of honor, dressed all in blue. The music swelled as Samantha slowly came forward, although it seemed to be taking much longer than it had at the rehearsal. I didn't recall the aisle being so long.

From out of the crowd came a harsh whisper, "What is that music? Why aren't they playing 'Here Comes the Bride'?"

Joanne, looking splendid in her gray and black ensemble, turned back and yelled, "Because it was written by that Nazi bastard Wagner."

As I wondered what was taking Sam so long to get to us, Frank leaned over and whispered in my ear, "You have the rings?"

Did I have the rings? Of course, I had the rings, I reached into my right jacket pocket and pulled out a slip of paper. "Inspected by No. 37," it read. I hurriedly checked my left pocket, my four pants pockets, and my inside jacket pockets. No rings. Had I forgotten to retrieve them from the vault? Oh no. I had to fix this quickly. There was no time to lose. I went running up the aisle. As I passed Sam, I shouted, "Start without me. I'll be right back."

Out at the curb, I pushed aside a lady with a walker trying to figure out just how she was going to get it and herself into a taxi. I made it easy by pushing them both away from the cab. "Sorry, this is an emergency."

Once at the bank, I needed to type in both analog and digital codes, offer up fingerprints and retinal scans, and then go through facial recognition. The last thing I was required to do before I could open the vault was to answer a security question: What was the name of your first pet?

"Chase." I typed in.

On screen appeared, "Really?"

"Yes, really."

"Funny name for a dog."

I could hear the gears and bolts and wheels of the vault moving and turning as the massive door swung open. I ran in and found my safety deposit box. Using the bank key on the first lock and my personal key on the second, I opened the little door and slid out the box, placing it on the table in the center of the space. Opening the lid, I began rummaging through the various items looking for the rings. There was the deed to my silver mine, a folded-up canvas of a long-missing oil painting, my stamp collection, and a treasure map. I'll have to dig that chest up someday, I thought, as I continued rifling through the contents, looking for those two small blue boxes containing the rings. At last I found them.

Carefully placing both of them in my right jacket pocket—after first making sure that they each contained the appropriate ring—I reversed the process of locking up: close the box, slide it in, close the door, turn the keys. Mission accomplished. Now to get back to the wedding.

I turned to the massive vault door and watched as it began to swing shut.

"No!!!!" I shouted as I ran to get through the opening before it was too late, screaming the whole while. If I was trapped in the vault, I'd not only miss the wedding, but I could die, as it was airtight. This couldn't be happening.

I was still screaming when I sat bolt upright in my bed, drenched in sweat.

It was 2 A.M. We were sitting in the kitchen as Joanne warmed a mug of milk in the microwave. What I wanted to do was open the bottle of scotch, but Joanne vetoed that. "Warm milk. It will sooth your stomach, calm you down, and help you get back to sleep."

"I may never sleep again."

"Don't be silly. Of course, you'll sleep. What you need to do is make a list."

I looked up at her, not quite sure if I had heard that right. "A list?"

"What do you think keeps me focused? It's all a matter of organization. As long as I'm following the plan, I know I have nothing to worry about. Everything's accounted for." She handed me a pad and pen. "Now, let's make your list. What do you have to do for the wedding?"

"Besides pay the bills?"

She gave me a pitying look, and then said, "Write it down."

I wrote, "Pay the bills."

She gestured that I should drink some of the milk. "Okay, what else do you need to do before the wedding?"

I thought about it a moment. "Pick up the tuxedos."

"Go ahead, write it down."

I was way ahead of her. After adding it to the list, I said, "Pick up the rings."

"Good. See how easy this is? Anything else?"

I really couldn't figure out if there was anything else... oh, yes, I almost forgot. I had another responsibility in my second role at the wedding. "Write the best man's toast." After I wrote that down, I put the empty mug on the table next to the pad.

"See how easy that was?" said Joanne. "Now that's your list. If you remember something else you need to do, you add it to the list. Once you've accomplished a task, you check it off. No more nightmares, because you know you won't forget anything." She picked up the mug and rinsed it off in the sink. "And now let's get back to bed, I've got a busy day tomorrow."

I turned off the light in the kitchen. Before heading upstairs, Joanne went into the dining room and turned on the light, looking at her master list against the wall. "Let's see: finalize menu with the caterer. Confirm times for Samantha, Susan, and myself at the salon. Make sure florist is all set."

I took her hand. "Thank you."

"Trust the list, dear, and nothing can possibly go wrong."

I finally got that drink I had wanted at the club after work on Wednesday. Joanne was helping Sam shop for some clothes for the honeymoon which, as it happened, was not going to be in the Carpathian Mountains after all. They were being cagy about where they had decided to go, but when Frank asked me about the Universal Studios tour, I wondered if he was still obsessing over old movie monsters.

I was looking for a place to sit in what might have been mistaken for the library but for the fact that a well-stocked bar took up a good portion of one side of the room. The rest of the space consisted of chairs upholstered in dark leather, dark wood, and dark curtains, all of which were winning the battle with the afternoon sun. Lamps started to be turned on here and there, but in spite of the walls full of shelved books, it was the sort of light that would get you yelled at by your mother if your tried to read by it. Indeed, I wasn't even sure if the books were real, or simply props from a theatrical supply house, consisting of nothing but the outer bindings.

A man of roughly my age was sitting by one of the windows, and when he saw me, he waved me over. I was fairly certain that I hadn't met him, but looking around the room, I couldn't see any other open seats, so I figured why not? If he got past the membership committee, he was presumably an upstanding citizen of the community and not some tabloid reporter.

He stood as I came over. "I'm pretty sure that we haven't met. I'm Oscar Mulvaney."

It took me a moment. Yes, of course, the liquor distributor.

"And I'm—"

"Yes, of course I know who you are. It's not possible to have been living in this town for the last few months without knowing that. But please, have a seat."

As we sat down, Oscar signaled the waiter to come over to take my drink order. I ordered a Manhattan on the rocks. It seemed a festive way to end the day.

When my drink arrived, he picked up his glass, containing something amber, and said, "To your daughter and prospective son-in-law, every success."

We tapped glasses. "Why thank you. I wasn't sure how you'd be feeling after that nonsense at the tasting."

Mulvaney waved his hand dismissively. "Think nothing of it. Ian said it had been quite an adventure, and he's now seeing that young woman from the university. All's well that ends well."

"Yes, she had mentioned something about wanting to bring him to the wedding."

"Young love, eh?" chuckled Mulvaney. "Of course, we have a few more miles on us. Married thirty years."

I raised my glass to him. "Thirty-two for me and Joanne. Doesn't matter. Your wedding day is the one day where you not interested in hearing the voice of experience."

"Isn't that the case? When my older son got married last year, I wanted to give him the benefit of my being in a marriage that endured, and what it takes to make it work. He wasn't interested. *He* was going to be different."

I laughed. "Of course. They're all going to be different. But weren't we just the same at that age?"

"I wonder about that sometimes," he replied. "If our kids are younger versions of us, have we turned into our parents?"

"Just as long I don't turn into my in-laws." That got a laugh. "Seriously, isn't it hard not to want to help your kids avoid the pitfalls?"

Mulvaney put down his glass. "When they're younger it's easier. Children think their parents know everything. When they're young adults they think their parents don't know anything."

"I have a good relationship with my daughter, but right now I think I'm at the stage where my opinion is more tolerated than respected."

"I don't mean to pry," began Mulvaney, "but are you happy about this marriage? I mean, is this the son-in-law you were expecting?"

Now I had to laugh. "I don't think anybody could have expected Frank. And when Samantha first brought him home, it was a bit of a shock."

"I'll bet."

"But as I got to know him, I saw a bit of what she saw in him: a smart, decent, caring man with, I have to say, an odd sense of humor. I suppose it would be the same if he had come from another country or culture. First you see the differences but then you see the person."

"And the fact that he's a corpse doesn't bother you?"

"*Reanimated* corpse, thank you very much," I answered. "Frank is very much alive. He's not a shuffling hulk or a zombie, shedding body parts along the way. His complexion is a bit on the gray side, and when you shake his hand for the first time you might feel the difference, but it passes."

"So, you're satisfied it's a good match?"

"As much as any father of an only daughter is ever satisfied that anyone is going to be good enough for his baby."

"Then I wish them well," he said, raising his glass only to notice it was empty. He looked to call the waiter over.

I felt a vibrating in my pocket, and between the Manhattan and the conversation, it took me a moment to realize it was my phone. How did we ever survive in a world where people couldn't instantly reach us where ever we were? I was going to let it go to voicemail, but then I saw it was Sam. "Excuse me," I said to Mulvaney. "It's my daughter."

"Of course," he said, still looking for the waiter.

"Hello, dear, what is it?"

"Daddy," she said, and I was instantly aware she had been crying, "We need you."

"What's the matter? Where are you?" Too many scenarios ran through my head, from a protester getting violent, to Frank suddenly recovering the memories of his past life and realizing he was already married, for me to even guess which would be the least stressful.

"It's Frank. We're at the hospital. I think he's dying."

CHAPTER FIFTEEN

The trip to the hospital went by in a blur. I parked the car and hurried to the entrance, with only one thought on my mind: my baby needs me. Waiting right inside the entrance was Joanne.

"What's the matter? What's going on? Is Frank all right?"

Joanne gave me a hug, as much for herself as for me, and then said, "He's okay for the moment. They're doing tests."

"Where's Sam? How could you leave her alone?" I was babbling, I admit. I was running on adrenaline and needed to get answers. So far, I was getting very few.

"Samantha is fine, dear. She's in the cafeteria with Mike and Evelyn. We figured it was easier for me to find you than for you to find us."

Joanne led the way to the cafeteria, which I'm certain I wouldn't have found on my own in my present state of mind. They were sitting around a table with lots of coffee cups and some half-eaten pastries. When Sam saw me, she ran over and threw her arms around my neck. I appreciated the emotional state she was in, but she was starting to cut off my breath. I gently disengaged without letting go.

"Daddy, I'm so scared."

"Tell me what happened."

We went back to the table and sat down. Evelyn and Mike made their greetings, and then mumbled something about having to check for messages. They could have easily done it at the table, but I suspected that they had been through this several times already and needed the break.

"Do you want some coffee?" asked Joanne.

"No, I don't think coffee is going to make this any easier."

"Well, I do," she said, and went over to the urn for a refill.

"So, what happened?"

Sam took a deep breath and let it out, as if steeling herself for the task of reliving the day's events. "We were in our seminar with Dr. Simonson this afternoon when Frank started complaining about feeling rundown and dizzy. Dr. Simonson looked at him and said he was looking a bit pale."

"Frank? Pale? How could he tell?"

"Actually, it was more that his eyes and skin had taken on a yellowish tinge."

"Yellowish? Like jaundice?"

"That's what they're thinking. Dr. Simonson asked him to stay after class, but Frank said it wasn't necessary. He was feeling fine."

"Typical man," said Joanne, who had come back with a fresh cup.

Sam ignored her. "Frank said all he needed was some water, and got up to get some, and then he collapsed."

"He passed out?"

"He kept drifting in and out. Dr. Simonson called an ambulance and ordered a bunch of tests. And now we're waiting to find out what's gone wrong."

"And Samantha is taking after your side of the family in imagining the worst. I say we let the medical professionals handle this." I could have taken offense, but as Sam and I took our seats, I realized this was simply Joanne's way of coping. It was clear that nobody knew, as of yet, what was going on. It seemed fruitless to speculate with so little information available.

While we were waiting with nothing else to do, I called Tom to give him a quick update, just in case anyone at the hospital turned out to be a blabbermouth and he started getting phone calls. Better safe than sorry.

"You did the right thing," Tom said. "If anyone asks, I'll say he's in for some routine tests, and that there's nothing further to say."

"What if they ask about the wedding?"

"It's going on as scheduled," Tom answered without missing a beat. He seemed a lot more certain than I was at this point.

"What if that changes?" I asked.

"We'll cross that bridge when we come to it."

Two hours later, Dr. Simonson found us in the cafeteria. He said Frank was resting comfortably and we'd be able to see him, but to keep it short. He obviously had more to say, but didn't want to speak in front of non-family members. So, Mike and Evelyn said they'd pop into his room to say hello and goodbye and head home. Sam hugged them both and thanked them for their support.

As if trying to delay the delivery of any bad news, Joanne asked the doctor if he wanted any coffee. At this point, they just should have set her up with a caffeine drip. It was now after 9 P.M., and she'd been here since the middle of the afternoon. He thanked her but passed.

The three of us sat expectantly, waiting to hear his verdict: do they know what's happened? More importantly, is it treatable? As in the story about Rabbi Hillel that Frank liked so much, everything else was commentary. Dr. Simonson sat up straight in his seat, put his hands in front of him, and tented his fingers. It was a gesture I was beginning to find extremely annoying.

"Let me give you the bottom line, and then I can fill in the details and answer your questions. Frank has jaundice. What's led to it remains unknown, so we are continuing with a variety of blood tests, scans, and a biopsy of his liver. The reason for this is that jaundice is a symptom of something else that's gone wrong in the body, and until we identify what it is that's taken ill, we cannot plan a course of treatment."

This sounded hopeful or, at least, like it could have been a lot worse. "How long do you think before you'll be able to identify the cause?" I asked.

"I would hope we would have some indication, if not a definitive answer, within the next twenty-four to forty-eight hours. In the meantime, I've had Frank admitted so we can deal with any immediate symptoms related to the jaundice, like severe itching or insomnia, while we await a diagnosis."

"So, he's not dying?" asked Sam in a very small voice.

"No, Samantha, not that we can tell. Jaundice, if left untreated, can be a serious and even fatal condition, but he's nowhere near that stage, and he's now going to get round-the-clock care."

For a change, I didn't have to worry about the cost. As part of the resolution of *In re: Frank*, the university had agreed to provide his medical insurance indefinitely.

"Can I see him now?" asked Sam, sounding a little more like her usual self.

"Yes, of course. Just don't tire him out. You can come back in the morning. He'll be getting some sedatives to help him get through the night."

Joanne, who had been quiet since offering him coffee, rose and shook his hand. "Thank you, Dr. Simonson."

"There's no need to thank me. Frank is an important part of my family—my university family—too. Our program needs him almost as much as you do."

Strings had been pulled, and Frank had a private room on the top floor of the hospital, the area reserved for special cases or, more usually, VIPs. He lay in bed with the back ratcheted up, flipping through the offerings on the TV protruding from the wall.

He smiled when we came in. Sam made it to the bed before he had a chance to move, not that he was going to get very far. He was getting oxygen through a tube to his nose, and he was wired to an array of monitors which were recording various metrics like his respiration and heart rate. She covered his face with kisses, and then stood back. "Honey, I was so frightened," she said.

"There's no reason to be afraid, they're taking good care of me. I've got three movie channels and all the gelatin I can eat. Who could ask for anything more?"

"You gave us a good scare," I said, trying to follow his lead in lightening the mood.

"Wait until you see what I have planned for Halloween."

Joanne went over and kissed his forehead. "No temperature," she declared.

"Well, I hope I have some temperature...."

"You don't have a fever, is what I meant."

"All this fancy equipment, and you can tell that with a kiss?"

"Now listen, smart guy," she said with a hint of a smile, "don't you give the doctors and nurses any trouble. Do what they say and let's get you out of here. You've got a wedding coming up."

"Mother!"

I stepped in. "Let's let the two of them say good night," I said, guiding Joanne to the door. "We'll see you tomorrow."

We gave them a few minutes to themselves, and then Sam came out, struggling to keep the smile on her face and the tears from overflowing her tear ducts.

"You'll stay with us tonight," said Joanne, as we headed downstairs toward the parking lot.

At breakfast, everyone tried to give the impression of business as usual. Joanne even opened the return cards for the wedding that had arrived in yesterday's mail, but I could tell her heart wasn't in it when she didn't immediately pull out the seating chart to figure out where she was going to place the late arrivals. I called the bank to let them know I'd be in later this morning. It wasn't until I hung up that it registered that my secretary had said she was praying for Frank. This was not good.

Oh, it was perfectly fine that my secretary was so moved by Frank's plight that she would pray for his well-being. What was not fine was that she knew that there was something that needed her prayers at all. It could only mean one thing. News had leaked. And that would mean things could get ugly when we arrived at the hospital to see Frank. If they knew he had been hospitalized, it was a safe bet that they knew where as well.

I didn't say anything to Sam about the call, but when she went to gather her things, I quickly filled in Joanne. Sam had enough on her mind worrying about Frank. She did not need rude questions being screamed at her while she was going in to see him. I told Joanne that they should drop me off near the hospital's main entrance, and then drive around and park on the other side of the building, where they could go in through one of the back doors.

When we arrived at the hospital, I got out and waited until the car turned the corner before sauntering up to the main entrance. As I suspected, there was a gaggle of reporters there, and even a camera crew from one of the television stations.

"There he is," I heard someone shout, and suddenly I was in one of those scenes you see in the movies, where the person leaving the courthouse is just trying to get to the taxi at the curb and is forced to hold a press conference in the middle of the street.

"Has Frank contracted the Plague?" shouted one reporter, "Is the public in any danger?"

"We saw Rabbi Wheaton arrive. Will the wedding be taking place from Frank's hospital bed?"

"Is the rabbi here to conduct last rites?"

"Is Frank dying?"

"Stop!" I shouted. "Frank is not dying. He's here for a routine series of tests. I have no idea why the rabbi is here, but it's not to perform the wedding and it's certainly not for last rites, which is part of the Catholic faith. Frank will be discharged when they're done with him, and the wedding will take place on schedule."

With that, I turned and pushed my way through the crowd toward the entrance. I made no eye contact with anyone nor did I engage in any further statement or even react to the questions being shouted inches from my face. I may have stepped on someone's foot. I certainly hope so.

When I got inside, I saw several security guards milling about, watching through the windows. "Big help you were," I said, annoyed that they had allowed this mob to congregate.

"We're sorry, but the hospital lawyers instructed us that we could keep them out of the building, but that the sidewalk is a public space and we should not engage with them there. They won't bother you any further."

I made my way to the elevators and headed toward Frank's room. When I got there, I was surprised by the sound of laughter.

"Thank you, Thing," said a familiar woman's voice.

Inside Frank, Sam, Joanne, and Rabbi Wheaton were watching an episode of *The Addams Family* on TV.

"I can't believe you've never seen this," Rabbi Wheaton was saying. "I used to watch this with my dad as a kid."

"We were a *Munsters* family," said Sam, as if she was expressing a preference for French impressionist painters over abstract expressionists.

I couldn't believe we were about to witness an argument over two half-century-old sit-coms about monstrous families. On screen, Lurch the butler entered, exclaiming, "You rang?" to great hilarity from the laugh track.

"Well, it doesn't matter to me," said Frank. "I like them both."

"Ah, a peacemaker, just like Moses's brother Aaron," said the rabbi, looking a little smug at getting in the last word.

Before we had a chance to debate the rest of the television schedule, Dr. Simonson arrived. Reluctantly, Frank turned the set off. Score one for Sam.

"Thank you for coming by, rabbi, I'm sure you have other patients you need to see," said Joanne diplomatically.

"Oh, yes, the work never stops," he said, clearly disappointed that he would not be in on the latest news. Turning to the bed, he addressed

Frank, "We will pray for *refuah shleimah*—a full and complete recovery for you, speedily and soon."

"Thank you, Rabbi Wheaton. I appreciate your visit."

The rabbi shook hands all around, including with a somewhat surprised Dr. Simonson, and took his leave. After he was gone, Frank looked at the doctor sternly, "If you want any more of my blood, I'm going to have to start charging you." He then turned to the rest of us, "It's a funny way to cure anemia—by seeing that you have *less* blood."

"All right, enough with the kibitzing," said Joanne, all business. "Dr. Simonson, do you have any news for us?"

"Yes and no."

"That's not good," said Frank.

"Well, yes and no," repeated Dr. Simonson. "We think we've figured out what the problem is, and we think it's treatable. That's the good news."

"And the bad news?" This was Sam, girding herself for whatever it might be.

"We're not quite sure of the extent of it, and thus, we're not quite sure how involved correcting it will be."

It was time for me to get everyone to the point. "You'll excuse my excessive curiosity, doctor, but what exactly is 'it'?"

"Oh, I'm sorry. We just got the biopsy report back a little while ago, and we're going to need further tests. However, we're fairly certain what's causing the jaundice."

"And that is…"

"Frank," said Dr. Simonson, "you seem to have cirrhosis of the liver."

CHAPTER SIXTEEN

The diagnosis was a bit of a shock to all of us, and for a long moment no one said a word. Finally, Sam broke the silence.

"That makes no sense. Cirrhosis is a disease that usually follows years of alcohol abuse. Even if Frank overindulged at his bachelor party"—he put up his hands in a "Who, me?" gesture—"that wouldn't have done it."

Joanne took this in, and then turned to Simonson, "Well, doctor?"

I hardly knew what to say. If it turned out that his present metabolism changed the way alcohol affected his body, I might be guilty of having set all this in motion.

Looking very much like the professor addressing his seminar, he turned to Joanne. "Samantha is quite right. It's highly unlikely that anything Frank drank since his, er, reanimation would have had the impact on his liver that our tests have discovered."

Well, that was good news. I was off the hook. And Frank had no reason to beat up on himself, since it was clear that his current drinking habits couldn't possibly have been a factor here.

"Well, I'll drink to that," said Frank, attempting to lighten the mood. "Except all I have here is a pitcher of room-temperature water. Dear, do you think you could get me some ice?"

Samantha stepped out of the room to ask if someone at the nurse's station could spare a minute to get Frank some ice. Fortunately, there were no Code Reds or other dramatic emergencies going on at the moment, and the ice was soon delivered.

Simonson had taken a seat and begun explaining that until they had surveyed the damage to the liver, it was hard to say what the next step would be. He was outlining several possible courses of action when Frank interrupted.

"Something doesn't make sense. If *I* didn't do this, that means the previous, um, owner of this body must have been a heavy drinker. But why would they have gone through all that trouble to reanimate a damaged body? For all they knew, I could have been brought to life only to immediately collapse."

Sam went over to the hospital bed and took Frank's hand, kissing him on the cheek. It wasn't a sexy kiss. It was one of affection, sympathy, and immense love. "Dear, I'm beginning to think that was the point."

"Go ahead, Samantha," said Simonson, "Connect the dots for us."

I could tell Joanne was as clueless as I about this turn in the conversation. I went over to be by her side.

Standing next to the bed, she addressed the four of us. "Look, we know the people doing these experiments weren't the most ethical people. They were working surreptitiously, stealing equipment, not to mention bodies and body parts from the morgue... it was not the sort of behavior that was going to impress the Nobel committee."

"So, they were scum," I said. "What's your point?"

"That they may be scum, but they weren't stupid. Beyond the innovations they came up with, they worked methodically. They started with small organisms and then larger ones, and then body parts, and then, finally, Frank."

"We know that, Sam," said Frank. "I was the culmination of all their experiments."

Sam took both his hands in hers. "No, dear, you weren't. You were merely the next step."

"I don't understand," said Joanne. "They wanted to bring a man back to life. That's what they said at their trials."

"That's right. And they failed."

Now I was confused. "How can you say they failed when the proof is right in front of us? They brought Frank back to life."

"Don't you see? They didn't. They brought someone's body back to life without any of his memories. Whoever that person was, he was gone. The experiment was only a partial success."

"But what does that have to do with Frank's liver?"

If someone had told me I was going have to a conversation like this someday, I never would have believed them. And then, as if it weren't already complicated enough, things got really strange. "It's like *The Jazz Singer*," said Sam.

"Who?" asked Joanne, even more at sea than I was.

"*The Jazz Singer*. The first talking movie. Except it wasn't."

"I have no idea what you're talking about," interrupted Frank. "But I can listen to you for hours. Please keep going."

She gave him a smile, and then turned to us. "When I was an undergraduate. one of my electives was in film history. And we saw *The Jazz Singer*, which came out in 1927 and achieved fame as the first talkie. Within two years, the silent movie was gone."

"If you say so," I responded.

"The point is that *The Jazz Singer* wasn't the first talkie and it wasn't supposed to change everything. But like Frank, it did."

"Does this mean I'm going to have to sing? I had enough trouble learning to chant all the blessings," said Frank.

"The movie was simply the latest in a series of experiments in synchronizing a soundtrack with motion pictures. There had been a series of shorts. Think of the experiments they did with animals. Then they did a movie that had a pre-recorded musical soundtrack. That was like the experiments with various human body parts. And then they did *The Jazz Singer*."

"And how was that like Frank?" That came from Simonson, who seemed to be following this with great interest, certainly better than the rest of us.

"Because it was supposed to be the next step. Al Jolson was going to sing on camera, and both the music and his singing would be recorded. It was still a mostly silent movie, complete with title cards."

"But…"

"But, apparently, they didn't tell Jolson to keep quiet. He started adlibbing dialogue. The other actors didn't know what to do, but he was on a roll. It was all recorded, and when they played it back, they realized they had a movie with singing *and* talking. And when it was shown to the public, they not only accepted it, they demanded more. I don't know what the next experiment with sound would have been, but it was no longer necessary."

Simonson nodded. "And when the authorities were called in on the illegal experiments, there was no chance to find out what further plans they had. In bringing Frank to life, they seemed to have come to the culmination of their project."

"Exactly," said Sam. "For them, Frank was likely only a stage. So, they didn't care if the body they had contained problems. They probably didn't think he would last very long."

"Or planned to terminate him when they were ready to move on."

A sickening silence fell on the room as the full realization sunk in of just how little Frank had meant to the people who had brought him to life. It was broken when Frank said, "I don't think I want to be a 'Jazz Singer'."

"Honey," said Sam, "what it means is that you didn't create the problem. They simply didn't bother to check very deeply what your condition was."

"Okay, I get what you're saying," I said, "but why wasn't this discovered afterward? There were all those tests…"

Simonson shook his head. "At the point when the authorities were trying to figure out what to do with Frank, the only question was whether he could be considered a living, sentient being. So, there were IQ tests and personality tests, and his life signs were checked, but as long as he was breathing and had a pulse, he would have passed. It's also not clear what effect the reanimation process had on his condition. It may have masked it or slowed it down so that it wouldn't have been immediately obvious."

Frank sighed. "This is all very disheartening."

"Oh, honey…"

Simonson rose out of his chair and strode over to the bed. "Frank, get a grip. None of this is a reflection on *you*. You are a remarkable person who has much to offer the world. You have a bad liver? So, what? We can deal with that. You are not responsible for the actions of the person you were, nor of the despicable people who ignored your condition when they enlisted you for their experiments. So, pull yourself together while we figure out what to do next."

Frank looked at the doctor. "That was quite an inspirational speech. What if I don't buy it?"

"Then I'll have no choice," said Simonson. "I'll have to give you a failing grade for the semester."

There was a moment as we all processed what he said, and then Sam started to giggle.

"Oh, all right," said Frank with great drama, "Fix my liver."

By the next morning, Frank was stable, and they had done all the tests they could. Dr. Simonson had him discharged. With no fanfare, he left the hospital at midday through a side entrance. By the time the reporters in front of the building realized that Frank was leaving, he was already home.

Frank and Sam came over for dinner that evening, which allowed her to retrieve her things from the nights she had spent here. I had asked Tom to join us for dessert and coffee. After making sure that Frank was doing okay—or as well as could be expected under the circumstances—Tom said to me, "You handled yourself perfectly in front of the hospital. You gave them something to work with, ignored their baiting questions, and cut it off without really telling them anything." He took in the family group. "Folks, I know this isn't easy for you. You didn't ask to be public figures, but the press isn't going away. No matter what they say to you, you don't have to respond. And if you're going to say anything at all, you should decide on what it will be beforehand and, even then, you really should run it by me first."

"Do we have to tell them about Frank's medical condition?" asked Joanne.

"Absolutely not. He's not a public official. The public has no right to know. Indeed, Frank, I don't know if your lawyer has gone over it with you, but your doctor is forbidden by law from revealing any confidential information without your permission. It's called the doctor/patient privilege."

"I get what you're saying, Tom," I said, "but if Frank requires hospitalization for treatment, I don't think they're going to buy 'routine tests' again."

The whole family was feeling rattled, and Tom was trying to calm us down. "One step at a time. The only thing *they*"—gesturing to the press and the outside world—"want to know about is the wedding. Are you considering postponing or cancelling it?"

"Dr. Simonson said as long as Frank does nothing to tax his condition, there's no reason it can't go on as scheduled," said Sam with what seemed to be as much relief as conviction.

"And Frank? You're on board with this?"

Frank told the publicist, "As sure as I know I'm not Al Jolson."

Tom looked puzzled. "Excuse me?"

"Private family joke," I quickly interjected. "Frank, the wedding proceeds, right?"

"Absolutely." He paused, and for a moment I was afraid he was going to break out into a chorus of "Blue Skies," but instead he said, "It's going to take more than a liver to keep me from marrying Sam."

The past several months had been a series of shocks, from our introduction to Frank to all the wedding preparations, plus having to deal with the press and the protestors. Every time I thought I had reached my limit and couldn't take any more, a new crisis arose. As we dealt with each thing, one after another, I kept thinking to myself, "This is it. One more thing and I'm going to crack."

I was reminded how I had worried before Sam was born whether I was capable of being a good father to her. Could I feed her and guide her and take care of her? I didn't even know if I would be able to change her diaper. One day I was talking to someone at the bank during lunch. I was not yet a vice president and was having a sandwich at my desk where I worked as a loan officer. One of the senior execs was walking by and stopped to say hello. He was one of the old timers, one of those Yankees with deep roots in the community who seemed to have been born with only last names: Graydon Emerson Cathcart III. I don't know what was stranger, that there were two other people with that name, or that a man several decades my senior was known as "Skip."

"I understand you and your wife are expecting. How far along are you?"

"We're entering the third trimester."

"You must be very excited," he said. Skip was a genial sort, but we had little to do with each other. He must have sensed something about me.

"We're very excited. It's our first. And, I have to admit, I'm a little nervous as well."

Skip gave a genial chuckle. "Well, a baby changes everything, that's for sure, but I'm sure you'll do just fine. Nothing to be nervous about."

"I'm not even sure I'm going to be able to change a diaper."

Skip came into my office and took a seat. He removed a small cloth from a vest pocket and took off his wire-framed glasses which he commenced to clean. "Let me tell you a story. When my daughter was born, I was scared to death. The men in my family worked. The women raised the children. I didn't have any other model growing up. My wife made it clear that that was not the way things were going to work for us."

"What happened?"

"One afternoon, shortly after my daughter was born, my wife was out, and I was left alone with the baby. She was asleep, so I figured I couldn't mess up too badly. But then she woke up and started crying. Really loud crying, where the baby lets you know that she's not going to stop of her own accord."

I was surprised he was sharing this story with me, as it went far beyond the rather arm's-length relationship we had had up until then, but clearly there was a point he wanted to make. "So, what did you do?"

"I said to myself, 'My daughter needs me.' And that was all that mattered. Change her diaper, warm a bottle, make sure she burped: I ended up doing it all. I had no desire to do this for anyone else's baby, but this was my daughter, and anything I could do to make her life a little better in the world I would. You'll see. It happens so quickly and naturally you won't even notice it until after the fact."

He was right. That was exactly what happened. Somehow, through some fatherhood network he sensed that this was the advice I needed at that moment. I never forgot it.

All through Sam's life, it had always come down to that: if my daughter needed me, it didn't matter what the reason was. I would be there. I never could have guessed that someday she would need my support because her fiancé was a reanimated corpse with a bum liver, but the details didn't matter and never did. My daughter needed me.

I could handle this. I *would* handle this. From a diaper to a scraped knee to the first broken heart to the academic challenges and choices she had set for herself, I had always been there for Sam. I think I was prouder of that than of anything else in my life. I had met the challenge.

And then the phone rang.

CHAPTER SEVENTEEN

We were seated in Dr. Simonson's office. It was an academic office, somewhat messy, with shelves of books rather than cabinets of patient files. He would occasionally be called in to consult, but his work was at the university, not dealing with people facing life-threatening situations and their families. He was trying to make an effort at a bedside manner. The strain was showing.

"Frank, there's no sense in beating around the bush. Your liver is on the way out. If we did nothing, my best guess is you'd be dead within the year."

Samantha gave a gasp. Frank, surprisingly, seemed unmoved. "And I'm guessing," he said, "that you wouldn't be so blunt about it if there was nothing we could do."

Simonson sat back in his chair, not used to being addressed in such a fashion by one of his students. Well, he'd best get used to it. Frank still hadn't developed that internal censor that keeps most people from blurting out what's on their minds. There was a part of me that hoped he never would.

"You're right," said the doctor, finally. "What you need is a liver transplant. Medically, it's something we know how to do, and we know how to treat its effects. With a new liver, you would have a new lease on life."

"And the wedding?" asked Joanne. I couldn't blame her. We were all thinking it.

"The only reason it couldn't happen as scheduled is if the operation was occurring on the day of the wedding. Since that's unlikely, so long as Frank takes care of himself now, you should be able to celebrate right on schedule—although you might want to postpone the honeymoon. And there would be more conditions and precautions if we performed the surgery immediately, but I see no reason you can't go forward."

Joanne heaved a sigh of relief. There would be no need to notify everyone of a change in plans, no need to renegotiate contracts with the photographer, florist, caterer, videographer, etc. The only small glitch was that if the groom didn't get a new liver, he wouldn't make it to their first anniversary. I hesitated to say anything at a moment when everyone was feeling as positive as they could under the circumstances, so I spoke as offhandedly as I could.

"That's wonderful, Dr. Simonson. I'm sure I speak for my whole family when I say we're grateful for all your efforts. But since we're in unfamiliar territory, could you tell us what happens now?"

I couldn't read the expression on Sam's face, but I suspected she wanted to know too, but was too afraid to ask.

As for Simonson, he was in full pedant mode, getting to explain a process that he knew well, and which was a total mystery to us. "Well, the first thing we have to do is register Frank with UNOS, the United Network for Organ Sharing."

"Can't we just put an ad on Craig's List?" asked Frank.

"I'm afraid it doesn't work like that. There's a waiting list. If there wasn't someone setting the rules, you'd have capitalism run amok, with organs going to the highest bidder. This prevents that from happening."

"Okay, sign me up."

"That's just the start of the process. Then you have to get scored. There are somewhere between fifteen and twenty thousand people waiting for a liver, and the average waiting time is nearly a year."

Sam looked stricken again. "But you said he might not even have a year."

"And that's why they use MELD."

"I'm afraid to ask," I said, "but what is MELD?"

"MELD stands for Model for End-stage Liver Disease. It's a system that assigns points based on the severity of your condition, your location in likely proximity to potential donors, as well as the results of several of the tests you've undergone. Depending on how all these factors play out, you may be selected for an eligible donor sooner, rather than later."

"Or later, rather than sooner."

"Yes, that's true, but that would mean your condition was far less serious than we currently believe."

There was a cool logic to it all, but that didn't mean it was reassuring. "This all sounds like a complicated and cruel game. What if Frank's condition does get worse?" That was Joanne, whose occasional bouts of pessimism had their place. Certainly, right now was more than appropriate.

"You're not locked into your score," explained Simonson. "If your situation changes, your score changes. While we're hoping it doesn't come to this, there's even an opt-out called Status One. Were we to determine that, unless Frank got an immediate transplant, he could suffer irreversible damage or die, he would automatically move to the head of the list."

Frank contemplated that for a moment. "I don't know that that's fair. This whole system seems to be set up so that no one gets to cut the line."

"You're right," agreed Simonson, "and that's why it's done only in the direst of emergencies. Less than 1% of transplant candidates are ever classified Status One."

"And meanwhile, other people are getting on the waiting list ahead of Frank. Let's stop talking and do it," said Joanne, in a tone that made it clear that the only response she was looking for right now was Simonson tapping away at his keyboard, getting Frank on that list.

With the wedding a month and a half away, there was plenty to distract all of us, plus which Sam and Frank were coming to the end of the academic year and were submitting various papers and projects. They had agreed to postpone the honeymoon until after the surgery and his recovery, and thus thought they were entitled to a getaway weekend. I had arranged for them to have access to a house on the beach several hours away, courtesy of one of the bank's clients. He had offered it to Joanne and me several years ago, in gratitude for the work we had done for them, and I decided to take him up on it on behalf of Sam and Frank. There was no objection. In fact, the only condition he put on it was that the two of them come back for a return visit when the client was in residence.

It was Friday afternoon when I dropped in at the grad students' lounge at the Bioethics department. I had the keys for the house, and the name of a local restaurant where I had arranged for their dinner that night, on me. The poor kids had had a rough few weeks and deserved it.

At this point, I recognized Mike and Evelyn, and the others looked familiar even if I couldn't remember their names. I was greeted as a welcome guest, and not some interloper into their domain. I handed Frank the keys and then told Sam that I had arranged for dinner.

"Oh Daddy, you think of everything," she said, giving me a hug.

Frank, looking a lot chipper than I'd seen him of late, gave me a hug as well, only slightly less painfully than in our previous encounters. I was hoping that was because he had learned to restrain himself, and not because he was getting sicker.

"Is this the grad student lounge?"

There was a guy at the door holding what looked like several pizza boxes. He was in his late 20s, with scraggly hair and very much in need of a shave.

"That is us," chirped Mike.

"I've got one pepperoni, one veggie, and one plain."

"Anyone order pizza?" asked Mike to the room. He was greeted with blank looks. "I think you've got the wrong address."

The delivery guy looked at a note pad and said, "Grad student lounge? Bioethics department?"

"That's definitely us," said Frank, "but none of us ordered any pizza."

"Well look," answered the delivery guy, "It's all paid for, including the tip. So, whether you ordered it or not, someone wants you to have lunch. Is it okay if I put these down? My arms are getting tired."

"If they're all paid for, I guess we can help you out," answered Mike.

With a grunt, the delivery guy came into the room and put the boxes down on the table in the center. Immediately, the hungry grad students were opening the boxes and digging into the pizza of their choice.

"Say," said the delivery guy, suddenly spotting Frank, "aren't you the one that Brad Pitt played in the movies?"

"Yes, I am. What can I do for you?" After all this time, Frank was no longer surprised by this. Having seen him handle himself at the bank with the teen girls I knew he was able to handle himself with strangers coming up to him. He walked over to the delivery guy with his hand out, hoping a shake would be sufficient.

"Oh no, Frank, it's what I can do for you." And with that, he reached into his pocket, pulled out an envelope, and thrust it at Frank. Before anyone could say anything, Frank did what came naturally, and took the envelope. "Consider yourself served," the delivery guy said, doing an about face and a quick exit as we all tried to understand what had just happened.

"That was weird. What was that all about?" asked Mike.

"I don't know," said Frank, opening the envelope. It contained several pages of papers stapled to a blue sheet. He started to read them, but quickly saw it was a form of English with which he was unfamiliar. He handed them to me. "It seems to be some sort of legal document."

I took the papers and started reading. By the time I got to the second page, I had to sit down.

"Daddy, what is it?"

"It's a class action suit against Frank, trying to get him thrown off the organ transplant waiting list, claiming he has no right to be on it."

"Who the hell would say that?" blurted Evelyn.

"Reverend W. Allen Twitchell," I said, reading his name off the document.

"Twitchell?" asked Frank. "Didn't he get laughed out of court because he had no standing?"

Mike looked surprised, "Whoa! They laughed at him because he was in a wheelchair? That's pretty harsh, man."

"No, Mike," said Sam, "Legal standing. It means Frank hadn't done anything that affected him, and therefore he couldn't sue." Turning to me she asked, "So why is he doing it again?"

"Because," I said, looking at the papers, "he's not a party to the case. He's the lawyer. Apparently, Reverend Twitchell is also 'Esquire'. He's suing on behalf of people, including members of his own church, who will be denied a liver if Frank gets one first."

"But that's how a waiting list works," said Sam. "What possible objection can he raise to that?"

"He's arguing that Frank isn't human and has no right to be on the list at all."

The room grew silent as everyone took that in. It was finally broken by the sound of half-eaten slices of pizza being thrown back into boxes. Everyone had lost their appetite.

At 5 P.M., we were ushered into Neal Kennerly's office. In addition to Frank, Sam, Joanne, and myself, it seemed most of the bioethics department was there, with everyone deferring to Dr. Simonson. It was a tight fit, and when people started moving files to make places to sit atop shelves and cabinets, Neal called a halt and suggested we reconvene down the hall in his firm's conference room.

When we finished moving and settled in around the long boardroom table, Neal was at the head flanked by Joanne and me on one side and Sam and Frank and Simonson on the other. Others filled in seats around the table and then against the walls. Having ushered us all in his secretary said, "You need anything, Neal?"

"No, I'm good."

And with that, she closed the door from the outside. Kennerly took out a legal pad and pen, and started scanning the papers with which Frank had been served. "You know," he said, "when I'm asked to advise couples getting married, it's either to negotiate a pre-nup or draw up their wills." He looked at Frank and Sam. "You've been a different sort of challenge."

"Can he really stop Frank from getting a transplant?" asked Sam. "What right does he have to do that?"

Kennerly put his fingertips together in an arch. "That's an interesting question." I was getting ready to break his fingers, but Joanne put her hand on my arm, bringing me back to reality.

"And are we going to like the interesting answer?" I asked instead.

"First off, it looks like he's met the standing issue. He's cobbled together a class that, he'll argue, will face real and potential harm if one of its members is aced out of a liver by Frank. Second, he may have found the Achille's heel in *In Re: Frank*. The court ruled he was alive and sentient. We have a subsequent decision that it's a fair read that he was also found to be an adult because no guardian was appointed. But the court never reached the question of whether he should be considered human. The record—and, of course, the experiences of everyone in this room—acknowledge that he's intelligent and articulate." Turning to Frank, he went on, "We could elaborate other traits, such as your generosity or your sense of humor, as being further evidence of that. However, all of that begs the key question: what does it mean to be human?"

"I saw a *Star Trek* episode about that," blurted out Mike.

"I've seen several *Star Trek* episodes like that," said Kennerly. "That won't help us."

Simonson got us back on track. "Mr. Kennerly, why is this important? Surely, he's human enough."

"Twitchell—or someone working with him—did his or her homework. Under state law, the transplanting of animal organs into human beings is limited, and done only in very restricted circumstances, subject to amendment by the legislature as medical science advances. There's much that can be done today that couldn't have been done twenty or thirty years ago."

"I don't understand," said Joanne. "What does any of that have to do with Frank?"

"According to Twitchell's reading of the law, there is no provision made for the opposite. In fact, it's pretty much banned."

All this talking in shorthand was getting to me. "What is?"

"Transplanting human organs into an animal. And he's arguing that, without proof to the contrary, Frank is an animal or, at the very least, a non-human, and cannot receive a human transplant."

"Can he do that?" asked Simonson. "I'm more than willing to take the stand and offer my expert testimony on Frank's behalf, including my considered opinion that the only person involved here who seems to be lacking the slightest trace of humanity is this Twitchell."

Sam and Frank turned to their mentor in gratitude. But Simonson's eyes were fixed on Kennerly's. The lawyer faced the doctor, "It's my job to see that he fails. But you have the tougher job. You have to keep Frank alive until we win."

There was nothing more to be said, and a lot of work to be done. As we exited the board room, Frank reached into his pocket and took out the keys to the beach house. He put them in my hand. "I think we'll have to take a rain check on this one."

It was more than raining. It was pouring.

CHAPTER EIGHTEEN

Tom was certainly earning his keep today. Court proceedings are, except in rare instances usually involving minors, public proceedings. And Twitchell had no reason to keep things quiet. Once word of the lawsuit got out, Frank's condition was a matter of public record. Rather than complain about being kept out of the loop thus far, Tom spoke with the family, Simonson, and Kennerly, quickly getting up to speed. He then held a press briefing explaining that none of the principals were doing interviews right now, and that he would be the conduit for information on the case. He then gave them everything Kennerly and Simonson thought would buttress our argument, which was a substantial amount of information. Reporters weren't complaining about our stonewalling. To the contrary, they were complaining about having too much to take in. This not only buttressed our claim that we had nothing to hide but had the added benefit of getting them to leave us alone. Even the tabloid reporters behaved, because they knew to do otherwise would cut them off from a major source.

Meanwhile, Kennerly had managed to convince the court that time was of the essence—as it was, with Frank's life in the balance—and get a preliminary court hearing for next Tuesday. We had filed a motion for summary judgement which, as Kennerly explained, meant that even if everything Twitchell was alleging were true, we would still prevail. It wasn't a slam dunk, but we had a shot at it.

The following Tuesday morning, less than a week after Frank had been served by the bogus pizza deliveryman, we were at the new court house where Judge Henry Chiang would be presiding. This was much different from the night court we had been in, which looked like a bus station that had seen better days. This was all blond wood paneling and track lighting. It would have made a nice place for a cocktail party or a poetry reading.

Twitchell appeared all business in a dark blue suit and gray tie, not betraying any of the nervousness we felt on our side. Kennerly and Frank sat at the defendant's table while Sam, Joanne, and I were seated in the front row of the spectators in the public gallery right behind them. The room was packed with people I assumed were mostly press, but several came over to shake hands with Twitchell. Kennerly said they were probably members of the "class" of people needing liver transplants which had been certified for the suit.

We rose for the judge's entrance, and then resumed our seats. "We are here to determine if there is a cause of action in this case, and I want to limit the discussion to those points. The issue is whether Frank"—and here the judge acknowledged Frank's presence, showing neither sympathy nor antagonism—"qualifies under applicable law to be placed on a list for a potential liver transplant. Mr. Twitchell, you may make your opening argument."

"It's Reverend Twitchell, but since I'm here in my capacity as an officer of the court rather than an emissary for the Holy Court, I won't object. May it please the court, Judge Chiang—" He said the name as if it were spelled "Chang."

"It's pronounced 'Chung'," said the jurist.

"Really? Are you sure?" asked Twitchell.

"Is Counselor suggesting to the court that I don't know how to pronounce my own name?"

"Of course not, Your Honor," said a clearly chagrined Twitchell.

"Then let's proceed."

Kennerly leaned over to Frank, and I could just barely make out his muttered, "Score one for our side."

"Your Honor," Twitchell began again, "our state law clearly permits organ transplants from animals to humans in certain limited circumstances, but not at all—and this is important—in the reverse direction. For the defendant in this case to be eligible, there would have to be a showing that he is human. Which means the question before this court is, 'What does it mean to be a human?'"

"I saw a *Star Trek* episode like this," interrupted Judge Chiang. Kennerly barely suppressed a giggle. "How do you propose to define 'human'?"

"It has to be more than has been raised in the legal proceedings so far. We readily concede that the defendant Frank exhibits signs of life and independence, as the court found in *In re: Frank*. We'll even accept that he is the adult version of whatever his life form is, as was determined in a subsequent legal proceeding. None of these attributes are determinative by themselves of humanity, which is the crown of creation. A housecat, for example, may be alive and independent and adult, but it is not superior to Man."

"I take it you have never shared a household with a cat," interjected the judge.

"Score two," muttered Kennerly.

"Your Honor?"

"No mind," said Judge Chiang. "Please proceed."

"Very simply, a human being has the Divine Spark—a soul, if you will—something that separates us from all other living creatures. Frank may be alive in the sense that a tree or a rabbit or a lobster is alive, but that does not elevate him to the highest rung of life, of humanity, and thus he is—as a matter of law—ineligible to maintain his own existence at the cost of human life. Were he to receive a liver transplant through the United Network for Organ Sharing list, the human who by right would be entitled to that organ might have his or her own life put at risk. This is unpardonable. We ask the court to find that the sanctity of human life is utmost and rule this… this *thing* ineligible for a transplant."

On that pompous note, Twitchell took his seat. There were some murmurings in the courtroom, although I couldn't tell if it came from Frank's supporters, opponents, or some combination of both. It stopped with a sharp rap of the gavel by Judge Chiang. He turned to Kennerly, "Very well. Mr. Kennerly?"

Before taking us on, Kennerly's most newsworthy case was defending a plumbing contractor who had delayed the opening of an elementary school. He was now being written up as a modern-day Atticus Finch, the lawyer in *To Kill a Mockingbird* who faced down deep-seated prejudices in a righteous cause. I hoped that he kept his eyes focused on the prize, rather than on his press notices.

"What is human?" he began majestically. "That is indeed the question. I agree with learned counsel that signs of life or independence or maturity are not enough. A snail is alive, but it is not human. A wolf may run free, but it is not human. A loyal dog may reach a ripe old age, but it is not human either." He paused, as if allowing everyone to feel the regret that a loyal old dog also fell short of the standard and might even, perhaps, be a cause to reconsider.

"There are other standards that fall short as well. Speech? There are birds that mimic speech. The ability to communicate? A pet may tell us it's hungry or needs to go for a walk or wants to play. There are even chimpanzees who have learned a vocabulary with which they can construct complex sentences, but even they are not human. No, the standard is much higher than that. To be human is to be a moral creature, to know the difference between right and wrong, and to act accordingly."

This seemed to be moving into Twitchell's territory and he looked ready to object, but the judge shut that down. "There will be no interruptions. If you feel a need to rebut afterwards, you may do so. Continue, Mr. Kennerly."

"Simply put, Your Honor, my client's expressed yearning for a moral code of conduct, exhibited by his embracing of one of our major faith traditions, shows without question that he is endowed with the same free will that is the inheritance of all humans, and no other creatures. A horse may strike the ground adding two plus two, but if it finds another horse's feedbag, it will not attempt to return it. A dog may be loyal to its owner, but if it meets another dog in heat, it won't stop to inquire if she is in a committed relationship."

I thought that last was a bit much, but Kennerly was on a roll. "Your Honor, I am prepared to present testimony from my client's rabbi and from his academic mentor, the founding head of the university's Bioethics Department, to demonstrate beyond any reasonable doubt that Frank has free will and uses his ability to discern right from wrong. Further, that there is ample evidence that since the court in *In re: Frank* ruled that he was entitled to live on his own, that he has made and continues to make value judgements which then lead him to act according to his moral guidelines. These are not reflexes. These are the actions of a human being. Your Honor, there is no question that my client is human. The real question—beyond the purview of this court, perhaps—is why does so much of humanity fall short of the high standards adhered to by Frank?"

He sat down to a burst of applause which Judge Chiang allowed to play out for a few moments before stifling it with several raps of his gavel. "That will be enough of that.... Now, Mr. Twitch... excuse me, Reverend Twitchell, do you have anything further to add?"

Seeing which way the wind was blowing, he simply shook his head. "Very well then," said Judge Chiang, "I will review your oral arguments and your written submissions. I'll have a ruling for you tomorrow morning at 10 A.M. Court is adjourned." And with a sharp rap of the gavel, he took his leave, faster than the clerk could intone, "Please rise."

The following morning, the courtroom was even more crowded. The entire Bioethics Department had shown up, as had several people from the bank. I was touched by their support, but I hoped someone was still there tending to our customers. Susan, Sam's maid of honor, had come in, telling her that supporting the bride-to-be in the weeks leading up to the wedding was one of her jobs.

Twitchell sat alone at his table, although his supporters were present in the room as well. When Judge Chiang took his seat, there was utter silence in the courtroom. Frank started to rise as if he was a criminal defendant hearing the verdict, but the judge indicated he should resume his seat. When everyone was settled, he began addressing the parties.

"In both your oral and written arguments, you boiled down the issue to its essential question: what does it mean to be human? We cannot turn to legislation or prior court decisions, because this is a question of first impression. What I have decided may be parsed and debated, but no one should think it's the final word on the subject. Reverend Twitchell argues that in the absence of any definition we must rely on our traditional understanding, and in that he's not wrong. What we must decide is what *is* that traditional understanding.

"It once was defined as 'a man who was to woman born,' as Shakespeare writes in *Macbeth*. But even there, the definition was challenged because Macduff was born by Caesarean section. He is deemed no less human for being so. Today, we have babies born through *in vitro* fertilization, through the use of sperm and egg donors, and through surrogate mothers, and no one denies that all of these result in the births of humans, no matter how much it may vary from the more traditional method.

"Mr. Kennerly argues that it is free will and being able to choose between good and evil that is what separates us from beasts, and he is persuasive. All animals, even our most beloved pets, are creatures of instinct. We may anthropomorphize their actions, but these are stories we tell ourselves. There is nothing in the record presented to this court that suggests that Frank is anything other than a sentient being making choices as to what religion to follow—if any, whom to marry, and what career to pursue, none of which can be explained by instinct.

"Therefore, it is the judgement of this court that Frank be deemed a human being for the purposes of the laws in this state governing organ transplants, that he may remain on the waiting list for a liver transplant until such time as his situation is resolved. Summary judgement is hereby granted to the defendant. That being the case, the action is dismissed. Court is adjourned."

There was a brief pause as the full meaning of the judge's remarks sank in, and then there was cheering and applause. Chiang, not quite succeeding in suppressing a smile, pretended not to notice the reaction as he left the courtroom. Frank and Sam embraced, while Kennerly accepted congratulations from anyone offering it. I turned to see Twitchell's reaction, but he had already left the courtroom.

Later that afternoon, we convened in the Bioethics department grad student lounge. Frank allowed himself a sip of champagne, not more, and accepted the congratulations and well wishes of everyone there. We all knew he was not yet out of the woods. He had won the right to apply for a liver. Now he had to get one.

Still, there was the sense of relief. People like Twitchell seemed to be suffering what Tom had dubbed "Frank Derangement Syndrome"—an inability to accept Frank's existence and get on with their own lives. Now, however, his attempt to block Frank from getting the surgery he needed had failed, and hopefully we had heard the last of him.

That hope lasted about five more minutes. At the top of the hour, someone turned on the TV hanging on the far side of the room, perhaps expecting that a news report about our triumph in court would inject new life into the party. Instead what we got was this:

"...Twitchell said he was disappointed but not surprised by the ruling."

Cut to Twitchell in front of the courthouse, *"A journey of a thousand miles begins with a single step. Some may think we took a step backward but, in fact, we are moving ahead. We will be appealing this unfortunate ruling and have already filed for a stay against the judge's order to put Frank back on the organ transplant waiting list."*

Cut to Tom shepherding Frank and Sam out of the courthouse. Before joining Sam in the car at curbside, Frank turned to the throng of reporters and unidentified spectators, *"We're grateful for all the support we've received. Now we just want to focus on my health and, of course, our upcoming wedding."*

Back to the reporter, *"This long-running saga may not be over yet, nor will it be for some time to come, with Twitchell saying he is prepared to fight this all the way to the Supreme Court...."*

If our celebration had any life left to it, that news report sucked it all out. *"Yer bum's oot the windae,"* shouted Ian at the screen. I had no idea what he meant, but it didn't sound good.

"I thought we won," said Joanne, who had started cleaning up the party's debris as much out of a desire to expend nervous energy as anything else.

Kennerly gestured to me to let the room clear out. He had something to say, but not something he wanted on the next newscast. At last it was what I had come think of as the inner circle in this fight: the family, Kennerly, Simonson, and Tom, who had made it clear that he needed to know what was going on if only to know what *not* to say. Simonson closed the door. We sat around the central table which, only an hour before, had been the site of a festive celebration.

"All right, Mr. Kennerly," said Frank, breaking the silence. "What does it mean? Won't we continue to beat him in the courts?"

"Let me give it to you straight, Frank. I'm convinced we will prevail in the courts."

"Then what's the problem?" asked Sam. "You're reacting like this was a death sentence."

"That's exactly what it is. Twitchell can't win. He knows that, and he doesn't care. He's just going to keep appealing and filing new motions, knowing that even if we succeed in expediting the process, this case could go on for three or four years."

Frank sat up with a start. "But I don't have three or four years."

With a look of profound sadness, Kennerly replied, "He knows that. He's counting on that. He's only interested in one thing."

"What's that?" asked Simonson, anticipating an answer that he hoped he wouldn't be hearing.

"Running out the clock."

CHAPTER NINETEEN

And there it was. Frank didn't have all the time in the world. None of us did, in the larger scheme of things, but Frank wasn't in a position to look at the big picture. He might be getting married in August, but if he didn't get a new liver, he and Sam would be celebrating their first anniversary at the cemetery, and there would be no reprieve from the grave this time.

"I'm sorry, Frank—" began Kennerly, but Dr. Simonson cut him off. I couldn't say what it was, but something about the professor's demeanor had shifted.

"Mr. Kennerly, Neal, if I may? You have nothing to apologize for. Your argument was masterful in court. You took a case I would have—at best—rated a fifty/fifty proposition and turned it into a sure thing. It was an amazing performance."

"I'm not sure I deserve that but thank you."

"No need to thank me for telling the truth," said Simonson, "but someday you'll thank me for what I'm about to do. I'd like you and Tom to leave."

"Wait a second," said the press agent, "I thought we agreed I had to know everything that's going on."

"I made no such agreement, regardless of what Sam and her family may have said to you. I'm asking you both to leave now for your own good. Later on, you will want to be able swear under oath that you had no idea about anything I'm going to discuss with the family."

Kennerly was a bit quicker on the uptake. "Discuss what?" asked Tom, "I can't do my job if I don't know what's going on."

The lawyer put his hand on the press agent's shoulder. "Let's go back to my office and discuss how we're going to spin the appeals." Tom wasn't at all happy about it, which he continued to make clear as they walked down the hall to the elevators.

"I'm confused," said Joanne. "What's going on, Dr. Simonson? Why did you send them away?"

He came closer to us and pulled over a chair, as if to make the conversation more intimate. "I have a confession to make, and I think it'll speed things up if you call me Herb."

"Dr. Simonson... Herb... what's this all about?" Sam joined her mother in bafflement. I couldn't be certain, but I'd gotten better at reading Frank in the last few months, and I think it was unanimous. None of us had the slightest clue what Simonson was going on about.

The doctor poured himself some scotch from the bottle Ian had left behind and swallowed it in one gulp. "I have some good news and some bad news and, ironically, they're the same thing. The bad news is that I lied. The good news, Frank, is that I think I can keep you alive."

"Dr. Simonson, it's been a long day. With your permission as my doctor, I'd like to have some of what you're having," answered Frank. Without another word, Simonson provided a bit of the scotch for each of us, including Joanne, and another for himself. He and Frank poured it down the hatch while I sipped about half of mine. Joanne and Sam's lay untouched on the table. "Now then," Frank continued, "what did you lie about, and how does that help me?"

"Remember when I said on TV that our experiments had consisted of mice and hamsters? That was only half true. We have been experimenting on human organs as well."

"Doctor, no," said Sam, with what were obviously mixed emotions. "How could you?"

"I understand your disappointment, Sam, but let me assure you that, other than not reporting it, we stayed within the limits we've been developing as our protocol. Nothing whatsoever to do with the brain. Nothing that might lead to organs operating independently. Our focus was on those organs that might someday be candidates for transplants: kidneys, lungs, hearts... livers. It is, after all, our ultimate goal, as we've repeatedly stated publicly, and there seemed no harm in simply finding out if we could actually reanimate those organs, or if it was just a pipe dream."

This was amazing, or it would be if they had actually succeeded. "I assume you're telling us this because your experiments were successful," I said. "Why not tell the world?"

Frank interrupted. "Because if he did, it wouldn't do me any good. Even if everyone agreed to overlook the unethical and possibly illegal experiments—especially at *this university* and coming so soon after my creation—it would be years before they would be allowed to attempt a transplant of a reanimated organ into a human."

"Exactly right," sighed the doctor. "There would be experiments on lower animals, and then on chimps, and then—maybe—we'd finally get permission to attempt it on a human. Frank's name would come up on the donor list sooner than we'd be able to operate."

"You said you had some good news," said Joanne.

"Well, yes. If the appeals court stays the order to put Frank on the list, it would be because they feel there's still some question in dispute as to whether he's human. That might just work out to our advantage."

"Are you working for the other side now?" Sam was not at all pleased at what she was hearing.

"Not at all. The reason I say it's to our advantage is because, so far as I know, there is no law in this state forbidding the transference of an organ such as a liver from one cadaver to another."

After I processed that image in my head, I didn't know how I was going to get to sleep that night or, indeed, ever again. Yet after I got over my horror movie moment, I realized that he was right. This was a moment that potentially changed everything.

"Honey, what are you going to do?" Sam didn't want to push Frank into something he thought was wrong. That was what all their talk of religion and free will was about.

"This does seem to be the solution we've been looking for," I offered.

Frank did not reply and looked at Joanne to see what she had to say. Finally, she looked him square in the eye and said, "If you don't do it, we're going to lose all our deposits, and you'll end up having to have Elvis marry you in Vegas. I haven't come this far to settle for that."

Frank rose. "Well, then, I guess I better get ready for an operation. I couldn't bear disappointing my mother-in-law."

And with that, Joanne picked up her untouched plastic glass of scotch, and swallowed its contents whole.

"Mother!" shrieked Sam.

"After what I've been through, I think I'm entitled," she said, putting her cup down. "And if you're not having yours, there's no sense in letting it go to waste."

I was delegated to call Kennerly and tell him not to fight the appeal too strongly for the moment. "Right now, if there was a delay of a week or two before pressing ahead with arguing the appeal that would be just fine. And if they put a stay on the order putting Frank on the list, we should say we're hugely disappointed, but not fight it."

"And this is what Frank wants?" the lawyer asked over the phone.

"Yes."

"And I shouldn't ask why?"

"It would be best if you didn't."

There was a long silence, and then Kennerly said, "And you have complete faith in Simonson?"

I sighed. "Yes, but even if I didn't, it's not like we have a lot of choice."

"All right," said Kennerly, "I'll try not to make it obvious that we're shifting tactics, which shouldn't be too hard, since I don't know why we're doing this."

"If things work out, you'll know soon enough."

"You know, I'm not a religious man, but do you think Frank would mind if I lit a candle for him at church and said a prayer for him?"

"No, he won't mind. If you can be as persuasive as you were in court this morning… Let's put it this way: right now, Frank can use all the help he can get."

Two nights later, Frank, Simonson, and a small, carefully selected operating team arrived at a private clinic outside the city. It was important to be away from prying eyes, including anyone at the university who might be willing to pull the plug the moment they learned the nature of the surgery being done under cover of darkness.

Joanne, Sam, and I were at our house. There was nothing we could do except share our nerves with everyone else, which was reason enough to stay away. Joanne and I took turns comforting Sam, who was so tense I was afraid she would snap something. She jumped every time the phone rang, even though I told her that Simonson would call me directly on my cell as soon as he knew whether the operation was a success. The problem was that this wasn't like changing a lightbulb. All the connections bringing blood to and from the liver had to be cut, as well as the bile ducts. Then, once the diseased liver was removed, the new liver would be installed, necessitating a total reversal of the process, as everything cut had to be reconnected to the new liver. A normal operation of this sort could take up to twelve hours, and this was no normal operation.

They began around 7 P.M. Simonson had some connection with the people who operated the facility, and they had granted him access, no questions asked. We couldn't expect updates, as there were no observers, and no one involved in the operation could be spared, so as the clock swung past midnight, we had no idea what was going on except that it was going on. Sam finally fell asleep around 1 A.M., snuggling next to an already unconscious Joanne on the couch. I started to fade myself when I woke with a start. I went to the den to fetch my recharger. Returning to the living room, I plugged it in, and then attached the phone. All I would have needed was for them to call us with some emergency while the phone's battery was dead. I then turned the volume up on the phone so that, when it rang, it could wake me up. It was the last thing I remembered doing.

At 5:25 A.M., the fireworks went off. The ringtone had been set to "Fireworks," so there were whistles and explosions, not to mention exploding lights on my screen. It took me a while to make the transition from deep sleep—where I had been dreaming I was at a deli where they were trying to transplant a pastrami sandwich from pumpernickel to a kaiser roll—to semi-coherent wakefulness. Lurching from the couch, I fumbled for the phone.

"Whazzzit?"

"It's Herb. Good morning. The operation was a success."

That snapped me awake. "It worked?"

"Well, that remains to be seen. The new liver seems to be functioning, but we want to make sure Frank's body doesn't reject the transplant. We're keeping him under careful observation. But so far, so good."

"That's wonderful," I said. Joanne and Sam were now awake and looking at me. I smiled and nodded. "When can we come see him?"

"He's out right now, but if you were to come for a short visit this afternoon, that shouldn't tax him. Make sure you're not followed."

"Of course." Of course. By now, I had become an expert in evasive driving.

"Now if you'll excuse me, I've been up for 24 hours, and I need some rest as well."

"By all means. Dr. Simonson? Herb? Thank you."

"Don't thank me yet," he said. "Even if it's a success, once the news gets out, there's no telling what the reaction will be."

"Well, one thing I know, they can't take the liver back. Possession is nine tenths of the law."

That afternoon, we followed the directions Simonson had provided us, and found ourselves in a lush rural area that seemed to be a mix of farmland and private estates. The clinic was apparently one of those estates that had been converted to other uses.

A wan Frank greeted us from his hospital bed with a small wave of his hand. Joanne and I took a few moments to wish him well and let him know that we were all pulling for him, and then left the room so he and Sam could say whatever couples have to say to each other after emerging from dire circumstances. While we were in the waiting room, Dr. Simonson came out to see us.

"We're going to keep him through the weekend, and then bring him back to the university hospital, which is better equipped to monitor and tend to his recovery. That also means this is going to go public. At that point, I can't say for sure if I will still have a career, or even my freedom."

"Don't you worry, Herb," said Joanne, newly resolute. "You were there for Frank. We'll be there for you."

"That's very kind of you, but right now my concern is Frank and Sam. Now that the operation is a done deal, you should let Neal and Tom know what's occurred, so they can proceed accordingly. I hope that you can hold off on any announcements until Frank is safely in the hospital, but after that, we'll have to let the chips fall where they may."

At that moment, Sam joined us. Without saying a word, she went over to Simonson and gave him a big hug. When she was done, she stepped back and quietly said, "Thank you for saving his life."

"How is Frank?" he asked.

"Sleeping."

"Good. That's what he needs a lot of right now, as his body repairs itself. I'm sure your visit did him a world of good, but I'm going to suggest you come back tomorrow morning before seeing him again."

"I understand."

I went over to shake his hand. "Herb, you did good. You did more than good. What you did is someday going to become a commonplace operation. We're not going to let you be a footnote to that. You're the hero here."

"I hope the university feels the same way."

It was Kennerly who decided, after he was fully briefed, that he needed to appear with Simonson before the university authorities. On Monday afternoon, Frank was quietly transferred to the university hospital. Simonson felt his recovery was going even better than expected, and he might be discharged by the end of the week. Once Frank was settled in, Simonson and Kennerly met with the university president. From what we learned of the meeting, he was shocked. He threatened not only to fire Simonson, but to have him lose his medical license as well, and then do everything he could except burn down his house and pour salt on the remains. When he was done, Kennerly quietly laid out an alternative set of facts.

By transferring an experimental organ from one cadaver to another, Simonson had not violated any state law, and since Frank's humanity was still being litigated, no one could show otherwise. Frank had fully consented to allowing himself to be the subject of this experimental procedure which was a.) a success, b.) something that—with proper testing—had the potential to save countless human lives, and c.) performed by a person who was now the world's leading authority on this cutting-edge medical science and who happened to be the head of the university's Bioethics Department. Kennerly further explained that several universities and major hospitals might be interested in Dr. Simonson's services, but he was inclined to remain where he was—bringing great honor and prestige to the university—provided that there were no repercussions. Also, the university would be assuming the mortgage on Simonson's house. After all, a medical genius should not have to bother with petty details such as mortgage payments. By the time Kennerly was through, Simonson was not only in the clear, but the president promised to look into finding someone to endow his chair.

By pre-arrangement, shortly after the university's announcement of Dr. Simonson's medical breakthrough, Tom held a press briefing in which he emphasized Frank's willingness to take a risk that would benefit all mankind. We now knew that organs could be reanimated and transplanted, although it would be some time before attempts would be made with actual humans. He also announced that Kennerly was filing a motion to dismiss Twitchell's case, as Frank no long needed to be on the waiting list. Twitchell was furious, not the least because the end of his appeal lifted the stay on the lower court which had, after all, ruled in Frank's favor.

Even with the 24-hour news cycle and the various social media, it would take some time for all this news to be digested by the pundits and the public. Reporters understood that Frank was recuperating and unavailable for comment, although Tom did issue a statement on his behalf on how grateful he was to Dr. Simonson and the university, singling out the president for his bold leadership. Meanwhile, at Tom's suggestion, Joanne and Sam fled town. They didn't merely flee town, they left the country. Joined by cousin Susan, the women went up to Prince Edward Island in Canada, where they could relax unrecognized for a few days. Sam didn't want to go, but Frank insisted, saying there was no reason for her to put up with the hounding of the press when she should be getting ready for the wedding, now just a few weeks away.

That left me. I gave no interviews, held no press conferences, but was a prisoner in my home. The bank allowed me to work remotely, and with no one around it was actually a bit restful. Polls showed our strategy was working. If you had told me several months earlier—or, indeed, at any time in my life prior to meeting Frank—that plans for my daughter's wedding would include national polling, I would have thought you insane. However, everyone had an opinion: 63% approved of Frank getting the experimental liver transplant, and that rose to 78% when told that humans might benefit from the procedure. Frank and Sam's marriage was still "controversial," with 48% "strongly approving" and another 23% "somewhat approving." Of the remainder, 19% "strongly disapproved," 8% "somewhat disapproved" and 2% were "undecided/don't know." Having ridden the whirlwind for several months now, I came to really admire that 2%. I like to believe that their non-answers were not due to apathy or ignorance, but were principled statements amounting to, "What business is this of mine?"

What all this meant, though, was that approximately one out of four people had a negative view of the wedding, which presumably included the one in ten who thought the operation that had saved Frank's life was an "abomination." And all of them, whatever their opinion, seemed to be congregating in front our house. While the police did an outstanding job of holding the crowd back, it was made clear to me that they really wouldn't mind if I left, taking my family with me, until after the wedding was over.

And after several days of living under siege, I had to agree.

CHAPTER TWENTY

"Welcome, welcome. We're the Cluskeys and we're delighted to be of service."

Tom, as it turned out, was not only an expert at getting the word out, but also at keeping things quiet. His firm had a long-standing and very discreet relationship with the Cluskeys, a middle-aged couple who ran a rustic bed and breakfast upstate. With the application of more money than I cared to think about at the moment, their guests had been relocated to other delightful inns in the area, having been told that they would be shutting down to deal with a leaking septic tank. Given that explanation, no one stayed long enough to check out the details.

Instead, I drove out there before sunrise, arriving some two hours later to the smell fresh coffee brewing in the kitchen. Tom had brought out the freshly discharged Frank late the evening before, and they were waiting for the arrival of Joanne, Sam, and Susan, who were taking a circuitous route back into the U.S. They were expected around lunch time.

The Cluskeys managed to avoid being walking clichés. They were no Ma and Pa Kettle. Cluskey, the only hair on his head covering his eyebrows and sticking out of his ears, was a retired tradesman who helped his wife run the inn, and also ran the small farm that was part of it. She was a hearty woman whose mostly brown hair was done up in a bun, and who knew her way around both domestic chores and running a business. She had cut a hard deal for us to take over the place for two weeks.

We would be living here until the wedding, far out of the public eye. Of course, that also meant we would not be enjoying the joys of antiquing in the village, dining at the picturesque roadside restaurants, or doing anything but staying inside and keeping a low profile. The Cluskeys would serve us breakfast and pick up our food for our other meals at what

I'm told was a charmingly quaint country store. In addition to our paying for all our expenses (plus a delivery charge), the gracious Cluskeys would also be allowed to take pictures of their celebrity guests but could not offer them on the open market until after the wedding. It wasn't like we had a lot of room to negotiate, but when Joanne heard about this she was not pleased, "Well I certainly hope these will be flattering pictures, and not an attempt to embarrass us."

Mrs. Cluskey looked appalled. "We are not barbarians. We're just simple country folk trying to make ends meet."

Nice try. Some simple country folk. I saw the Lexus parked in the driveway. The two women then entered into their own negotiations on what access the Cluskeys would have and what would be off limits, and Mrs. Cluskey came to see the logic of how their inn could only benefit from photos that showed preparations for a fairy tale wedding.

Meanwhile, Cluskey was giving Frank and me what he described as the "two-dollar tour," which ended in the barn behind the house. They had some chickens and cows, so their eggs and dairy products were fresh. "Not like that stuff you city folks get," chuckled Cluskey, in a line I suspect he had delivered hundreds of times to his guests. I wouldn't be at all surprised if the animals were all props, and he got his food at the supermarket, same as we did.

Then he pulled out something that really was different. I don't know if the container had been selected to impress his guests, but it was just like you see in the cartoons: a big jug marked "XXX" on the side.

"You fellers ever have real moonshine?"

If this was an act, it was really well thought out. He took us outside to the back of the barn, and pulled the tarp off what he said was his "still." I wouldn't know if it was or not, but there was a kettle and lots of copper tubing. Whatever concoction came out as a result of the process would have been finely aged for a day or two before being shared with the other connoisseurs of fine corn liquor in the region.

"Frank, I don't know about this. This is pretty strong stuff."

Cluskey poured a small bit into three tin cans which, I'm glad to say, looked like they had been washed. Ambience only took you so far.

"Dr. Simonson said a little alcohol in moderation would be fine. Besides, we want to hide the evidence before the revenooers get here."

Cluskey let out a laugh. "Where'd you hear about 'revenooers'?"

"One of the stations I was watching at the hospital did a day of binging on *The Beverly Hillbillies* and *Green Acres*."

Just when I thought my life couldn't get any weirder.

Cluskey raised his tin can, "To the bride and groom." And he chugged it in a single swallow. I tipped my can to the other two and then did the same, and immediately felt as if my throat was on fire.

"Yep, this batch has a real kick," he said, hitting me on the back, and filling my can with plain water which I gratefully swallowed, holding it out for some more.

"Here's looking at you, kid," said Frank, who I realized had not yet drunk this deadly potion. Before I could say anything, he brought his can to his lips and upended it. There was a long pause, and then he sneezed. He looked at Cluskey and then me and said, "You know, I think this is the first time I can remember that my sinuses are clear."

After a few days, the protestors seemed to realize no one was coming or going from the house, and even the mailman had stopped delivering, as I had arranged to temporarily have our mail forwarded to Tom's office, where he could send on those items we needed to see. As the media speculated where we might have "vanished" to—at least one cable host wasn't ruling out that we had been picked up by aliens—the resulting quiet allowed people working on our behalf to quietly pick up those things we had left behind in the hurry to escape. There were the wedding clothes, the rings from the safety deposit box, the marriage license, and the contact list of all the people with whom we had contracted for services, so that Joanne could go over any last-minute instructions with them. This was all done by cell phone, so it was untraceable unless the guy making the wedding cake also worked for the Justice Department.

"Samantha, come sit with me," Joanne said, as she prepared to start making calls.

"Why? You have it covered."

"Samantha," said Joanne, in a tone of voice suggesting that there would be no arguing about it, "this is your wedding. There are things where you have to take charge. What shots do you want to make sure the photographer gets? When do you want to dance with your father? Someday I may not be here you to help plan a wedding, and you'll be glad to have had the experience."

Sam and Joanne sat in the parlor, several sheets of paper on the table in front of them, as they began going down the list of things to do. "Uh oh," Sam suddenly blurted out.

"What is it?"

"We have to cancel the rehearsal dinner. We won't be going back into town until the day of the wedding."

I guessed I could kiss that deposit goodbye.

"Well, we're a small wedding party. In fact, we're all here," noted Joanne. "We can do the rehearsal right here."

Frank was sprawled in a chair across the room. "Honey, maybe we don't have to cancel the dinner, just postpone it. We're not leaving on our honeymoon until Tuesday."

Samantha perked up. "You're right. Mom, do you think we can convince them to change our reservation from Saturday night to Monday?"

Joanne looked at Sam in a new light. "I don't see why not. Monday's the slowest night of the week. They'll probably be grateful for the business. Do you want to make the call?"

And with that, Sam showed she was ready to engage in the mundane negotiations of being an adult. It might not be as dramatic as the breakthroughs in bioethics she'd have in her future, but for Joanne, it was a marker that her little girl had grown up.

The inn was turning into what looked like backstage at a Broadway musical about a wedding. Sam's dress arrived, and she tried it on to make sure all the alterations had been done properly. Joanne and Mrs. Cluskey took turns suggesting different poses, the one to test the seams and the other to get a few more shots for that future payday. Frank and I trying on our tuxes didn't generate anywhere near the excitement.

Joanne had managed to find the magical wedding checklist online using the Cluskeys' computer. She printed out the last weeks' worth of activities. The food was set. Rabbi Wheaton was contacted and told everyone was doing just fine and we looked forward to seeing him on Sunday. A long conversation—involving much passing of the phone—was held with Mike, who had the idea of including "Beauty and the Beast" in the playlist for the wedding. We found a copy of the animated film in the Cluskeys' video library and had to play the song a few times before Joanne relented. Frank wanted to hold out for "Be Our Guest," but finally agreed that dancing cutlery and china was probably beyond our capability of the things we'd be able to pull off.

I reverted to my earlier role of writing the checks, glad that I had had the presence of mind to throw in the next book of checks when I was packing. Joanne went through the mail for any late arriving R.S.V.P.s and, fortunately, there was nothing necessitating reconfiguring the seating plan. Finally, on the Wednesday before the wedding, when everything seemed to have fallen into place and we were getting just a bit complacent, a new crisis arose. I was hoping against hope this would be the final one, but at this point, who was I kidding?

"Dear," shouted Joanne as we were finishing breakfast, "we forgot about the salon."

Mrs. Cluskey came out from the kitchen to see what the fuss was all about, and when she realized what the matter was, said, "Never you mind. I'm sure I can get you squeezed in at my local beauty parlor."

I saw several expressions pass Joanne and Sam's faces as they contemplated that prospect and was proud that what came out of Sam's mouth was, "That's so generous of you, Mrs. Cluskey, but you know how personal the relationship is between a woman and her stylist. I've been seeing Naomi since I was sixteen; she fixed me up for my first prom. I'm sure you feel the same way about yours."

"Women and their hair," laughed Cluskey from the parlor. "I haven't worried about mine since I went bald at forty."

"And not for twenty years before that," chuckled Mrs. Cluskey, in a voice pitched so as not to carry.

"What are we going to do?" asked Joanne. "Naomi is coming to the wedding, but we won't have enough time once we're there for her to do your hair and makeup."

"There's only one thing to do," piped up Susan, who had been staying in the background.

Joanne looked at her. "Yes, dear, what's that?"

"Have her come here, do you and Sam, and go in to the wedding with us. It's only a few more nights, and she can stay in my room."

"Oh, Daddy, can she?"

I didn't answer. I pulled out my phone and hit Tom's number on the speed dial. When I got him on the line, I said, "I've one more task for you, and I can't even promise this is the last one. I want you to call the Bonne Chance salon in the village and ask for Naomi…"

Naomi arrived late Friday morning with three suitcases. She had not only come for the weekend, but brought her dress for the wedding, and all the tools and concoctions she should need to transform Sam and Joanne into the fairy tale princess and the Queen Mother. Her arrival was also a reminder that our stay with the Cluskeys was drawing to a close. Sam and Frank decided that they would like to host a Friday night Shabbat dinner, and that the Cluskeys would be our guests.

Of course, we were in the middle of nowhere, which meant that there was a certain amount of improvisation involved. Frank had contacted Tom, who delivered three bottles of good kosher wine—not the stuff that tastes like cold medicine—along with Naomi. The candles that would be lit after the appropriate blessing had no specific requirements, and Mrs. Cluskey produced a box of candles left over from a power outage the previous summer. The side dishes were local vegetables, and Joanne suggested this might not be the occasion to introduce the Cluskeys to the world of gefilte fish and horseradish, so we would do without that course.

That left the chickens and the challah, the traditional braided bread brought out for festive occasions. Cluskey offered up two of his hens, but Frank insisted on doing the slaughtering himself, after spending a few hours on a website for kosher butchers. "It may not be ideal," he said, "but it's the best we can do under the circumstances." I absented myself from that part of the preparations, and went into the kitchen, where Sam was holding a class in bread baking.

She had made the dough early in the morning to give the yeast time to do its work. The ingredients weren't a problem: flour, yeast, oil, water, sugar, salt, and, of course, eggs. All were readily at hand. It was when Sam started to work the dough that Mrs. Cluskey became fascinated.

"Why are you separating it like that? How many loaves are you baking?"

"Just the two," said Sam, "These are for braiding." She then proceeded to wrap the coils of dough around each other, topping each loaf off with an egg glaze. After placing them in the oven and closing the door, she turned with a flourish, "And that's how you make challah."

"Can't wait to try it," said our hostess. "I don't think I've ever had colla bread before." She pronounced it as if it were part of a shirt.

"Not 'colla.' Challah."

"I don't know if I can pronounce it like you do."

Sam smiled. She was a born academic and was ready to engage a potential student on any subject. "Sure, you can. Think about what you would say if you saw something really icky. Can you say, 'Yecch'?" Sam emphasized the guttural "ch" sound.

"Yech!" said Mrs. Cluskey, having no trouble at all.

"Great. Now take the 'ch' sound and put it at the front of 'challah'."

It took a moment for Mrs. Cluskey to figure out what she was being asked to do, and then she said, "Yecchhhallah."

"There you go."

As the discussion turned to the question as to whether there would be any other linguistic surprises on the menu, I slipped out of the kitchen. The whole downstairs was filled with the delightful smell of baking bread, and it occurred to me that this might be one of the few times in the next few days of which absolutely nothing was expected of me. I may have already been asleep when I made it to the couch, because the next thing I remember was Joanne gently waking me and telling me I had better freshen up for dinner.

Much of Jewish ritual is set up to educate, both how to understand what it signifies and how to do it again in the future. This is especially true of the Friday night home blessings. Sam lit the candles, and then covered her eyes as she said the prayer so that the Sabbath light would be revealed to her. Sam explained that, just as night is separate from day, so is the Sabbath separate from ordinary work days, and the lighting of the candles marks that separation.

Then Frank, a dark purple yarmulke pinned to his hair, poured himself a glass of wine. His fancy kiddush cup was back in their apartment, but any container would suffice. While the rest of us poured our wine, Frank handed skullcaps to me and Cluskey.

"Why do I have to wear a beanie?" he asked.

Frank explained it was called a yarmulke or kippah, not a beanie, and was worn out of respect for God. When you wear a hat—there was no ritual significance to the skullcap itself—it is a constant reminder that there's something, or Someone, over you.

Cluskey chewed on that for a moment, and then turned to his wife. "Makes sense to me. A lot more than the reverend at your church telling us we have to take our hats off."

We seemed to have stepped into a long-running discussion as to the merits of Mrs. Cluskey's church. "What is the wine for?" asked Mrs. Cluskey, ignoring her husband.

"Ah, we drink wine at festive occasions and thank God for creating the fruit of the vine. We are reminded that once we were slaves in Egypt, but now we are free and may enjoy the Sabbath."

"When do we eat?" muttered Cluskey.

"Another traditional question," Frank answered with a laugh. "After the *kiddush*, the blessing over the wine, some of us will engage in a ritual handwashing, and then we will say the blessing over the challah"—indicating the two loaves on the table that were currently covered with a napkin—"followed by dinner."

Frank raised his glass of wine and, to our amazement, Mrs. Cluskey raised hers and said, "*L'chaim!*" with a perfect expression of the gutteral "ch." It wasn't the traditional Jewish toast—"To life!"—that surprised us. It was that the woman who couldn't pronounce "challah" suddenly sounded like she had come fresh from the *shtetl*.

"Hold on," I said. Frank was starting to get annoyed at the interruptions, but I couldn't help it. "How is that someone who struggled with 'challah' comes out with a '*l'chaim*' like her grandmother came from Minsk?"

Mrs. Cluskey seemed startled. "Did I do something wrong?"

"No, you did it exactly right. How do you come to know '*l'chaim*'?"

She looked a bit flustered. "The local high school did a production of *Fiddler on the Roof* last year. My nephew played the butcher. That was his big number."

"We may be in the sticks," said Cluskey, "but we're not rubes."

There was a moment of silence, which Frank rushed to fill with the blessings over the wine for Friday night. Then he and Sam headed into the kitchen for the ritual washing of the hands. After a moment, Susan and Naomi followed them. That left me with Joanne and the Cluskeys.

"Come," I said, heading to the kitchen, "let me show you another one of our customs."

*   *   *

After dinner, I got a taste of what attracted Frank and Samantha to observing the Sabbath. After a week of tension and anxiety, and with Sunday looming as the payoff for months of planning, organizing and, frankly, dealing with crazy people, having a respite with my family and our guests/hosts, with good food and friendly conversation, was a blessing. That was exactly the word for it. I didn't know if I could do this every week, but right now, it was what this family needed and, more than that, deserved.

I offered to help pack up the leftovers, but Mrs. Cluskey made it clear in no uncertain terms that that was not going to be happening in her kitchen. I left her with Joanne and Sam, who were trying to teach her how to pronounce the word "chutzpah." Out in the parlor, Cluskey was offering a nightcap out in the barn of the latest "blend" from his still, which had been "aging" since mid-afternoon.

I passed, but as I made my good nights, I admonished Frank, "In all things moderation."

He smiled and said, "*L'chaim.*"

On Saturday, after a leisurely lunch, the women announced they would spend the afternoon packing and organizing for our move back into town. As it would take me about five minutes—the tux was already in its carry-all bag, the rings I kept on my person so as to not lose them—it wouldn't take long to pack my "civilian" clothes and toiletries.

Having survived months of figurative and literal trials, Frank was a bit giddy. He announced that he was going for a swim in the Cluskeys' pool, which we had ignored up until then. Only he didn't call it a "pool." He insisted on calling it "the cee-ment pond." It took me a moment to get the reference. He was still feeling the effects of binging on *The Beverly Hillbillies* in the hospital, and that's what Jethro had always called their built-in pool.

Sam looked at me and started to giggle.

"What? I didn't bring any bathing suit and have no intention of going swimming."

"No, Daddy, that's not it. I was just thinking that, since you're a banker, that makes you Mr. Drysdale."

At this, she and Frank both burst out laughing. I looked to Joanne for support. "If you call me Granny, you can sleep in the barn tonight."

This led to a new round of laughter. I got up to devote my five minutes to packing, but Cluskey came in abruptly with a strange look on his face. It could have been bad news, or it could have been indigestion. "Folks, I don't know what to make of this, but I figured you'd want to see for yourselves."

He led the way into the parlor, where the TV was tuned to an all-news channel. Sam had told me that she and Frank were trying to use the Sabbath to tune out electronic and social media, but it wasn't always easy. In this case, the choice had been taken out of their hands, and when they saw who was on screen, there was no pulling them away.

"Turn the sound up," said Joanne.

"...and while *People* magazine isn't ordinarily known for their investigative reporting, they've certainly got a scoop here. The revelation that the woman calling herself Frieda Guerrero is, in fact, named Lois Turner, who has a record as a con artist across five states, suggests that her claims to be sister to the reanimated being known as Frank is open to question."

"Open to question?" shouted Sam. "It makes her an out-and-out fraud."

"She was picked up for questioning outside the hotel where Frank and his intended, Samantha Levin, are to be married tomorrow. The police are looking at a possible violation of a restraining order under which Turner is allowed to be no less than a thousand feet from him. Her lawyer told us earlier they would challenge the arrest on the grounds that there was no evidence that Frank was even at the hotel at the time, but this new revelation suggests that her motives were more about financial reward than familial bonds."

The perky blonde anchor turned to her equally perky male counterpart. "And of course, no one has seen hide nor hair of Frank for the last few weeks."

"That's right. And this has led some to speculate that they have cancelled the elaborate wedding plans and gone off to elope. We have this report from Las Vegas...."

The reporter was standing in front of the Chapel of the Eternal Elvis, but we were no longer paying attention.

Frank looked a bit confused. "What does it mean?"

I was thrilled. "It means that we no longer have to worry about Frieda or Lois or whatever her real name turns out to be. She was a scam artist."

"So, this is good news?" said Cluskey.

"This is excellent news," I replied. "And if there's any of your moonshine left, I wouldn't mind a bit, heavily watered."

That was language Cluskey understood, and he went to fetch his jug.

Meanwhile, Frank looked a bit sad. "I suppose it is good news if she's a fake."

"What's wrong?" asked Samantha.

"Part of me was kind of hoping she would help me find out who I was and where I came from."

I put my arm around Frank. "That's a question that no one of us ever really gets a good answer to. C'mon, let's see if Cluskey has an extra pair of trunks, and I'll join you in the cee-ment pond."

CHAPTER TWENTY-ONE

I was not planning to get up at 5 A.M. on the day of the wedding, given that the ceremony was scheduled for late afternoon. Joanne and I were woken by a pounding at the door. It was a very frazzled Mrs. Cluskey.

"Bob says you have to leave immediately," she said, with just a touch of fright in her voice.

Barely awake, I wasn't quite sure I was hearing correctly. "Who's Bob? And why does he think we have to leave?"

"He says he's the head of security for the wedding, and that they know you've been staying here."

This shed little light on the matter. Who were "they" and how did "they" find out where we were? Indeed, who was Bob? Having not hired any security detail, how did he come to be in charge of it?

I put on my bathrobe, and headed downstairs, Joanne in my wake. Frank and Sam were already there.

There was Bob. "About time you got here. We have no time to waste. You need to relocate immediately." Who was Bob? He was the head of security, all 6'3", sandy brown hair, mirrored sunglasses, and electronic earpiece of him.

I was now fully awake, and even though he had several inches on me and what looked to be several concealed weapons beneath his bulging jacket, I was in no mood to be pushed around. "Who the hell are you? And how did you find us?"

Bob took no offense. "I was hired by Neal Kennerly to provide security for this operation. My team is ready to move you and your party to a secure location while we figure out if the wedding can go on as scheduled."

"What?!" shrieked Samantha. "This wedding *is* going on as scheduled."

"We'll do everything in our power to make that happen, but right now you've got to relocate. Yesterday there was something like a thousand people around the city block of your hotel, with more expected to arrive today. Even assuming we could get you and your party inside, there's no guarantee we would be able to ensure your safety."

A thousand people? That meant something like five protestors, counter-protestors, police, and members of the media, not to mention the simply curious, for every one of our guests. The odds were not in our favor and, as it turned out, it was getting worse.

"Why do we have to leave here?" asked Joanne. "There are no protestors outside."

Instinctively, we all glanced out the window where several black vans and at least a dozen members of Bob's "team" were securing the area. At that moment, two of them were marching a very unhappy Cluskey in through the front door.

"We found him lurking around outside, boss," said one of them to Bob.

"Unhand him at once," I demanded. "He's our host here."

Bob nodded, and Cluskey stepped away from his captors. "Just when I had them where I wanted them."

Frank, who had been quiet, asked the obvious question. "How could anyone know we were here? It was strictly on a need-to-know basis."

"Apparently, someone was on Facebook last night, and it reported their location."

I heard a gasp behind me. It was Naomi from the salon. "I'm so sorry. I can never figure out how those various settings work. I was just checking for messages and letting people know I was away. I didn't say where I was."

"You didn't have to," said Bob. "Facebook did it for you. And apparently enough people knew you were involved in the wedding to piece it together."

"I feel awful."

"It's all right," said Sam. "We know you didn't mean to give us away."

"You can kiss and make up later," said Bob, "There are protestors being led by Twitchell who are in the vicinity, and it's only a matter of time before they find this place. You've got five minutes to get dressed and get in the vans."

"What about our clothes for the wedding?" asked Joanne.

"Just put everything on your beds. I'll leave a team here to bring your belongings. Now, let's move."

As we all rushed to get dressed, Cluskey ran to get his camera. As we were saying our goodbyes and heading to the vans, he took a few pictures. One of the men made a move on him, and I stopped dead in my tracks. "He's taking pictures with my cooperation. I don't care what your orders are, you're to leave him alone."

The team looked to Bob, who was mumbling into his wrist. It turned out he had a microphone there and a connected earpiece. "Got it... Okay, Mr. Cluskey. You can take your pictures, but you do not have permission to use any photo where my men are identifiable. Got it?"

Cluskey looked ready to argue the point, but his wife figured out that their deal with us had just been given the stamp of approval by whatever power had sent this armed force into her front yard. "We got it, no problem," she said. She shot her husband a glance that made it clear that if he had anything to say, he should save it for later. She came over to exchange hugs with Joanne and me as well as Frank, and then gave Sam a kiss on the cheek. "You're going to be a beautiful bride, honey, don't you worry."

Sam was then hustled into one of the vans with the rest of us, and we took off while Bob's men loaded up the luggage we had left behind. Ten minutes later, they were following us. Five minutes after that, I was later told, Twitchell and several cars of protestors pulled into the Cluskeys' front yard to find Cluskey alone on his porch, cleaning his shotgun.

The windows in the van were tinted, so it was hard to tell where we were, but I got the sense we were heading back toward home. However, after forty-five minutes or so, we veered off the main road onto a bumpy, unpaved path. When we finally came to a stop, much to our relief, the doors were flung open, and we found ourselves at a rustic cabin in the woods. There was no indication as to who owned it or what they might have used it for, or even if it had ever been used prior to this. We were brought inside, where there was fresh juice and coffee, and some bagels and cream cheese. Not exactly a deluxe breakfast, but at the moment we weren't complaining.

To my surprise, the cabin was also equipped with electricity and either cable TV or a satellite dish, because there a television set that was showing what looked like refugees trying to flee ahead of the invading troops. "This was the scene outside the hotel where the most controversial wedding of the year is scheduled to take place this afternoon."

The sign-wielding protestors seemed equally divided between those for and against the wedding, but this made the protests in front of our house seem like a walk in the park. It was utter bedlam. Even though the police had made sure the entrances to the hotel were clear, it would take a brave soul to walk through this mob scene to attempt to get inside. We watched as reinforcements were brought in to widen the space around the entrances while doing what they could to hold the crowd back.

So, this was how Joanne, Sam, and I ended up in a cabin in the woods, awaiting the arrival of Rabbi Wheaton. While Bob determined what the best course of action was, and I sat quietly, trying to determine how many pieces I was going to tear Kennerly into for hiring this guy without my permission, Naomi was still profusely apologizing. "I had no idea Facebook would do that," she was saying.

"What's done is done," said Frank.

"Let me make it up to you," she said.

"How?" asked Susan.

"After I take care of you and your mother, I'd like to work on Frank."

"I've already had my haircut, thank you," he said, "I'm quite all right."

Naomi, though, was insistent. "I don't want to do your hair. I want to do your makeup."

Frank gave her a puzzled look. "I don't wear makeup."

"Precisely," she answered as if that explained everything.

"Naomi, what are you talking about?" said Sam.

"Those of us fortunate enough to have met Frank know what a catch you're getting," she said to Sam, "but the general public notices his gray, leathery skin, and some part of their brain starts screaming, 'Monster!' I think I can do something about that."

"I'm not going to look like a clown, with my face painted," objected Frank.

"Look at your bride-to-be, dearie. Do I look like I don't know what I'm doing? I may be a klutz online, but I'm an artist when it comes to appearances. I'm talking a little color in your cheeks and a few subtle highlights. If you don't like it, you'll have plenty of time to wash it off. I want people to look at you and Sam on your wedding and say, 'There's something different about him. I don't know what it is.'"

"I don't know…" said Frank.

"Try it, honey. Like Naomi said, if we don't like it you can wash it off."

By mid-morning, the situation hadn't improved, and Rabbi Wheaton was quietly notified that he was needed on urgent business. When he hesitated, he was told it involved some congregants he was scheduled to see later that afternoon. At that point, one of the agents sent to pick him up handed him a phone. I was on the other end.

"You probably know what's going on the hotel. At this point, I don't know how we're going to get around this, but I think it would be better if we were all together."

"And you're not under duress?" asked the rabbi, perhaps having seen too many movies where the kidnap victim makes a phone call with a gun at his or her head.

"Rabbi, I'm under nothing but duress, but my wife and daughter would kill me if I tried to call off the wedding now."

"I'm on my way."

It was early afternoon when Frank entered the cabin, announcing, "He's here." He was followed by Rabbi Wheaton, Cantor Eisenstein, and another young man who was a stranger to me.

"We need to have two witnesses for the *ketubah*, the marriage contract. They need to be unrelated to the parties or their families. So, I asked Hermie to join us. He teaches in the Hebrew school."

Hermie went to help himself to the remains of our breakfast and looked despairingly at the bagels. "No pumpernickel?"

Before I could answer, Bob turned away and began talking into his wrist. "That's a roger. Bring the van around."

"What's happening?" I asked.

"We're going to Plan B."

Not only had I not been told about any Plan B. I was beginning to wonder how many other plans were locked in place, waiting to be activated. I was soon to find out.

I was in a daze. "This is not exactly how I envisioned my daughter's wedding day. And what about all our guests?"

Bob, who had joined us, turned away to listen to the voices in his head. "Operation Shell Game is a go. I repeat, Operation Shell Game is a go," he said into his wrist. Then, turning to us, he announced, "We're relocating the wedding to an alternate location across state lines."

"There's a problem with that," said Rabbi Wheaton.

"No, there's no problem. The situation at the hotel has gotten totally out of control. We can no longer guarantee the safety of the participants."

This sounded ominous. "So, what are we going to do?" I asked.

"Kennerly has made arrangements for this space to be used as a backup, all of the vendors—including the caterer and the florist—have been made aware there could be a change of venue, and that the new location would be divulged on a need-to-know basis at the proper time. We have transportation lined up for everyone. No problem."

"Well, except with the state authorities," said Rabbi Wheaton. "The marriage license is only good in this state. I'm just visiting clergy once we cross state lines."

"I'm sure we can get a justice of the peace…"

"No." Frank clamped his hand on Bob's shoulder. "Sam and I are getting married by our teacher and friend, and not some stranger dragged in at the last moment."

"I can't help that…"

Frank did not release Bob as his voice got very low and serious. "This is not subject to debate."

"We've got to be on the road in thirty minutes," said Bob.

"Well then, we'd best get started," said Rabbi Wheaton. "Could you bring in some of your men to hold the *chupah*?"

"The what?"

"The marriage canopy."

"What?"

"Go get your men, Bob," I said. "We can answer your questions afterwards."

It felt good to be back in control again, if only for a moment.

The marriage rituals were performed in record time. Frank and Sam signed the *ketubah*, a document in Aramaic in which, traditionally, the husband spelled out his obligations to provide for his wife. I'm told modern marriage contracts are more egalitarian. I couldn't tell without a translation. The ceremony itself was done with no frills, from the groom unveiling the bride to the traditional seven blessings chanted by the cantor to the exchange of rings to Frank stomping on a glass (it may have been plastic). When it was done, there was little of the excitement and celebration one expects from having witnessed a wedding. Indeed, it seemed like the air had been let out of the room.

"It's time to go," Bob said, preparing to load the vans.

"No, hold on a moment. I have a few words for the bride and groom," said Rabbi Wheaton. Bob rolled his eyes in impatience, but he seemed to realize that things would move a lot faster if he just kept quiet and let the rabbi have his say. "Frank and Samantha, I know this was not the way you envisioned your wedding. And you may be feeling disappointed. You shouldn't be. First, no one knows better than you what the two of you have had to endure to reach this moment. With everything being thrown against you, you persevered and prevailed. Revel in your triumph."

The newlyweds smiled as if they appreciated the effort being made to pick up their spirits, but it wasn't quite working. "Second," the rabbi continued, "we're about to join your friends and family, who will have literally risked their well-being to perform one of the sweetest of *mitzvahs*, rejoicing with the bride and groom. That there are so many people who were determined to celebrate your special day is a blessing."

Bob started tapping his watch. The rabbi gave him a benevolent smile, and turned back to Frank and Sam. "And lastly, what we have really come to celebrate is the union of two souls who have shown over and over how devoted they are to each other. Your every Shabbat will be a celebration of your marriage. Don't let this day be about how difficult others have tried to make it for you. Make it a celebration of how you wouldn't let anyone, or anything, stop your love and what you knew was the right path."

"Amen," said Joanne. I have to admit that Rabbi Wheaton rose to the occasion. It was a beautiful statement and watching the vein pulse in Bob's neck as he delivered it made it all the sweeter. We were now ready to head out when Susan interrupted.

"One more thing. This wasn't a ceremony that fell short. It was the most romantic statement I've ever seen between two people. Couples for generations to come will look to you for inspiration. And if you two don't write a book about it, I will."

"And maybe Brad Pitt can get another Oscar for playing me," said Frank.

"Who needs Brad Pitt?" said Susan. "You and Samantha can play yourselves."

Sam and Frank gave her hug, and then turned to Rabbi Wheaton. Sam exchanged kisses with him, and then Frank embraced him in a bear hug.

And that's when Bob announced, "The guests are leaving the hotel now. Can we please get going?"

How the guests left the hotel without encountering the now 2,000-plus demonstrators and press was a neat trick. Bob's counterpart at the hotel had gotten the wedding guests and vendors, along with their goods and equipment, down to a parking garage via a service elevator. The hotel was part of a large shopping complex that included another hotel on its far end. Of course, since everyone knew which hotel we had selected for the reception, no one was bothering to watch the other hotel. When several busses and trucks—carefully spaced—emerged from a driveway two blocks away, no one noticed.

Meanwhile, we were being loaded into vans, and Sam's gown took so much space we lost a seat. She and Frank, Joanne and I, along with Susan managed to squeeze in, but there was no longer room for Naomi. "That's okay, I'll ride with the rabbi," she said, taking Hermie's arm and following the rabbi and the cantor. As the van doors were being shut, I heard her say, "So you're only teaching to earn some money while you're in medical school…" I was afraid Hermie was going to have to fend for himself.

Once we hit the highway, Joanne passed out some cheese and crackers, and filled some plastic glasses from a single bottle of champagne, allowing us to have at least a hint that this was part of a celebration and not a funeral procession. I didn't know how all our people would work at a new venue we had never seen, but the die had been cast.

The van had Wifi—ah, the modern age—and Bob was in the front seat with the driver, monitoring the situation. Once we had confirmed that all our people had gotten out without incident, I lost interest in the protests which no longer affected us. Those people had nothing to do with the wedding. They didn't know us. They really had no right to interfere in our family's affairs. I shut the partition between the front seat and the passenger section, shutting out the news reports as well as Bob's coordinating everything with the rest of his team. For the moment, I wasn't even concerned what all this last-minute security and logistics was costing me. Instead, I raised my plastic glass of champagne and said, "To the bride and groom."

The van continued into the afternoon sun.

CHAPTER TWENTY-TWO

We pulled into the parking lot a little after five. We were at what seemed to be a luxury ski resort which, this being August, was readily available on a moment's notice. The owners were probably looking at this as a windfall. Well, so be it. I hadn't really planned on ever retiring.

Sam, Frank, Joanne and Susan were met by Naomi, who hustled them off to the Bridal Suite—or the "Apres Ski Lodge" as it said over the door—to freshen up. I was apparently either perfect or beyond repair and was sent in to tell our guests that we had arrived. I went into the restaurant which was decorated with moose heads, a décor that would certainly make the wedding photos distinctive, and made my way toward the bandstand where Mike and his band were doing sound checks. I was stopped by a frazzled looking woman who I recognized as a hotel liaison.

"We made it," she began without introduction. "The food, the vendors, the servers, it's all here. We did have a problem with the cocktail franks when the truck hit a pot hole and they spilled over into the Swedish meatballs. But since we're going by the contract which charges by the tray and not by the item, we're going to count those combined hors d'oeuvres as single trays. Consider it our gift for the wedding. No need to thank me."

Believe me, I wasn't planning on it. I continued on my way, going past the videographer, who was yelling at the lighting person, "Keep those mooseheads in shadow as much as possible. What kind of place is this for a wedding?"

Making it to Mike, I asked for a microphone, and said to him, "We're all here. When will you be ready to play us in?"

"Give me five minutes and we'll be ready to bring down the house."

"That won't be necessary. Just bring in the wedding party."

He handed me a live microphone, and I turned to our guests. "Ladies and gentlemen, can I have your attention please?" It took a moment, but they quieted down, eager to see what would happen next in this bizarre adventure. "For those of your who may not know me, I'm Samantha's father. I want to thank you all for putting up with the ridiculous demands that have been made on you, and to let you know that Frank and Sam are here. That's the good news. Unfortunately, because we had to cross state lines, we were required to conduct the wedding ceremony before we got here."

There were murmurs of disappointment across the room. Something within me said I needed to keep everyone's spirits up, and so I blurted out, "However, if absolutely necessary, I think we can convince Frank to step on another glass."

This got a big laugh and a round of applause. "If you'll excuse me now, I'm going to rejoin the wedding party, and we'll be coming out in a few minutes. I know I speak for my wife and myself, as well as for Sam and Frank, in saying that we are honored by your presence and look forward to celebrating this marriage with you the way it should be celebrated: as the union of two people who are deeply in love. Thank you."

I handed the microphone back to Mike and began to make my way out to the Lodge. Mike took the microphone and exhorted the crowd, "Eat, drink, and be merry. And be ready to party."

When I walked into the makeshift bridal suite, it was clear that Naomi was worth whatever confusion she had inadvertently caused. Samantha looked absolutely radiant in her white gown. Joanne and Susan were made up to perfection, with every hair in place. I turned to look for Frank and gasped. I couldn't put my finger on it, but he looked different. His complexion was a little ruddier, and his features seemed more relaxed. If I was forced to put a word to it, I'd have to say he looked more human, not that he had looked otherwise. Maybe it's that he seemed less inhuman. No one seeing him for the first time would think, "Oh, that must be the reanimated corpse guy."

"What did I tell you?" said Naomi to Frank.

"What do you think, Daddy?" asked Sam.

"I think my daughter and new son-in-law may be the two most beautiful people on the planet right now. Certainly, within the confines of where ever it is we are."

Before anyone could say anything further, the door burst open, and Evelyn came rushing into the room. She stopped short when she saw Samantha. "Sam, you look beautiful and Frank…" she said turning to him, "…you look amazing."

"Just some artful highlighting," said Naomi.

"We have a problem," said Evelyn.

I didn't even want to guess what problem was arising at this late moment, and it's just as well, because it was beyond anything I could have imagined. "What is it?" I asked, dreading the response.

"Mike says we're a person short."

"Someone didn't show up for the band?"

"No, for the wedding party."

Joanne looked around the room. "He's mistaken. We're all here."

Suddenly, it clicked. "I'm taking two roles."

Evelyn turned to me. "Yes, that's exactly it. You can't walk in with the bride's mother *and* the maid of honor."

"I knew we had overlooked something," said Joanne. "If it wasn't on the checklist, I just went on to the next item. All right, I'll just go in alone."

"Over my dead body you will," I said. "We're Sam's parents. We brought her into this world together, and we're going to marry her off together."

"It's all right," said Susan. "I don't mind going in alone."

"Why don't you get your fiancé Gary?"

Susan frowned. "Because he's stuck at O'Hare Airport in Chicago, where a thick fog has grounded all flights."

Meanwhile, Sam, Frank, and Evelyn were huddling during this round of "who can be the biggest martyr," and Evelyn then ran off shouting, "I'll be right back."

"Nobody's going in alone," said Frank. Before he could explain, Evelyn returned with a somewhat confused Dr. Simonson.

"I understand there's an emergency…" he began before stopping short as he beheld Frank. "Frank, you're looking exceptionally healthy. I guess the healing process has taken hold." Taking in the rest of us, he asked, "So if it isn't Frank, what's the emergency?"

"Dr. Simonson," said Frank, "I asked Sam's father to be my best man, as he has done so much to bring me along in the world. But that means if he escorts Sam's mother into the reception, there's no one to take his place to escort Susan, our maid of honor. Sam and I would like it if you could do it. If it wasn't for you, I might not even be here today."

"I'm honored. I don't know what to say."

"Say 'yes,' Dr. Simonson, so I can tell Mike to start the music."

"Okay. I mean, yes, of course."

Evelyn said, "Go ahead and line up outside the doors, and I'll go tell Mike we're all systems go."

As we were a small wedding party it didn't take look to line up. First Joanne and me, then Susan and Simonson, and then Frank and Sam. Naomi wished everyone luck, and headed into the reception with Evelyn.

"...and now the moment you've been waiting for. Let's greet the wedding party. Here's Phil and Joanne Levin, Samantha's parents."

With that, Mike cued his band into a festive arrangement of the theme from *The Munsters*. As people caught on to what the music was, there was laughter and applause. Joanne and I made our way to the bandstand. Joanne leaned over and hissed, "I don't know what possessed me to let you use that music."

"Smile, dear. We're on camera."

A beaming smile returned to Joanne's face, and only the occasional twitch of an eyebrow betrayed her feelings about the music.

"And since Phil is also the best man, we've asked Dr. Herb Simonson, faculty mentor to the bride and groom, and the man who saved Frank's life, to escort Susan Fine, the maid of honor."

A generous round of applause, with some cheering from the grad student table where Barry, Herb's husband, was carrying on with the members of the BioEthics Department. Ian was there with Evelyn, in full Scottish regalia. He waved in our direction as the doctor brought Susan in.

The music stopped, and there was a hush across the room as everyone knew who was next. "Ladies and gentlemen, appearing for the first time in public since their exclusive engagement—and wedding—at a cabin in the woods, let's welcome Frank and Samantha Ben Abraham."

The room erupted in pandemonium, which only grew as the guests got their first look at the newlyweds. Simonson leaned over to me, "You know, I can't put my finger on it, but there's something different about Frank."

"It must be the country air," said Joanne, before turning to give me a wink.

It was a joyous moment, and on the video, you can see some tears on my face. Joanne insists they were tears of joy. I maintain they were my body's reaction to the pollen the truckload of flowers that had been carted in were spewing into the air.

Amazingly, the reception went off as planned. Courses were brought out on schedule. The first dance (to En Vogue's "I Want a Monster to Be My Friend") of bride and groom was of storybook caliber. The traditional Jewish folk dance of the *hora* led to the usual free-for-all on the dance floor, including Sam and Frank hoisted on chairs by their friends. And then came time for the best man's toast. I took the microphone from Mike and waited for the room to quiet down.

"It's unusual for the bride's father to be the best man, but then everything about this wedding has been unusual. If I knew then, when Frank told me of his intentions, what I know now, I would have put a stop to it. Not to the marriage. There was nothing that was going to stop that. But I might have been more insistent that elopement was the way to go."

"Too late now," someone shouted.

"Indeed, it is. Right now, as we celebrate this happy occasion, there are more than two thousand people demonstrating in front of the hotel where we were supposed to meet. To those who object to this wedding, I have this to say: it's none of your business."

This was greeted with cheers. I went on, "To those who were there to support Frank and Sam, I say, Thank you, we appreciate it, but it's really none of your business."

More cheers. "And to the members of the media who were covering both sides—and the wedding plans—I have this to say: It really, really isn't any of your business."

I waited again for quiet. "An heir to the throne or a president's daughter might expect that their wedding would become news. But two private citizens, who did not ask for this attention, deserve that their privacy be respected. Thanks to all of you for making that possible."

And the toast? "When I first met Frank, I could not imagine him marrying my baby. Now I can't imagine my family without him. Sam and Frank are a special couple, and I believe they are going to be one of the great married couples, possibly because I'm going to be paying for today's events for the rest of my life. But today the focus is rightly on them, and so I ask you all to raise your glasses in honor of Sam and Frank." Turning to them I said, "May your road be smooth, your successes many, and your love eternal. *L'chaim!*"

When I returned to my table, Joanne kissed me and said, "That was beautiful. I didn't know you had that in you."

I looked at the rest of the people at our table. "And that's the secret to the success of *our* marriage."

I decided I didn't need to see the hoked-up shenanigans of Sam and Frank slicing the wedding cake and pretending to feed each other, largely for the benefit of the cameras. I went over to the bar and ordered a Chivas. I was paying for it, so I might as well have the best.

As I was savoring the first sip, Neal Kennerly came up with a big smile on his face.

"Ah, the man who tripled the cost of the wedding by bringing in the Marines. What other surprises do you have in store for me? When do the paratroopers arrive?"

Kennerly laughed. "Bob and his team? Didn't cost you a red cent."

I was confused. "What about the vans and the trucks and the buses?"

"Not a dime. While you've been in the bubble of getting to this wedding, things have been happening in the rest of the world."

"Such as?"

"Such as my firm's business taking off due to the publicity we received for representing Frank. I've had to take on two associates and a paralegal to handle all the new work. When I saw what Twitchell was planning in front of the hotel—oh, yes, we've kept up monitoring him—I knew that any attempt to hold the wedding there was going to be a disaster. So, I called in a few debts. Bob owed me big time for some work we did for him. There will be no charge for any of his services."

I could hardly believe my ears. While I ordered a Chivas for Kennerly, Tom Hammer came over. "Ah, another dependent," I greeted him. "Can I offer you a drink?"

"Yes, and a thank you for getting this venue for the wedding at the last minute at no cost to you."

"What do you mean 'no cost?' They're giving us this space for free?"

"Yes," said Tom. "This is one of our clients. How busy do you think a ski lodge is in August? But after I told them whose wedding it was, and how you'd have no objection to their using that fact—and some photos—to promote themselves as not only a ski resort but a year-round venue, they jumped at it. There's not only no charge, but as a wedding present, they've invited Sam and Frank back this winter for an all-expenses paid two-week holiday."

"Tom, I don't know what to say."

"'Thank you' and 'Here's your drink' will suffice."

It was a magical moment. It wasn't so much the money, although these two revelations were much appreciated, as the fact that, in spite of everything, we had been favored with good news. The wedding had taken place, the party was a huge success, and in just a short while life would return to normal. Oh, Sam and Frank would face challenges, some of them unique to their situation, but many of them typical of any newly married couple. However, it was now *their* problem to solve. Joanne and I would be rooting for them and helping when we could, but now it was their story, not ours. No more checklists. No more family meetings. It was finally done.

"Ladies and gentlemen, it's now time for the traditional dance of the bride with her father. Can they please come to the dance floor?"

I clinked glasses with Neal and Tom, finished off the Chivas, and headed for the dance floor. There, Sam and Frank awaited me. "I am proud to be part of your family," Frank said, as he stepped back for Sam and me to take the floor.

Yes, of course the music was "Sunrise, Sunset." And yes, I was never a great dancer. However, I took Sam in my arms, and we whirled around the dance floor. People who saw me there would later talk about how I was beaming. Some said I seemed overwhelmed with happiness at the successful culmination of the day's events. As we danced, I could see the photographer and videographer fight over who would stand where to get their best shot. I saw Naomi and Hermie slip out of the room to who knows where. I saw Joanne sit back in her chair, amazed that everything had fallen satisfactorily into its place. I saw Cantor Eisenstein and Mike arguing over whether the band could work in a solo number for the cantor, so he could do his specialty, *"Bei Mir Bist Du Schoen."*

Even on the video, one can see the dazed look at my face which everyone would chalk up to my being so happy and so proud. I was, but none of that explained the glazed look I was wearing, since only I heard what Samantha whispered in my ear as we spun around the floor.

"Daddy, I think I'm pregnant."

AFTERWORD

Probably the hardest question for any writer is, "Where do you get your ideas?" After all, even if one can point to something tangible as the inspiration for a story, others may have experienced the same thing or something similar and were not so inspired. Or were inspired differently. I've had some success in the past few years with short stories, particularly for themed anthologies, but were you to pick up one of these anthologies (and you should), you'd find a wide range of stories as different writers brought different things to the task.

Perhaps the easiest example I can give for how my mind works is to point to an anthology called *One Star Reviews of the Afterlife*. As a film critic of many years, I instantly thought of a film critic giving a negative review to heaven, and what would be a critic's idea of heaven but the perfect screening room? From inspiration to writing to acceptance took a week. This was a personal record not likely to be matched, as a short story usually takes me one or more weeks, and the submission and acceptance process often takes months. The story, "Cinema Purgatorio," is a personal favorite, and because the book went out of print very quickly due to some personal matters for the publisher, I'm happy to include it here as a bonus.

Which brings us to *Father of the Bride of Frankenstein*. It began life as what was, for me, a longish short story. I eventually realized there was much more to tell and expanded it into the novel you've just read. The beginning and the end are more or less the same, but what happens in between often was as surprising to me as it was as I was writing it as it may have been to you as a reader. What got me going was the odd resonance of the title, a mash-up of two classic films, *Father of the Bride* (1950, remade in 1991) and *Bride of Frankenstein* (1938). The plot and characters are original, but the notion of inserting a reanimated corpse into a domestic sitcom was just too weirdly funny to me to pass up.

Writers are told to write what they know, although others advise to write about what you don't know and to let your imagination run free. I've done both here. Without getting into the nuts and bolts of it, things like the details of wedding preparations, Jewish rituals, and legal matters were things with which I had some familiarity, while organ transplants and the music of En Vogue were totally new to me. A tip of the hat to Google for letting me easily access information during the writing process, rather than making me stop dead while searching for what I needed to know.

I always knew what the last line of the story was going to be, both in its short form and at novel length. To me, it was the perfect punchline. Interestingly, both versions of "Father of the Bride" led to sequels focusing on a baby being born, but there is no present intention for a sequel here. Still, never say never. If the right inspiration strikes (hint: a check for a large amount of money might do it), it could happen.

Which gets back to why I write and where I get my ideas. Having been a lawyer, a college professor, a film critic, and non-fiction author, I'm finally getting to do what I've dreamed of doing since I was a kid: make people laugh. My message to readers is that if I've made you laugh while reading my stories, then I've done my job. I don't mind if my writing elicits other reactions as well, but my primary goal is to write an engaging and funny story. There's enough stress and misery in the real world that an escape into a world that makes you laugh or smile can be a relief. That's not a criticism of more serious fiction. It's a recognition of where my own strengths lay. I'm the author of *Shh! It's a Secret*, not *The Great Gatsby* or *Grapes of Wrath*.

As to why science fiction, it's a genre I enjoy and where I'm comfortable. I don't know if I would do a credible job trying to write a comedy set in 17th century France or during World War II. Instead, I take our present world and add aliens or time travel or a reanimated corpse, and then see what happens. We humans have an amazing capacity to assimilate the most fantastic or horrific things into our mundane, everyday lives, from the triumph of man landing on the moon to the horrors of the 9/11 terrorist attacks. In short order, we go from shock to "this is the way the world is" and move on. Perhaps that's the real source of my inspiration. Is it so far-fetched to think that if an experiment produced a real-life Frank, he wouldn't quickly go from being the top news story of the day to "our guest tonight" on some talk show?

As long ago as my college days, when I did a humor column for the student magazine, I used to say I could never top real life in terms how strange the world can be. However, as long as I have appreciative readers and an indulgent publisher, I'll keep trying.

—Daniel M. Kimmel
October 2017

ACKNOWLEDGMENTS

A few thank yous are in order. First, to Kilian Melloy, one of the dedicatees of this volume, for bringing me into the "Writers Reading to Writers" group he was part of, and where—over time—I found the encouragement to try my hand at fiction and to discover my "voice." (Interestingly, I have been told I write the way I speak, which is not true of all authors. I don't know if that's a good or bad thing, but I seem to be stuck with it.) So, thanks to Iory Allison, Michael Cox, William Kuhn, Robert LeCates, Linda Markarian, Arnold Serapilio, and Jamie Simpson —the other members of the group—who first heard the original story and have been incredibly supportive. I hope I've done the same for them.

Thanks, too, to Rabbi Charles Simon, Jesse Gordon, and Naomi Lichtenberg, for providing some real-world employment opportunities while I was writing this novel. I may write for the love of it, but I've got to eat as well.

I'm also appreciative of Temple B'nai Brith of Somerville, Massachusetts, where I am a member, and Temple Beth Sholom (the "Tremont Street Shul") in Cambridge, Massachusetts, where I am a regular at Monday morning services. Their friendship and support has been especially important in the last few years, although let me add that the fictional Rabbi Wheaton is entirely a product of my imagination.

If you don't know any authors personally, you may not have heard of "beta readers," but as you might guess, these are people who read an early version of the manuscript and do annoying things like point out plot holes and other problems that the author then has to fix. They do it so that you don't have to. Special thanks to Bonnie-Ann Black, Michael A. Burstein, and Michael Devney.

As usual, thanks also to my friend, editor, and publisher Ian Randal Strock, and to my agent Alison Picard. Let's see if we can get the mega-movie deal on this one, so we can all retire.

And finally, a heartfelt thank you to my daughter Amanda, who turned 21 while I was working on this, which doesn't seem possible as she was just born. She was certainly the inspiration for some of the father/daughter musings in the novel, but Frank is in no way, shape, or form a reflection on any of her boyfriends, past or present.

BONUS STORY:
CINEMA PURGATORIO
by Daniel M. Kimmel

I had not been looking forward to this screening. After all my years as a film critic for a major metropolitan daily, I still did make the effort to keep an open mind before going into a movie. I wasn't surprised very often by something I had been dreading turning out to be something that was good. More often than not, it was the other way around. Still, I made an attempt to start off with a clean slate.

This was going to be a tough one. It was a modern dress version of *Hamlet* starring Adam Sandler, trying to reboot his career by tackling the Bard. My money was on Shakespeare going down hard. Sandler had a lot of recent films to atone for: *Pixels*, *That's My Boy*, *Jack and Jill*. In fact, his films were no longer drawing the audiences of his heyday, and most of them were now going out directly through Netflix. It wasn't clear if this new film was being released or had simply escaped.

I nodded to a few of my colleagues as I entered the screening room, ignoring the young punks who were making it harder and harder for people like me to earn a living. Why should anyone pay a professional film critic—in spite of our depth of knowledge and finely honed writing skills—when a bunch of children were giving it away for free on their "blogs?" Worse yet, they wanted to be considered peers. It was almost enough to make me wish I was dead. And then I was.

I had closed my eyes for a moment, steeling myself against the purveyor of *Happy Gilmore* and *Little Nicky* as the tortured Prince of Denmark. When I opened them, I was somewhere else.

It was still a movie theater or screening room of some sort, with dark red curtains framing the screen, and houselights just dim enough to make it impossible to read. I looked around, but I was all alone. At first, I thought I had blissfully slept through the entire film, but that my colleagues would leave without waking me seemed strange. Then, a door at the back of the room opened, and a man walked down the aisle. I couldn't make out his features because he was backlit, and I was shocked when he came down front—where I usually sat—and I saw that it was none other than Clark Gable, the legendary actor who had died in 1960. He had won an Oscar for *It Happened One Night*, and was the only choice for Rhett Butler in *Gone with the Wind*. This Gable seemed older, the craggy but still macho presence of one of his late films, like *Run Silent, Run Deep*.

I would have been happy to conduct a career retrospective but, for the moment, I was at a loss for words. "Why you're…"

He chuckled. "Yes, I am. And, no, you're not dreaming."

"Then that means I'm dead?"

"I'm afraid so," he said sympathetically, before favoring me with a broad smile. "But look at the bright side. Now you're ready for your eternal reward."

"But why are *you* here?"

Gable looked hurt. "Don't you think I belong here?"

"No, I didn't mean it like that. I meant why are *you* greeting me? Shouldn't I be seeing the King of Kings, Lord of Hosts?"

Gable let out a good laugh at that. "Do you know how many beings die across the universe every day? Even the Omnipotent One would be hard-pressed to find time for His other tasks if He had to greet each one individually. Oh, sure, He'll make an exception for Mother Teresa or Kurt Cobain—"

"Kurt Cobain?"

"He really dug his music. Can't say I care much for it myself."

This was too much to take in all at once so, as with my reviews, I focused in on what was important. "So why are *you* here to greet *me*?"

Gable gave me a big grin. "Because I'm the King. At least, that's what they called me in Hollywood. And you're a movie critic. If you were a musician, you would have been greeted by Elvis. If you were a comedian, you'd be welcomed by Alan King. If you were an author, it would be Stephen King—"

"Hold on. Stephen King is still alive."

"Well, in his case it's a Stephen King impersonator. And let me tell you, Edgar Allan Poe is none too happy about it. It's only until the real King comes along."

We were getting off track again. "So I'm dead and Clark Gable, the King, is welcoming me to heaven. I suppose we should we get on with it. Where do we go?"

Gable gestured to the room. "We don't go anywhere. You're already here. This is the screening room of your dreams. Any movie you've ever wanted to see is ready for your viewing. Alfred Hitchcock's lost film *The Mountain Eagle*? We've got it. Uncut versions of von Stroheim's *Greed* and Welles' *The Magnificent Ambersons*? You only have to ask. Complete, uncut, and without commercial interruption."

Well, I had to admit, that did sound like heaven. Yet something was odd. "Where's everyone else? Where's Roger Ebert and Pauline Kael and Judith Crist and Richard Corliss…"

"They're in their own screening rooms. You'll see them in the lobby after the movie, but you each get your own space to see what you want to see when you want to see it. So why don't you take a seat and let me know what you'd like to see first?"

I started to walk over to a seat in the center of the row, my preferred spot, when I noticed how sticky and gummy the floor was. "I would have thought the theaters would be in better shape than this."

"Sorry about that. Here, have some popcorn." The star of *Mutiny on the Bounty* tossed me a sealed bag of pre-made popcorn.

"It's not even freshly made?"

He shrugged his shoulders. "You're here for the movie, right?"

The shoddiness of it all was off-putting. Then something occurred to me. "I'd like to see the projection booth."

Gable looked surprised. "Why?"

"I'd like to see the equipment you're using."

"There's no need for that. I can tell you. We've got a state of the art digital projection system with all the latest bells and whistles."

I threw the bag of popcorn to the floor. "Digital? You're not even showing actual film?"

When Gable didn't reply, I decided I had had enough. "I've been in third-rate grindhouses that were in better shape than this. I assume you answer to somebody? I want to speak to him or her immediately."

The actor gave me a look I couldn't quite read, and then snapped his fingers. He vanished, and was immediately replaced by a short, rotund guy with gray hair and a receding hairline. It took me a moment to place him.

"I'm Louis B. Mayer. What seems to be the problem?"

I quickly recovered, and decided that, unlike the actors he terrorized at MGM in the '30s and '40s, I would not be intimidated. "I've devoted my life to the art of cinema, and *this* is my eternal reward? A crummy screening room with sticky floors and ersatz popcorn that can't even project actual film? What kind of racket are you running here?"

Mayer was utterly unruffled. He could be tough as nails heading up the studio that was the top of the food chain, but he could also be avuncular and paternalistic. At times, he could leave the people he was manipulating with the impression that they had put one over on him. "My dear boy, you're absolutely right. You deserve far better than this. I don't know what they were thinking."

Mayer snapped his fingers, and we were suddenly in a very plush space. The seats were wide and cushioned. When I sat down, I found I could lean back and a leg rest came up. Mayer motioned me to follow him up the aisle. We were in a lobby that would have put Radio City Music Hall to shame. He led me over to the concession stand.

"Some fresh popcorn?"

The smartly uniformed attendant scooped the popcorn right out of the machine and into a tub. She added a generous helping of what was labeled "fresh creamery butter."

Mayer handed me the tub. "No need to worry about cholesterol now, eh, my boy?" he said with a wink.

The concessionaire then gave me an ice cold bottle of Dr. Brown's Cream Soda, my favorite. In my entire life, I had never been in a movie theater that offered it.

"How—?"

Mayer wouldn't let me finish the question.

"Everything is possible now. Shall we return to your theater?"

We went back in, and I took my seat. There were holders for both the soda and the tub of popcorn. As I settled in, Mayer was giving his spiel, "We can project at both silent and sound speed, provide the proper aspect ratios, and have the means to project anything from Super8 to Cinerama and IMAX. Every film is shown precisely as its maker intended it to be seen."

"Now you're talking," I said as I settled in. "This *is* heaven."

"Ah, not quite." With that, metal clasps emerged from the seat holding my arms, legs, and head in place. My soda and popcorn were just out of reach.

"What's going on?" I demanded.

"You get optimal screening conditions, my boy, but you lose the right to select the films. You'll have to watch what we show you, for as long as we choose to."

"But I'm dead. That could be forever."

Mayer gave me a wan smile. "Yes, it could."

He started to walk up the aisle. I could not turn my head to see him, but I shouted after him, "So what am I going to be watching?"

Mayer came back down the aisle and stood in front of me where I could see him. He had a clipboard which he looked at before looking up at me. "It's a special retrospective that has been curated just for your benefit. All new pristine prints of the director's extended editions. It's a fifty film look at the works of…" He paused to glance down at the sheet on the clipboard. "Ah yes, Adam Sandler. Enjoy. Remember, movies are better than ever."

CPSIA information can be obtained
at www.ICGtesting.com
Printed in the USA
BVHW030328090119
537386BV00001B/10/P

9 781515 423799